Praise for Roxanne St. Claire and her sizzling novels of romantic suspense. . . .

KILLER CURVES

"[A] page-turner. . . . You don't have to be a NASCAR fan to go for this sexy, exciting, and poignant romantic suspense."

—*Booklist*

"Roxanne St. Claire dazzles. . . . This wildly exciting romantic suspense offers a breathtaking blend of mystery and sexuality as well as elegance and romance, a style that is Ms. St. Claire's inimitable trademark. Be prepared for an incredible spin through the world of NASCAR racing, you won't want to miss it."

—*The Winter Haven News Chief* (FL)

"St. Claire sets a sleek, sexy, and very American romantic suspense novel in the high-pressure world of auto racing . . . emotional . . . compelling."

—*Publishers Weekly*

"Grab onto your seat because once you open the cover of this book, *Killer Curves* will take you on the ride of your life . . . the perfect combination of suspense, intrigue, and romance . . . a first place winner."

—*Romance Junkies Reviews*

"Fun . . . intriguing . . . a great adventure."

—*The Best Reviews*

FRENCH TWIST

"St. Claire has created a truly compelling romantic hero, an enticing mix of sophisticated French seduction and solid, all-American male. With its clever plotting, evocative settings, and vivid sensuality, this offering is sure to set tongues wagging."

—*Publishers Weekly*

"Full of heart-stopping romance and mystery."

—*Old Book Barn Gazette*

"Intriguing suspense that crackles with sexual tension. The novel is a tour de force of the heart that will leave the reader breathless and yearning for more."

—*Winter Haven News Chief* (FL)

"Simply wonderful! Fast-paced action, red-hot romance and a healthy dose of danger combine for an addictive and wholly satisfying read, further solidifying Ms. St. Claire's place as one of the hottest voices in romantic suspense today."

—*Romance Reader's Connection*

"You are in for a real treat."

—*A Romance Review*

TROPICAL GETAWAY

"A tour de force of sizzling suspense and scorching sensuality!"

—Teresa Medeiros, *New York Times* bestselling author

"Romance, danger, and adventure on the high seas in just the right combination make St. Claire's debut a very impressive one."

—*Booklist*

"Four Stars. Sizzling romance and tangible suspense make *Tropical Getaway* a most enjoyable read. Get ready for adventure, passion, and danger!"

—*Romantic Times*

"Virtually impossible to put down . . . filled with twists and turns."

—*Romance Reviews Today*

"Captures the essence of paradise . . . heated passion . . . compelling suspense."

—*Romance Reader's Connection*

"Intrigue, danger, secrets, lies, and romance. . . . Roxanne St. Claire packs a punch."

—*The Word on Romance*

An *Original* Publication of POCKET BOOKS

 POCKET BOOKS, a division of Simon & Schuster, Inc. 1230 Avenue of the Americas, New York, NY 10020

ISBN-13: 978-1-4516-5554-4

First Pocket Books printing October 2005

10 9 8 7 6 5 4 3 2 1

POCKET and colophon are registered trademarks of Simon & Schuster, Inc.

Cover design by Jae Song; photo credit ©Index Stock Richard Gross

Manufactured in the United States of America

For information regarding special discounts for bulk purchases, please contact Simon & Schuster Special Sales at 1-800-456-6798 or businesss@simonandschuster.com.

KILL ME TWICE

Roxanne St. Claire

Pocket Books

New York   London   Toronto   Sydney

Also by Roxanne St. Claire

KILLER CURVES
HIT REPLY
FRENCH TWIST
TROPICAL GETAWAY

ACKNOWLEDGMENTS

Very special *gracias* to a team of experts who assisted in the research and story development:

Kelly Craig, Miami NBC-affiliate anchorwoman extraordinaire, who generously shared her life and profession with me, took me into her studio and opened doors that would otherwise have been locked. (And special thanks to Tammi Leader Fuller for making that happen.)

Robert Gonzalez, who gave me the insider's tour of the Cuban-American male psyche and offered patient and rapid responses to my questions, always making me feel comfortable enough to ask uncomfortable questions. (And thanks to Cori Rice for letting me borrow one of her best employees.)

Ileana Portal, for not only providing in-depth information about the geography and landscape of Sunset Key, but for unknowingly offering inspiration from the moment I saw a true Latin beauty.

Barbara Ferrar, a talented writer who assisted with the language of love, and gave me months of bilingual laughs in the process.

Jason Trask, Assistant Chief Pilot of Northeast Helicopter, for the guidance in helicopter rescue techniques.

Gavin De Becker & Associates, experts in public figure protection and threat assessment, for a glimpse into the life of a bodyguard.

As always, my deepest gratitude to Micki Nuding, an editor who is unfailing with her praise and unflinching with her pencil. I'd be lost and overwritten without her.

And, most especially, love and appreciation to my husband and children who lose me every time I go traveling in my mind, and always take me back when I've finished the journey. I love you guys the most.

Dedicated with love to Colleen Bidden, who read my first twin story in eighth grade and has been encouraging me to write another ever since. I'm so glad you laughed at the ribbons in my hair and became the rarest kind of friend . . . the one that lasts a lifetime.

Love, YBF

KILL ME TWICE

KILL ME

TWICE

PROLOGUE

"Inside this dossier is your penance." Lucy Sharpe stood to her full six feet and handed the folder down to the man who looked far too big for the delicate chair he sat in. Height was never a disadvantage to a woman who knew how to use it. "She's gorgeous, rich, smart, and built like a centerfold. Do you think you can manage to keep her alive *and* keep your hands off her?"

Alex Romero set the manila folder on the chair next to him, without opening it to verify *gorgeous* or *centerfold*. And to his credit, he didn't attempt another defense of his behavior in Switzerland. Lucy gave him one point for patience and another for recognizing that she'd just placed his world-class backside on probation.

"Is she a new client?" he asked.

"Actually, she's not the client who has retained the Bullet Catchers." Lucy crossed her arms and settled her hip against a massive Victorian writing table that filled one corner of her library. "The client is her employer, Kimball Parrish."

"The media mogul?"

Alex might look like he belonged in full leathers weaving through the Pyrenees on a Ducati, but he read *The New York Times*. And he had the memory of a supercomputer.

"Yes, he's the owner of Adroit Broadcasting Group," Lucy replied. "And as the master of sixty-five network-affiliate TV stations, a satellite radio network, a chain of theaters, a billboard company, and one of the most popular search engines, *mogul* definitely applies."

"He's the one who needs a bodyguard. The guy's a one-man right-wing conspiracy who's amassed as many enemies as dollars."

"He was referred by a friend." Though "friend" was too small a word for the person who dragged Lucy from the depths of hell and given her a reason to live again. Taking this unorthodox assignment was the least she could do in return. "Kimball Parrish is a Bullet Catcher client now. Our clients' politics are not our business; their security and safety is." Her gaze dropped to the dossier, giving him silent permission to open it. "He's hired us to protect an anchorwoman at WMFL, a Miami television station Adroit recently acquired. She's being stalked and threatened by a viewer, and he wants round-the-clock security. As you have proven repeatedly, there are few executive protection experts of your caliber in the world."

Alex's eyes burned as black as the Cuban coffee that fueled his Latin blood. "You're sending me to Miami to babysit a newsreader with an amorous fan?"

She knew he'd hate this job. The Bullet Catchers weren't overpriced bouncers hired to fend off the paparazzi, nor were they hourly-wage night-shift guards hired to impress friends of the wealthy. Her elite organization was comprised of first-rate security specialists, and she selected both her employees and her clients with tremendous care. Though she hadn't exactly *selected* this one—but Alex didn't need to know that.

She responded to his babysitting complaint with a silent, simple nod.

"No way. Huh uh. Get somebody else. I don't do newscasters."

"Nor will you *do* this one," she volleyed back. "You've been given this assignment because no one else in this operation can handle it as well as you." She had several covert surveillance professionals, an undercover master, two deadly marksmen, an explosives expert, a few hostage negotiators, and three counter-terrorism specialists on the Bullet Catcher payroll. But none could touch Alex for his ability to case a room, anticipate trouble, and get his principal out of harm's way.

"Why don't you send Max Roper? He could scare the nastiest stalker away."

"He's just back from Cannes." Lucy smiled. "I should think you'd love an assignment in Miami. This is your chance to go home, eat some black beans, and bounce your nieces and nephews on Uncle Alejandro's lap."

His swarthy complexion darkened, telling her he was working to control his temper. "Look, I joined the Bullet Catchers because I don't want jobs like this. If I did, I'd be a contract bodyguard for some white-bread security company. I work for you because I prefer to protect presidents, princes, and the head of Scotland Yard."

"You work for me because I pay you a ridiculous amount of money, let you wear your hair like a rock star, and usually ignore it when women are willing to risk marriages to multibillionaires just to serve you strawberry scones off their breasts."

The hint of a smile tipped his full mouth. "Raspberry."

"Unfortunately, that multibillionaire was one of my best clients and paying us a fortune to protect him."

"I *did* protect him. I told you, she had a knife and some interesting pictures of her husband and his boyfriend. She'd have carved him to the bone if I hadn't distracted her long enough for him to escape."

"I read the report." She picked up the manila folder and placed it in his hands. "This one's more important than it looks on the surface."

"Because you want more of Parrish's business?"

Let him think that. "I would very much like to impress him, regardless of his political leanings, and I'm counting on you to make that impression. And, of course, to be sure no one lays a hand on one of his favorite employees. Including you."

"Aw, Luce. Don't tell me you believe all those rumors." An irreverent smile broke across his face. "I'm telling you, it's all propaganda."

Lucy laughed softly. "There's truth in propaganda." She never could stay angry with him for very long. Five years ago, when she'd left the Agency with a plan to target the most powerful people in the world as her clients, Alex Romero had been one of her first hires. His intelligence and fearlessness had knocked her socks off. He had that effect on most women; unfortunately their underwear and common sense were invariably knocked off along with their socks.

"This subject is not an ordinary news anchor," Lucy told him. "When she's done in Miami, she's New York bound, being groomed to be the next star of the Metropolitan Network."

"And I'm supposed to get excited about that."

"No, Alex. That's just the point: you're *not* supposed to get excited about that. Your excitement was the cause of the debacle in Geneva."

He fingered the edge of the folder, and read the tab. "Jessica Adams. What's her deal?"

"She's an ambitious thirty-year-old workaholic who lives in a high-rise off Brickell Avenue in Miami. She rarely dates, loves to cook, reads the classics, collects antique glass, has an identical twin sister, chairs a breast cancer foundation, exercises regularly, and drives a BMW convertible. She'll be an easy client."

"Fine." His tone told her it wasn't. "I'll leave right away."

"Mr. Parrish requested that you arrive no sooner than tomorrow night. That way he'll have an opportunity to brief Miss Adams on his decision to hire a bodyguard. Evidently she's not taking the stalker threats seriously."

"That'll give me time to bounce some nieces and nephews when I get to Coral Gables."

Lucy smiled as she circled back to her chair. "You do that. And when you meet the principal, make sure she understands that the danger to her is real. She needs to know that complacency is the enemy." Picking up her electronic assistant to check messages, she added, "Don't let me down, Alex. You know the rules."

"Jeez, Luce. It's insulting that you think I'm such a dog that I can't resist one measly news—"

She heard the folder flip open, then his long, slow whistle.

"Those are real," she said without taking her attention from her handheld device. When he didn't answer, she finally looked at him, seeing a glint in his eyes that was both threatening and amused.

"You're evil, Lucy. Truly black-hearted and evil."

CHAPTER
One

Jasmine Adams peered through her rental car windshield at the gaudy glass and brass high-rise, then back to her cell phone to try her sister one more time.

This is Jessica Adams; please leave a message and I'll get right back to you.

Jessica's chirpy TV voice usually made Jazz smile, but hearing the message for the umpteenth time simply made her boil. Or maybe it was Miami's 200 percent humidity, which had long ago melted the spunk out of her new spunky hairdo and wrapped her whole body with perspiration. Back home in San Francisco, she'd need a leather jacket on a November evening; here, a thin cotton tank top was plastered to her skin.

"Come on, Jessica," she told the answering machine. "I'm not even late, for once. Where are you, Miss Never Met a Clock You Couldn't Beat?"

As night darkened the skies, the towering buildings came magically to light, spilling rivers of white and gold over the blackness of Biscayne Bay. Jazz scanned the deepening shadows under the palm trees and hibiscus bushes around the manicured grounds. What kind of self-respecting private investigator sat in the downtown Miami darkness unarmed?

But she wasn't here as a private investigator. And Jessica had gone all whiny at the idea of Jazz bringing a Walther P99 Compact into her brand new condo. Because this whole outrageous plan was for Jessica, Jazz had agreed. That was her mantra this week: *This one is for Jess.* Her chance to help her sister, after all the times Jessica had covered for her.

So where the hell was she, anyway?

Probably hung up at the TV studio, unable to answer her cell phone, and the station switchboard was closed now. Well, she had a key and knew the alarm code to Jess's condo—but what about the doorman?

Don't tell anyone, her sister had warned in a brief e-mail a few days ago. *No matter what, don't tell anyone that you aren't me. We'll talk when you get here.*

The doorman would be the first test. If the trendy new haircut—complete with oxblood highlights for that perfect anchorwoman-red—didn't fool him, it was better to find out now, *before* they tried to pass her off as Jessica Adams for the six o'clock news tomorrow night.

She climbed out of the car and headed toward the entrance. Squaring her shoulders to match that self-assured walk her sister had mastered when they were fourteen, Jazz opened the smoky glass doors into a lobby sparkling with marble and a two story glass-beaded waterfall.

Behind the high-gloss reception desk, a uniformed

young man looked up from a newspaper and nodded to her. "Hello, Miz Adams," he said with a Spanish accent.

She flashed her best TV-trained smile.

"Have a nice evening," she called out as she strode toward a bank of elevators, exuding Jessica's natural warmth, but not enough eye contact to invite conversation. Then she realized she had no flaming idea where she was going.

She slowed down near the elevators, faking a dig for her keys while reading the brass placard to figure out which one took her to the thirty-seventh floor. She glanced back at the guard, who openly stared at her.

It was the clothes, no doubt. Jessica would endure physical torture before she'd ever wear a skin-tight wife-beater tank, Army-Navy store cargo pants, and biker boots. The bell dinged and in a moment, she was safe in a marble and mirrored elevator car, staring at her reflection in the smoky glass.

She stabbed her fingers into the "modified spikes" her hairdresser had re-created from Jessica's publicity shot, and stifled a giggle of anticipation. Leaning closer to the mirror, she dabbed at her lip gloss and brushed a smudge of melted mascara from under her eye.

As long as no one saw them together, they could pull it off. Next to each other, they were easily identifiable. One had perfect hair, tailored clothes, a confident tilt to her chin, and that elusive sparkle in her eye that wowed the camera and anyone else within a five-mile radius. The other . . . well, that would be *Jasmine* Adams.

But one week with Jazz filling in at the anchor desk of WMFL Channel Five News would not ruin Jessica's charmed career. In fact, Jess was certain her career would catapult because of what she was doing *off*-camera while Jazz was *on*. She'd refused to give a single detail about what it was, but tonight, Jessica would explain.

As the elevator doors opened, Jazz stepped into a wide hallway lit by wall sconces casting indirect light that exuded wealth and exclusivity. She walked down the carpeted hall, slid the key into the door of apartment 3701, and opened into pitch blackness. Flattening her hand against the wall, she felt around for a light switch or the alarm pad.

Suddenly, the door was yanked from her hand and slammed closed with a rush of air. Terror punched her stomach and every muscle in her body tensed up for a fight. "What the—"

A hand slapped over her mouth so hard she choked on a gasp. She could feel the heat of a man against her back, a solid, sizable man who'd pinned her right arm with a paralyzing grip. Hot breath warmed her ear; the smell of raw masculinity filled her nostrils.

"That was stupid." His voice was a low, lilting growl that vibrated from his chest through her body.

No, leaving her *gun* at home was stupid.

Her teeth snapped over his palm and she slammed her left elbow into his solar plexus with a resounding *thwumpf*.

Alex cursed his amateur mistake of leaving her left arm free; he'd intended to be gentle in his warning. Her fist flew up at his nose, barely giving him a millisecond to stop it. He grabbed her forearm and saved his face, but she managed to get a handful of hair and yank for all she was worth.

The newscaster could fight.

He tightened his hold, squeezing her body against his and wrapping one leg around her calves. "Let go," he warned, shaking his head to loosen her grip on his long hair.

She pulled harder, then smashed a boot heel onto the top of his foot and crunched his toes.

Ignoring the pain, he swiped the foot she was balanced on and knocked her to her knees, going right to the floor with her. He used his right hand to break their fall, covering her whole body with his as they grappled to the carpet.

Her butt jutted into his stomach as she landed facedown. He finally managed to free his hair from her death grip and slid his hand back over her mouth to silence the inevitable scream. She obviously knew the basics of self-defense, which would make his job easier. As soon as she stopped practicing on him.

"I'm not going to hurt you."

She kicked a leg and grunted furiously, and he cupped his hand to avoid another bite. He pinned her legs under his, but she kept shoving her rear end up against his crotch as though that could push him off. He'd have to train her not to dilute her excellent self-defense skills by offering her ass to an attacker.

His groin tightened as she slammed her round backside into him one more time, and testosterone replaced the adrenaline rushing through him. *Carajo!* She'd never stop fighting if she felt a boner in her back.

"Hold still," he insisted, raising his body to lessen the contact that had suddenly become more arousing than aggressive. "I only wanted to show you how vulnerable you are."

She froze. *"Wh—what?"* Though the word was muffled by his hand, her indignation came through loud and clear.

"Sometimes a good scare can help you take a threat more seriously."

All the tension and steely defense dissolved as she went limp under him. Was that a trick? Could she be that good? It took years of training to learn how to stop the adrenaline dump and appear to drop your guard so your opponent did the same.

He didn't fall for it, but eased his hold on her.

"Listen to me," he whispered, surprised that his breath had quickened from that little bit of wrestling. "Someone who wants to hurt you could glide right by the boy downstairs, pick your lock, use the last four numbers of your social to disarm the alarm, and have a knife at your neck in a matter of minutes."

He could feel her whole body pulse with a rapid heartbeat, and fast breaths warmed his hand. Sex demons teased him again as he imagined those same responses for a different reason.

He eased back, removing his hand from her mouth, but ready for her to flip and fight again. "It only took me six minutes to get in here," he added, his tone completely unthreatening now. "Of course, I'm a professional. We don't know if your stalker is."

"What . . . are you talking about?" She turned her head toward him.

"I'm talking about your personal security liabilities."

He slowly inched to her right to try to make out her features in the darkness. "In your situation, you need to listen. And look. And get the doorman to escort you up here instead of sitting on his rear end reading *El Nuevo Herald*. And for God's sake, get a little creative on your alarm code."

Silver eyes flashed at him, giving him just enough warning to flatten his arm over her before she launched herself up. Instantly, all of the steel returned to her well-toned muscles, but he held her in place.

"Get off me," she ground out.

"Have you learned your lesson?"

"Yes," she whispered, her voice strained with effort as she tightened under his arm.

"And you believe I won't hurt you?"

"Yes," she insisted. "Let me up, damn it."

"Will you scream and attack me again?"

"Attack *you*?" She nearly choked at that.

"I'm demonstrating a point. You, on the other hand, are attempting to rip out my hair and break my foot."

"Excuse me, but you jumped me, asshole!"

Good, she wasn't afraid anymore, just mad. That made her a little safer. He eased off her and balanced on the balls of his feet before he stood to his full height. She stayed perfectly still on the ground, her head turned to watch him warily.

"I'll get the light," he said, sidestepping toward the living room without taking his eyes off her.

He knew exactly where the lamp was. He'd already scoured every inch of the apartment, searching for security flaws and learning that his principal was absurdly neat, had expensive taste in everything from clothes to art, and planned on marinated steak for dinner. He hoped he could change her opinion of him before she cooked it and refused to share.

As light bathed the room and she stood, he took his first long look at the newscaster.

The picture had not done her justice. It hadn't captured her . . . energy. There was something so alive about her, she seemed to glisten with vitality. Her eyes were like polished platinum, sparking at him. Her slanted cheekbones flushed as much from anger as a graze with the carpet. He'd smeared her lipstick with his palm, leaving her full lips stained and parted as she stared back at him, a dangerous combination of threatened and pissed off.

She placed her hands on her hips in a classic confrontational pose that accentuated the feminine, defined shape of her arms, and the rise and fall of her chest.

His gaze dropped over her tight ribbed top just long enough to confirm Lucy's assertion. They *were* real; he could tell by the softness of the flesh and the natural shape of her cleavage. He was, after all, an expert.

But something didn't fit. He'd just searched her closets and drawers, and nowhere had he seen evidence that she'd slide into a cotton undershirt and camos. Where had she been, dressed like that? Certainly not in front of the cameras, trilling about a bank robbery in Liberty City.

More likely committing one.

"Who the hell are you?" she demanded.

"Alex Romero. Mr. Parrish hired me."

She opened her mouth, and then closed it again.

"You did meet with Kimball Parrish today?" he prompted.

She shrugged and nodded, a mixture of such noncommitment that he almost laughed. "Briefly," she added.

It seemed a little silly after they'd had full horizontal body contact, but he extended his hand.

She took a step backward, her expression still dubious, refusing his handshake. "Alex Romero," she said slowly, as though flipping through a memory bank.

"Your bodyguard."

"My *what?*"

Son of a bitch. Parrish hadn't told her. He dropped his hand. "Mr. Parrish has arranged for personal security for you. Evidently he believes there is validity to the threats you've been receiving."

"Threats?"

Jesus, was she so immersed in her job that she didn't even consider the letters threatening? Doubtful, after that near pounding he just took. "Obviously you've bothered to learn a thing or two about self-defense already."

"Who hired you again?"

"Mr. Parrish."

She didn't react to the name. No light of recognition, no response to the mention of her new boss—one of the most powerful men in her business.

"Which threats are you referring to, exactly?" she asked, shoving her hands into the back pockets of her pants. A move that did nothing to lessen the impact of the skintight tank top. Still she didn't venture one step farther into the room.

"I'm referring to the letters you've received from a fan. Six, as far as I know. And several untraceable e-mails."

Her frown deepened. "How do I know *you're* not some kind of a stalker? And that's why you know all this? Not to mention your rather bizarre idea of a welcome. "

"You don't," he conceded. "But Mr. Parrish was supposed to have told you his decision to hire security today."

Still she didn't move. He waited for her to take control of her environment, to waltz past him and wrap herself in the familiarity of her home. She remained . . . cautious.

"As a matter of fact, he didn't tell me," she said. "And until I have that conversation with him, you'll have to leave."

"I'm afraid I can't do that."

She managed a tight smile. "Yes, you can. And it will be much simpler than all the trouble you took merely to scare the shit out of me and *make a point.*"

She stepped to the door, but he stopped her with a look. "I'm not leaving, Miss Adams."

"Excuse me?"

"Would you prefer I call you Jessica?"

She pointed to the door. "I'd prefer you get the hell out of here. Then I can call Kendall Parrish and discuss this with him."

Kendall? Her error set off a loud warning bell in his head. He took a step closer and her shoulders tensed visibly.

"Why don't you call him while I wait?" he suggested.

"No, I'll call him later. Then we can discuss this tomorrow."

"Please call him now, Miss Adams. This could be a matter of life and death."

"Can the drama. I'm perfectly safe here. . . . " Her voice faded into uncertainty. "Okay. I'll call him." She bent to retrieve her purse, but as she lifted the shoulder strap, the top opened, spewing out papers, makeup, a mirror, and roll of mints.

He crouched down and flipped his cell phone open for her. "Use mine."

She rose from the disarray and gave him another suspicious look, then studied the keypad as she punched in a number.

Why didn't she just pick up her cordless phone from the table in the living room?

She pressed his cell phone to her ear and looked away. "Hi. This is . . . Jessica. I need to talk to you. It's very important. Call me. On my cell." She snapped the phone shut with finality and handed it back to him. "If you just leave me a number where I can reach you, I'll call you after I've heard back from him. I'm sure you understand my reluctance to have a complete stranger in my home."

Nothing added up right. There was no way this woman would have misremembered the name of the man who'd recently bought her TV station. And she hadn't had a clue where to find the light switch or alarm pad when she'd walked in. Alex's gaze dropped once more over the revealing top, down to the black boots surrounded by the chaos of her handbag. Something was definitely wrong with this picture.

"Let me try him myself," he said as he flipped the phone open. "I have his private line."

He faked thumbing of a phone number, but simply pressed redial. He held her gaze while he listened to the taped message.

Hi. This is Jessica Adams. Please leave a message and I'll get right back to you.

"Well, what do you know," he said, dipping his head so close to hers he could almost kiss the smeared lipstick from her mouth. "I jumped the wrong Miss Adams."

CHAPTER
Two

He was so close that Jazz could see her reflection in his inky-colored pupils. Leave it to her to get assaulted by a guy who looked like Antonio Banderas, had the body of a personal trainer, and a mind like Sherlock Holmes.

"The wrong Miss Adams? I have no idea what you're talking about."

"Oh, yes you do."

"I can't imagine what you mean."

He pinned her with another black-eyed glare. "Where's Jessica?"

Good goddamn question. "I *am* Jessica."

"You *are* full of shit. You're her twin sister."

Jazz stifled a sigh of surrender. "What difference does it make who I am?"

"It makes a huge difference. Your sister isn't safe."

A sobering uneasiness spiraled through her. "How do you know that?"

"Because I've been hired to protect her. And someone

wouldn't go to that expense and trouble if the threats to her security weren't legitimate."

Damn it, he was right. "She never mentioned any threats to me."

He leaned against the back of a sofa that framed a magnificent living room, which Jazz hadn't even noticed yet. Her focus had been riveted on Alex Romero, and for good reason. There was just so much of him, and all of it so . . . riveting.

"Let's try this again," he said, a smile softening the angles of his face as he reached his hand toward her. "My name is Alex Romero. And you are . . . Jasmine Adams?"

This time, she shook his hand. His fingers were as long and strong as the rest of him, his palm warm. "Jazz. Are you a stalker or a bodyguard?"

He laughed softly as he let her hand go, then ran his fingers through the straight black hair that fell over his eyebrow and hung well past the collar of his black shirt. She'd had a handful of that hair, and it had reminded her of a thick, silky mane on a thoroughbred stallion.

"I am her personal security professional."

Only Jessica could win the Lottery of Bodyguards.

Jazz lifted her foot from the quagmire around her purse, and stepped past him. Time to check out the apartment instead of the man. "Do you always attack your client?"

"Principal," he corrected.

She felt his gaze follow her as she took in the utter whiteness of the vast living room, uncluttered but for a few choice pieces of Jessica's collection of precious antique glass bowls and decanters. The cranberry-colored

Victorian candy basket that Jazz had sent for their last birthday enjoyed a place of honor at the middle of a coffee table.

"I told you," he said, "I was trying to make a point."

She walked toward the sliding doors to the breathtaking nightscape of downtown Miami and the lights winking on Biscayne Bay. "There are easier ways," she said. "Like telling someone they are in danger. That really cuts down on the physical strain."

"I wasn't strained."

She cut him with a menacing look. "You're just lucky I left my weapon at home."

He chuckled, and she bridled.

"I'm a licensed private investigator, qualified to carry and not afraid to use. The only reason I don't have my gun on me is that my sister is terrified of them. So I agreed to leave it at home."

He seemed more surprised than impressed. "A private investigator? I don't remember reading that."

Uneasiness rolled through her. How much did he know about *both* the Adams sisters? "Then maybe you don't have all your facts, Mr. Romero."

Of course, even a thorough background check might not reveal that she'd hung her own PI shingle six weeks ago. The year before that, she hadn't technically been on anyone's payroll, even though she'd helped Elliott on at least twenty cases.

"A PI, huh?" He moved into the room and dropped onto the sofa, creating a contrast of long dark hair, ebony eyes, olive skin, and jet black clothing against the white silk. Six feet two of solid bad-guy black.

"Is that why you're here?" he asked. "To investigate? Or is it a social visit?"

"I'm here to visit my sister." *And pretend to be her for a week or so.*

What if this guy was in cahoots with one of Jessica's competitors, trying to beat her to whatever story she was working on? The secrecy of Jessica's project was key to its success; that was why she had to disappear without any-one knowing, and the reason she needed Jazz as a secret stand-in.

"So where is she?"

"She said she'd be home after the six o'clock newscast. I expected her by seven thirty. It's almost nine now."

"Doesn't she have to be back in the studio by ten?" He leaned forward and picked up the candy basket, its delicate scalloped edges looking out of place in his pow-erful hands. He gently set it back on the table as though he realized how fragile it was and wanted no part of handling it.

"She arranged to have someone cover the eleven o'clock newscast tonight, so she could be with me," Jazz said. "How do you know so much about her schedule?"

"I have a complete dossier on my principal," he said. She could have sworn she heard the softest lilt of an accent in his speech. *Romero.* In Miami, of course, the majority of the population was Latin. "That's the way we do business," he added.

"Who's *we*?"

"My employer."

"This Parrish guy?"

"*Kimball* Parrish." He emphasized the first name, and she cringed at the obvious mistake she'd made. "Your sister has never mentioned him?" He sounded doubtful.

Sliding into a creamy club chair across from him, she closed her eyes and visualized the e-mails and messages. A photographic memory was a great asset for a person who spent 90 percent of her day tracking down obscure computer data. It saved on printer paper and ink.

"No, but I've heard the name."

He leaned forward, a slight crease in his forehead. "She never mentioned that her television station had been recently acquired by Adroit Broadcasting Group?"

"Of course she has," Jazz replied. "She was over the moon when Adroit bought the station. WMFL is a Metro-Net affiliate and now that Adroit owns the station, Jess is certain that Yellowstone—the conglomerate that owns the network—will want to keep Adroit happy and pay more attention to the Miami station."

Whatever story Jessica was working on, it was one that would get her noticed by the higher ups at Adroit and Yellowstone. That had been clear from her e-mails. "So who's Parrish?" she asked.

"The owner of Adroit."

"The *owner*?" Jazz raised both eyebrows. "The guy that just bought her TV station hired a bodyguard for Jess because of an overzealous fan?"

"This one's gone past overzealous. As I said, Jessica has been receiving threatening letters."

Jazz shook her head. "That's so weird. She never mentioned that to me."

"Are you close?"

A pang of guilt shimmied through her. They certainly loved each other, but distance and differences had taken their toll. "We're close enough that she'd tell me about a threatening fan."

"Maybe she didn't want to worry you."

"That's possible," she agreed. "She's pretty self-sufficient." Which was why Jazz had jumped at the opportunity to be the one providing assistance for a change.

"Something is keeping your sister," he said. "Have you considered all the possibilities?"

"Jessica's late, that's all." Even as she said it, a clammy finger of apprehension clutched her. The words *Jessica* and *late* didn't occupy the same sentence. "If she thought it was something to worry about, she would have told me."

"Has Jessica recently broken up with someone?"

"On the contrary," Jazz said without thinking.

He raised his eyebrows, interested. "She's dating someone?" Was that another fact that didn't make it into his dossier?

"I don't know how serious it is." But she could visualize the words Jessica had written not so long ago. *I've met someone amazing, Jazz. He could change my life. He's smart, connected, and, best of all, he has a heart of gold.* The "best of all" part had really stuck with her.

"What about work? Is she working on anything in particular?"

"Actually, yes." Jazz said. "And I'm sure that's why I can't get hold of her. She'd turn her phone off during an interview with a source."

"A source for what?"

He asked entirely too many questions. That was *her* job. "I thought bodyguards stood at the door with their arms crossed, listening to an ear transmitter."

He grinned. "Not the one you got."

"Me?" She laughed. "I don't need a bodyguard, pal. I think I've proven that I can defend myself."

"I had you on the floor in three seconds."

"You couldn't have kept me there."

"You were pinned and . . . writhing."

The way he said it sent a rush of heat to her face. "I was not writhing. I was defending myself."

His gaze slid down her body, doing nothing to cool off the hot flash. "Remind me to teach you how to disengage, not stimulate, your attacker."

She'd *stimulated* him? Her throat went dry and she pushed herself out of the chair. "Consider yourself disengaged, Mr. Alex Romero. Nice of you to come and protect my sister, but since she's not here and I don't need you, why don't you mosey along now? I'm sure she'll show up any minute and if not, I can track her down. I'm pretty good at that; I do it for a living."

"I've been hired to be here." He crossed his ankles and spread his arms across the back of the sofa.

"So you said. When Jessica gets in, I'll have her people call your people and if she agrees, you can protect her. Although I have to warn you, she probably won't want you any more than I do."

He just stared at her, a teasing little smile pulling at his lips.

"I mean, she won't want your services." Jeez, the guy was distracting just sitting there. Imagine if she had him on top of her again. "Well." She stuffed her hands deep into her pockets. "Good-bye."

"I'm not leaving."

God save her from macho control freaks. "Yes, you are."

"No, I'm not." He gave her a nearly imperceptible shake of his head, just enough for one shiny lock to almost cover his eye. God *really* save her from macho control freaks with great hair. "I'm either going to find her, or wait here for her."

"All right. Let's find her." She glanced around the room. "Let's start with her computer. I bet she keeps her calendar on it."

"She has a laptop on the dresser in her bedroom." He stood and towered over her.

"Have you been through this whole apartment?"

"Would you like a tour?"

Before she could answer, the phone on the end table rang. Thank God. Jazz swooped over and picked it up. "Hello?"

"Where the frick *were* you tonight?"

The man's question and tone sent a shiver through her. "I'm sorry, who is this?"

"It's me, Ollie." He sounded put off that she wouldn't know. Could this be Mr. Amazing? All Jess had said was that there was someone new, someone special.

"Are you sick or something?" he demanded. "Why didn't you call when you couldn't come in for the six o'clock?"

Another shiver went through her. Her sister had missed a newscast? Never. "What happened?"

"Are you kidding? Jon Boy stepped in faster than we

could change the TelePrompTer. I gotta go; we're getting the chopper out to a small plane crash in the Everglades. But listen: Metro-Net is knocking, and I think it's in your best interest to be the one who answers the door. Just in case, you know?"

"What do you mean?"

"They've scheduled a live satellite feed with Rodriguez on *American Sunrise,* but he doesn't want to do a video-hosted interview. He wants a real person across from him asking questions. Enter Jessica Adams, eh?"

American Sunrise was Metro-Net's hot new national morning show in New York—the one that still needed a permanent anchor. But who was Rodriguez, and where *was* Jessica? "What exactly is the segment?"

"They asked the mayor to talk about the Latin American global conference that starts here next week. I don't care if you have flippin' appendicitis. Get your can over here tomorrow morning before Jon Boy sets up camp in the studio, all right?"

What would Jessica say? "Of course I'll be there."

"You up to speed on the conference?"

"I'll need some more information." Like what the hell it was. "Could you get me some background?"

"I'll e-mail you a link right now. You'll need about five hard-hitting questions. Keep it global, not local. Forget the Miami impact, think world economy, U.S. trade with Latin America, blah blah blah. You've got three minutes. They're running it as the second segment after the seven o'clock news. Get here an hour early. We go live at seven sixteen."

"A.M?" she almost croaked.

He laughed. "Very funny, doll. See you then."

As Jazz hung up the phone, her gaze shifted to the bodyguard, who'd moved closer to her to hear the conversation.

"So she didn't make the six o'clock broadcast either," he said simply.

Good God, could something have happened to Jessica? Otherwise why would she miss a broadcast, and not call when she knew Jazz would be here waiting for her?

"She'll be here any minute," she insisted. "Because she has to be at the studio tomorrow morning for a chance to be on network TV."

Another possibility suddenly took shape. Jessica had said her window of opportunity was brief, that she'd have to do her story research as soon as Jazz arrived. She must be interviewing a source earlier than planned—that had to be the answer.

"What if she *isn't* here any minute?" Alex asked.

Jazz swallowed. "Then I'm interviewing Mayor Rodriguez on network television tomorrow morning at seven sixteen A.M."

Alex cooked the steak himself. It was nearly eleven and by then, Jazz Adams had demonstrated an array of personal skills from brilliant deductive reasoning to some impressive hacking techniques using a laptop she'd retrieved, along with some luggage, from her rental car. However, nothing indicated she was interested in cooking.

Sitting cross-legged and barefoot on her sister's bed, she looked up from an open laptop when he tapped on the door announcing dinner.

"I'm not hungry," she answered.

"Then sit with me and we'll go over what we have so far."

"We have nothing," she replied. "No calendar, no information, no leads. In the meantime, I have to chat intelligently with the mayor tomorrow." She scooped her hair into a tousled auburn mess. "Did you know that Bolivia may be sitting on the second biggest natural gas reserves in the whole hemisphere?"

"Are you serious?"

"And yet the people are convinced they have no resources."

"I meant are you serious about doing this interview."

She gave him a "get real" look. "That's the whole reason I'm here: to pretend to be Jessica." She tapped a few keys, closed the laptop, and bounded off the bed in one graceful move. "I guess I could eat something. What did you make?"

"Your sister left steak and salad. For two. Which leads me to believe she expected to be home tonight to entertain you." He placed one arm on the doorjamb to block her way. "What do you mean, you're here to pretend to be Jessica?"

She ducked under his arm and slipped past him. "I'm covering for her while she does something else."

He watched her walk away. The loose military pants did nothing to diminish the sway of her backside. When she disappeared around the corner, he followed.

He had to remember whom he'd been hired to protect. If Jessica Adams was doing "something else," then so was he. "What will she be doing while you cover for her?"

"She's working on a special project." She stood in the dining room alcove, surveying the table. "You made this? Just now?"

"Your sister did most of the preliminary work. And the table was already set."

She looked up, a little surprised, when he pulled out a chair for her. "She's too much, isn't she? Talented, successful, respected, and she can cook."

"That was mentioned in her dossier. But it didn't indicate that she was on a special project. In fact, I got the impression she never did any investigative reporting." He sat next to her.

"She doesn't. And that's why this one is important." Lifting a glass of ice water, she made a mock toast. "To our missing hostess."

"She left two wineglasses out, all ready for action," he said. "But no wine."

She shrugged and shook out a linen napkin. "Listen, I don't mean to sound callous, but my sister's a big girl and she's working on a hush-hush story. If some wacko was really scaring her, she'd have told me. I know that like I know my name. She would never have suggested I stand in for her if she thought it would put either of us in danger."

Alex cut his steak. "I should think having a novice stand in for an interview televised all over the country would qualify as dangerous—to her career."

"We weren't expecting network time," she said, without a note of defense in her voice. "But I can do it. I've done television news before."

"I thought you were a PI."

"I am. Now." She flicked the salad with her fork. "Look at this junk. The lettuce in California is way better." Selecting a cherry tomato, she continued, "I decided to put my investigative skills to work in a different field. But I did TV reporting and news up until a year ago."

"In San Francisco? That's a sizeable market."

She smiled. "In Fresno. Not such a sizeable market."

"Why did you quit?"

"I sucked at it."

He looked questioningly at her. "Yet you think you can handle your sister's job?"

"I didn't suck on the air," she said. "I sucked at the politics. So I got involved with a start-up PI firm, and found I really liked the business. Much better than all that backstabbing in TV news. And that was in a tiny market." She took a bite and waved her empty fork toward the view of Miami while she chewed. "I can only imagine what goes on in a place like this."

"Your sister doesn't tell you?"

She shrugged. "She's so far past that stuff. I mean, she blew through every lower level job in television. In the time I went from Lubbock—now *there* was a dump—to Fresno, she propelled herself through four markets and ended up in Miami in the top anchor job."

"Then she must have made some enemies along the way. Perhaps her 'stalker' isn't a fan, but a jealous coworker."

"It's hard to hate Jess. Trust me, I've tried."

He couldn't help but smile at her honesty. "You're identical twins, correct?"

She grinned. "Yep. Same DNA. Proof positive that

ambition and discipline are not programmed in the gene code."

He had no idea how ambitious she was, but no one studied self-defense that thoroughly without discipline. "Why does she need a stand-in? Isn't working on a story part of her job?"

"If anybody at the station got wind of it, she could lose the exclusivity and ownership of the story. If I show up as Jessica, no one knows she's off investigating."

"Surely someone at the station knows. Her supervisor? A news director?" She couldn't be working in a complete vacuum. That didn't make sense.

"I don't know," Jazz said. "In her last e-mail, she was adamant that I not tell anyone who I am. Whatever she's discovered, she thinks it'll guarantee her national exposure, which is what she wants. And she doesn't get a lot of support for investigative reporting. They want her in the studio, looking perfect, reading news somebody else wrote and being the 'face of Channel Five.'"

"Doesn't sound very challenging."

"It's not. That's why she wants to get to network." She rolled her eyes. "Speaking of challenging, I hope tomorrow morning's interview is not."

"You'll be figured out in five minutes," he predicted.

"Thanks for the vote of confidence, Romero."

Alex set down his fork and pushed the chair back on two legs, releasing a long sigh. He had no idea where the principal was, and he could very well end up protecting the wrong sister. How the hell would he explain this to Lucy? "The whole thing is juvenile, if you ask me."

She sliced him with a silvery gaze. "I didn't ask you."

"You don't think anyone who works with her won't figure out that you're not her? It didn't take me very long."

"You caught me off guard."

He let the chair hit the ground. "That was the idea."

She rested her elbows on the table and watched him cut another piece of steak. "I don't suppose I can get rid of you by tomorrow morning."

Now, *there* was something he didn't hear often from a beautiful woman. "Why would you want to? Jessica's boss hired personal protection for her. If she shows up at work without a bodyguard in tow, won't Parrish know something's up? If you are hellbent on keeping this secret, you better think more deviously." He deliberately let his gaze drop over that lovely cleavage. "And you'll have to do a wardrobe makeover."

She didn't flinch or blush under his gaze. "Does that mean you'll go along with this?"

He wiped his mouth with a napkin as he considered the consequences. If he announced to Lucy that he had no real principal, Parrish might pull him off the assignment. With the current shakiness of his job security, he didn't want to create any white water. "For the time being. I've been hired to protect Jessica Adams. I'm most interested in finding her. At her office, I might be able to figure out where she is."

"I don't think it would be appropriate for her bodyguard to dig through her desk and computer files."

"No, but you can." He eyed her untouched plate. All she'd eaten was a few bites of the limp salad. "What's the story she's after?"

"I don't know." At his skeptical look, she added, "Really, she didn't tell me. Just that it was mega-juicy and breakthrough."

"If it's network attention she craves, you'd think nothing could keep her from tomorrow morning's opportunity to interview the mayor of Miami on *American Sunrise.* Doesn't that worry you?"

She dropped her chin onto her knuckles and flashed him a fake smile. "Do you live to be the devil's advocate?"

"Someone has to." He pointed to her steak. "Aren't you going to eat that?"

"I'd love to, but I really don't like it."

He nodded, his own plate still full. "For a gourmet cook, she overmarinated."

Jazz shook her head, a slight frown on her face. "So, tell me about this crazy fan. Have you seen these letters she's received?"

He stood and headed into the guest bedroom, where he'd left his bag and files. "I'll get the copies of the letters and show you."

While she put the dishes in the sink, he spread six letters over the counter. Wiping her hands on a towel, she glanced at them. "I was picturing words cut out of magazines, all different sizes, like in the movies."

Alex stepped behind her, trapping her between him and the counter, forcing her to stop and read the words. "These were generated on a computer. Standard font. Standard printer. Standard ink. Same for the envelopes. Postmark was downtown Miami, the same zip code as the TV station."

Her body fit right into his, the memory of her derriere

pumping against him still fresh. He concentrated on the letters instead of the warmth of her female curves.

The notes were short, no more than a few lines, but each one grew more ominous. The first one read, "I love to watch you," then the author moved to "You turn me on," and "I have to taste you." The last letter was the most explicit. "I'm going to fuck you while you scream at my camera."

Alex waited for her to recoil, but she just nudged the letter away and pivoted to face him.

"That's a relief," she announced. Her breasts were inches from his chest. She looked right up into his eyes and practically dared him to back away.

He didn't move. "A *relief*?"

"It's not exactly the fan mail you want, but not really vicious. This wouldn't set Jessica into a fear frenzy. She'd be on her guard, sure, but a television personality is a prime target for losers who sit at home and jerk off to the local news." She placed one finger on his chest, pushed him back, and walked away. "We've had worse than this, both of us. That's why she didn't tell me."

The phone rang again, and he grabbed her arm to keep her from answering. "Let's see who it is. It might give us a clue to where she is."

"Are you crazy?" She tugged from his grip. "It could be Jess."

"Then you can pick up." He knew an audio recorder was built into the cordless phone; he'd heard it ring earlier. And now he knew whose voice he'd heard while he waited in the dark, who had demanded Jessica to pick up.

After a digital tone, there was a second of staticky

silence. Jazz glared at him, but he just shook his head. "Wait. Listen."

"Hi, um, it's me." He knew immediately that it wasn't Jessica; the feminine voice was tinged with too much timidity to be a newscaster. "Sorry about tonight. Listen, I did get some more. And I think these will have what you're looking for. At the, um, end, you know? I'll wait for you to call me so we can meet again."

Another beep ended the connection.

Jazz seized the phone and peered at the digital read-out. "It was a pay phone. I can probably find it, though."

"Why did she say 'sorry about tonight'?" he mused.

She shrugged. "Maybe she didn't have the information Jessica needed when they met."

"Or maybe they didn't meet. Maybe Jessica was tied up. . . ." He waited until she looked at him expectantly. "By her stalker."

She waved toward the letters like she was swiping cobwebs away. "Trust me, that bullshit is not going to keep Jessica in hiding. I can't believe the station would hire protection for something as inconsequential as that."

"Inconsequential or not, I'm not going anywhere until we find her."

"Fine. She'll show up or call any minute. Until she does, don't forget, I'm not your principal. I don't need protection."

"Too bad. You're getting it."

Denise Rutledge hung up the pay phone and watched a Hialeah patrolman circle the perimeter of the secluded park, cruising for kids who'd climb the fence and swim in the public pool. When his headlights were safely aimed in the opposite direction, she pulled her backpack a little tighter and walked to her car, cursing herself for trusting that newslady. And for starting her stupid message with "sorry."

Why did she always take the blame? Out of habit, probably. She had nothing to be sorry for. She'd been right across from the racetrack, like they'd planned. Waiting, like a fool. Getting totally blown off by Jessica Adams.

The newscaster had been all sweetness and honey the first few times they'd met, all sympathetic to the cause and shit. But she'd gotten all she'd wanted from Denise; or else she'd have made their meeting tonight.

All that bullshit about following her around with a camera to get an "insider's" view. Puhlease.

Sliding into the ancient Plymouth Reliant, Denise grabbed a Marlboro and cupped her hands to light it. She'd been an idiot to think that newslady was going to help her, to help any of them.

Visibility will help your cause. You have rights.

What a crock of shit. She'd have said anything to get her hands on that stuff, and Denise, like a complete moron, had handed it over without getting a fucking dime. Now the bitch probably had everything she needed to take down half the residents of Cocoplum, and win some kind of news Oscar in the process.

And all Denise got was stood up. The priss probably thought she'd get cooties just being so close to someone who did what Denise did for a living.

She should have taken money the first time they

met—then she'd at least have something. Her ass was grass if Howie Carpenter ever found out what she'd lifted from that warehouse. She'd always been so damn careful never to break a law. Nothing she'd done so far was illegal . . . except stealing company property.

Blowing out a long puff, she flicked the butt out the window. That phony bitch had held Denise's hand, looked her in the eyes and acted like, well, like they were connected somehow. And Denise, like a blubbering fool, had told her about Grady and how she couldn't get custody of him until she had insurance.

Denise threw the backpack behind her, where it crunched an empty Big Mac container. Damn, she shouldn't have eaten that crap while she was waiting for Adams. All that salt would show tomorrow.

Tonight she'd have to take a laxative and a water pill. She shook her head at the shit she was willing to do just to look good and keep her lousy job. But it was the only way to get back to Minnesota before her boy was all grown up and didn't give a rip about having a mother. The thought made the greasy food roll in her stomach.

She glanced back toward the Hialeah Park Racetrack one more time, but there was no sign of the woman who'd promised to meet her there.

Jessica Adams didn't understand what it was like to scrape and crawl and beg for basic human rights. And she sure as hell didn't understand what it felt like to have your son ripped from your arms.

Well she'd just lost herself a fan. And her *exclusive* little story.

CHAPTER
Three

The bed dipped with the weight of a body and Jazz curled toward the warmth, lost in the quiet blackness of sleep. She heard her name whispered, felt her cheek feathered with a fingertip's touch.

She nuzzled into the hand, unwilling to climb out of the depth of her dream. *Touch me.* She tried to say the words, but all she managed was a soft moan from her throat.

Fingers tunneled into the hair at the back of her neck, sending a spray of delicious sparks over her skin. Beautiful, heavy sleep mixed with the first easy wave of arousal and she arched into the pleasure, wanting to drown in sleep and sex. She wanted both. She needed both. Deep, fierce, intense sex, and endless, dreamless sleep.

"Ahora no, querida. Despiértate."

That powerful hand slid over her shoulder, down her arm. She rose to meet it, to brush her breast against his fingertips. Lost in the dream, she laid her hand over his, guiding him to her aching nipple. Pleasure shot through her, sending heat between her legs. She lifted her hips at the sound of sweet, soft laughter.

"Despiértate, querida." The exotic sound intensified the warmth low inside her, pulling at her.

What did that mean? Desperate? Of course, she was. She stretched again, another plea rumbling in her throat. Breath warmed her face and she turned toward it, to kiss the mouth that spoke such sweet, sexy words. A silky strand of hair tickled her cheek and the strong hand closed over her breast. She could see his hand in her dream. Narrow, long, tanned fingers poised to tweak her swollen nipple.

She opened her mouth for a kiss.

"Jazz, you're going to be late."

She was *always* late. She sucked in a breath of frustration, the fog dissipating just as the hand abandoned her breast.

"God, I hate you, Lucy," he whispered.

Lucy? No. *Wake me in Spanish, Alex.*

Alex?

Awareness punched her awake and she jerked, her limbs tingling from a double shot of indignity and lust. She blinked at the size and closeness of him in the shadows. The bodyguard in black.

She yanked the silk comforter over the sheer nightgown she'd taken from Jessica's drawer. "What are you doing?"

"Trying to wake you up." He picked up a travel clock next to her bed. "This thing finally gave up after ten minutes of beeping. I waited, but you were comatose."

Had she dreamed he touched her? Or . . . had he? The idea shot more liquid through her veins.

"Did you just speak Spanish?"

"Sí, señorita."

"What did you say?"

"Despiértate. Wake up."

"What else?" Had he touched her? And, good Lord, could she have enjoyed it any more?

He leaned over her and a lock of his long hair brushed her cheek, feeling just as sensuous and erotic as it had in her dream. "Estás tan rica que te quiero comer," he whispered.

A toe-curling shiver cascaded over her body. "What does that mean?"

"You're going to be late for the mayor."

Somehow, she doubted that was a literal translation. "No word from Jessica?"

He shook his head, the teasing glimmer in his dark eyes suddenly gone. "I tried her cell phone again. Still getting voice mail."

"What time is it?"

"Five thirty. You promised to be at the studio by six."

She gave a frustrated moan. "Five thirty is inhuman. I hate waking up."

His smile was shameless. "I could tell."

Despite the heat that rushed through her, she pulled the comforter higher and forced her eyes to adjust to the predawn darkness. "I don't know where the studio is," she said, seizing on any change of subject. "Do you?"

"I grew up here. I know every street in Miami."

So he was probably Cuban. That explained the Spanish. *Estás tan rica que te quiero comer.* She could feel the mysterious words warm against her ear. "Are we very far?"

"About ten minutes or so." He strode across the room to the walk-in closet. For a large man, every move was as graceful and loose-limbed as a panther. "You have time to take a shower and dress."

Dress? Her heart tumbled a little. She was supposed to have tried on Jessica's anchor wardrobe last night. They'd planned that she and Jess would share a bottle of wine, pick clothes, go through a list of who's who at the station and practice for this charade. It was going to be fun, a little wild and crazy, but not . . . dangerous.

It certainly hadn't involved a whispering Latin lover. Or a predawn network satellite feed. Where the *hell* was her sister?

"Shit," she mumbled.

"Does that mean you don't like it?" He held out a yellow tailored suit, as bright as the sun.

She curled her lip. "It's so *Jessica.*"

He lifted his other arm, offering her a royal blue number with an Oriental collar and embroidered frog buttons. "More like you?"

Oh, please. She shook her head.

He went back into the closet and returned with a straight, short-sleeved khaki sheath. A tag dangled from the side and he flipped it over for her to see. "Here you go. Never been worn." He threw it on the bed.

Indignation prickled at her. "Thank you very much, but I don't need a personal valet to pick my clothes."

He started to the door and threw a look over his

shoulder. "If it weren't for me, you'd still be moaning in your sleep."

Damn him. "I'm awake now, so you can leave."

When the door closed, she picked up the dress and looked at the Neiman Marcus tag. *Café au lait. Size six.*

Nah. If she was going to be Jessica, she had to really look the part. She went directly to the closet and snatched the yellow suit.

Jazz wanted to resent the presence of a bodyguard at her side as she sailed through the reception area of WMFL, but part of her was eternally grateful. Not only did he know his way around Miami, driving a badass Cadillac Escalade with a nifty GPS system in the dash, he also magically produced a printed layout of the station and the newsroom, with proper names in each office and a list of key individuals who worked there. A "service of his company."

It was as much a godsend as the heavy-duty espresso in a plastic shot glass he bought her at a sandwich shop. By the time she stepped into the cavernous two-story newsroom, she was as awake as she'd ever been at this contemptible hour, and had memorized nearly every name in the Channel Five newsroom. She also knew where the offices were, and which one she should call home.

It was no surprise that Jessica had one of the few glassed-in offices that surrounded the giant pit of workstations where the writers, reporters, and producers toiled away. An anchor at a TV station this size would be the Queen Bee. Jess's office was in the back corner, right next to someone by the name of Jonathan Walden. Could that be "Jon Boy"—the person who'd replaced Jessica last night?

She'd skimmed the list for Ollie, the man who'd called last night, and found an Assignment Manager named Oliver Jergen. That meant he ran the assignment desk, the main artery of the newsroom. In this ultra-modern facility, the "desk" was a centrally located circle of gleaming wood and technology, currently managed by a tall, lanky man in his thirties, with shaggy blond hair and Hollywood stubble.

As Jazz approached, he looked up and his hazel eyes widened in surprise.

"Jessie!" he exclaimed. "I can't believe you would ever put that on again after the lemon drop comment."

She recognized his voice as the man she'd talked to last night. "Always want to keep you guessing," she said with her very best Jessica smile.

His gaze shifted to her right and he raised his eyebrows in question. "And you are? . . ."

"This is Alex Romero." She made a concerted effort to keep her voice at the lower, slower inflection that Jessica had learned from an overpriced voice coach. She'd taught Jazz for free.

"Are you with the mayor's PR staff?"

Right. As if he looked like a flack from City Hall. "It seems the PTB have decided I need a bodyguard," Jazz explained.

The man's eyebrows lifted in another surprised expression. The two men shook hands and exchanged names, confirming her guess that he was Oliver Jergen.

Oliver pointed a finger to the second floor, toward an entrance to far more private offices. "Just so happens that those same Powers That Be decided to come in early to watch your network interview. Mr. Parrish was so pleasantly surprised that you nailed the assignment that he decided to come in and give you moral support."

Just what she needed—the station owner watching her performance. "Then I'll have to be flawless."

Ollie rolled his eyes. "He sure seems to find plenty of excuses to stay in Miami. Don't they need him up in New York?"

She shrugged, hoping it was a rhetorical question. "I better go over the interview I've prepared."

"Yvonne'll be here to do you at six thirty," he said, raking her with a look that could be teasing or insulting, depending on the nature of their friendship. "Looks like you could use her magic concealer."

Without thinking, she touched under her eyes. It was three A.M. West Coast time, and she hadn't bothered with makeup; she knew a professional would be here for her.

"Nice of you to notice," she said with the light sarcasm she'd heard from her sister a million times, and continued to her office. Her shadow, naturally, was right behind her.

"You can wait out here," she said to Alex at the office door. "I can't escape."

He shook his head and opened the glass door, holding it for her. "You have to go through the computer files and tell me what you find."

"First I have to interview the mayor of Miami on network TV," she answered in a hushed whisper as they entered. "Give me some space, will you?"

"Nervous?" he asked as he closed the door behind them.

"Just preoccupied, and I don't need you breathing down my neck." *Like you did in my bed this morning.*

He took a chair across from her desk, adjusting it so that he could observe the newsroom through the glass walls. "Boot up your computer as fast as you can," he instructed. "See if you can find her calendar and address book. I want both printed out."

She switched on Jessica's computer and it whirred to life. Her sister's desk was as immaculate as her home. A neat stack of file folders on one side, an antique glass container holding some pens, a notebook open to a blank page, paper clips, tape, a few business cards, a stack of unopened mail, and two framed pictures.

While Alex perused the business cards, Jazz studied the pictures.

One showed their parents twenty-fifth wedding anniversary in Hawaii. Jazz had that picture, too, somewhere. Looking at it made her heart twist a little. Jessica was so good about keeping in touch with them, sending little packages and gifts, and e-mailing Dad since he retired from the university. Jazz hadn't been home to Chicago in four years.

The other snapshot was of Jessica and Jazz together, waving their diplomas from Northwestern's Medill School of Journalism.

Jazz grabbed the frame with a little gasp. Who here knew that Jessica had an identical twin? Although they looked very different in the picture—Jazz's hair flying

well past her shoulders and Jessica's in a neat little bob—
it made her uneasy.

"What is it?" Alex asked, immediately alert.

"A picture of the two of us." She pulled open the bottom file drawer and slid it in the back. Turning to the
computer, her prayers were answered when there was no
password to contend with.

"The address book," he reminded her.

"Give me a second." She clicked away, finally finding a
version of Outlook and an intracompany address book.

"I want the personal stuff, contacts and sources," he
said, leaning over to watch the screen. "And see if she
keeps another calendar here."

Damn, he was demanding. He reminded her of her
ex-boyfriend, the way he barked orders at her. Elliott
Sandusky had elevated control to an art form—but the
resemblance ended there. Elliott was blue eyed, blond
haired, uptight, and lily white. And suddenly that
seemed incredibly . . . unsexy—even though Elliott had
been a perfectly satisfying lover. A pain in the ass boss
and a suffocating boyfriend, but he generally got the job
done in bed.

"What are you waiting for?" Alex asked. "There's a
personal address book right there."

She stabbed the enter key and shot him another dirty
look. "Let me remind you *again* that investigation is my
job. I don't need your help." Unless she was sitting there
comparing former lovers to him. Then, she evidently did.

"Here it is." Jessica's entire address book flashed on
the screen. "With every entry complete and up to date.
God love that woman."

"Print it." He settled back into his seat. "And brace yourself, here comes your new boss."

Across the newsroom, the second most handsome man she'd seen that day strode toward them with the raw determination of a hunter. Although he had a powerful build, a flawlessly attractive face, and a smile that teeth whitening companies could use for commercials, it was the possessive gleam in his slate blue eyes that told Jazz exactly who he was. She was about to meet her sister's Mr. Amazing.

Kimball Parrish whipped open the office door and wasted no time claiming his turf.

"I love you in that color." He barely spared a glance at Alex, his gaze locked on his female prey; he all but pissed in the doorway to stake his claim. "Remember what I said last time you wore it?"

Something about a lemon drop, Alex guessed as he stood to offer a handshake to his client. "Pleasure to meet you, Mr. Parrish. Alex Romero."

He nodded, finally giving Alex a brief flash of attention. "Don't let her out of your sight unless I tell you, Romero. Not for one minute."

"I don't plan to, sir."

Dismissing him, Parrish turned back to Jazz, who had copped a remarkably cool demeanor. She stayed in her chair, relaxed yet watchful. A confident woman who knew at least one man in the room had serious hots for her. She tipped her head at an angle that accentuated the upward tilt of her blue-gray eyes, a clever little smile on her face. She suddenly looked softer, more ladylike.

"No need to worry," she said with a charming laugh. "I can't shake him off even to prepare for a network interview." Her voice was modulated, practiced, even a touch raspier.

Holy shit, she'd just become a different woman. *Alex, meet Jessica.*

Parrish turned to him. "Give us a few minutes, Romero."

Even though he wanted to witness the exchange, Alex moved to the door. "I'll be right outside if you need me."

On the other side of her door, he couldn't make out their words, but he noted that Parrish settled one hip on the corner of Jessica's desk. Friendly, but oddly formal. He hasn't been in her bed yet, Alex decided. Maybe he thinks hiring a full-time bodyguard will melt her heart.

How had he found himself in this low-level position, protecting the *wrong* person? With the man actually footing the bill for his high-end services just five feet away, holding a conversation with an *imposter*?

Jesus, what a mess.

Had Lucy ever fired a Bullet Catcher? Perhaps. There was a lot of mystery in her organization, but black ops came naturally to the woman at its head. He didn't know if she'd make good on her subtle threats and didn't want to find out. The loss of Lucy's generous paychecks would mean the end of a hefty, steady stream of illegal cash to a wretched little fishing village just ninety miles from here.

Not that he would ever tell his ex–CIA agent boss that he needed his job so he could continue breaking federal embargo laws. All he wanted to do was remain indispensable to her, and keep that cash headed to San Tomás, Cuba.

From here he could easily observe Oliver Jergen, whose attention shifted constantly from a police radio to several two-way communications systems firing calls and information at him. Jergen threw a few looks Alex's way as well.

A tall, dark-haired man talking on a cell phone sauntered up to Jergen's circular stage and paused, his suspicious gaze falling on Alex.

"Hey, Ollie, who's that?" he asked, snapping the phone shut with an air of self-importance.

"Jessica has a bodyguard now."

The other man snorted. "Why don't they just hire a team of professionals to floss her teeth and wipe her backside?"

"Don't let that green-eyed monster blind you, Jonathan," Oliver said. "You'll be the top dog when she goes to New York."

"Hell, we could all go to New York if we were willing to suck Kimball Parrish's dick."

Oliver glanced at Alex, who kept his eyes straight ahead as if carefully watching the crew hustling around the studio set at the other end of the newsroom. "You could give it a shot, Jon. I hear he's an equal opportunity prick."

"I'll pass." Jonathan slipped his phone into his pocket. "Never let it be said that Jonathan Walden didn't earn his stripes the old-fashioned way. When I need a promotion, I fuck a woman."

Oliver laughed and handed over a piece of paper. "Here are the A.M. crew assignments. And what the hell are you doing here at this hour, anyway? Our first live update isn't until three-thirty this afternoon."

"You think I'd miss a network feed?" Jonathan jutted his chin toward Jessica's office but kept his gaze on the paper in front of him. "Plus, you never know when La Primadonna is even going to show up for work, now that she can smell the big time. I have to be here—it's the curse of the understudy."

With an unfriendly look at Alex, Jonathan proceeded to the office next to the one where Jazz sat.

Evidently Jessica Adams had a few enemies, after all.

On the other side of the glass, he heard Jazz let out a raspy laugh, a little deeper than anything he'd heard from her so far. Unable to resist, he shifted his position to see into the room.

Parrish's whole body leaned toward her, as if he could just inch forward without warning to plant one on her pretty mouth. Jazz—*Jessica*—was animated as she flirted right back.

An odd resentment coiled up in him, the sudden impact of her parted lips and twinkling eyes surprising him.

What was he? Jealous? Horny? Or just all around stupid?

This whole assignment sucked, and he cursed himself for getting stuck with it. He never should have used sex to distract that wild woman in Geneva. And he should never have accepted this babysitting job.

He glanced again at Jazz, whose head tipped back in another throaty chuckle.

Worst of all, he should never have agreed to this charade.

CHAPTER
Four

Once again, Jessica had scored the biggest man on campus. That girl had a magical touch with men.

As Jazz made small talk about the interview and engaged in harmless banter with Kimball Parrish, she observed the delight in his blue eyes and his body language. This handsome executive was no different than the countless football heroes and company presidents and political masters of the universe who invariably dropped to their knees when faced with a chance to be with Jessica Adams. She just had that effect on men.

He perched on the side of her desk, obviously at ease with her, but distant enough to keep tongues from wagging.

"Seriously, Jess, are you ready for Mayor Rodriguez?" Parrish asked, crossing his arms over his barrel chest in a move that made him look bigger than he actually was. "I want to blow them away in New York with this one."

"Have you ever known me to be less than one hundred percent ready?" She gave him one of Jessica's signature winks. "Don't come in here and wave doubt at me."

"I would never doubt you, Jess." He dipped his head and lowered his voice. "But you don't look like you slept well. Are you okay?"

She shrugged casually. "I have a virus or something. That's why I missed the broadcast last night."

"You missed the broadcast last night?" Parrish's looked turned wary. "Thank God I didn't know that while I was at the Economic Development fund-raiser."

"I assumed you'd heard the buzz by now," she said, adding a flippant wave to send him out the door. "And I do need some time for last-minute preparations, or New York will *not* be impressed. Let's talk later."

"Yes," he agreed. "Tonight. At dinner."

"Dinner?" There was no way she'd be able to spend a whole evening with him and not have him figure out that she wasn't Jessica. "I have the eleven o'clock broadcast," she reminded him with relief.

"Let Jonathan do it. He's chomping at the bit to get more solo air time. I have to leave for New York tomorrow and I won't see you for . . . days." He made it sound like a stint in purgatory. "Anyway, I know you want to give me hell about the bodyguard."

Oh. So Jessica and Kimball *hadn't* talked about the bodyguard. "You know it's unnecessary," she said, purposefully vague.

He reached over and took her hand. "It most certainly is necessary. You aren't safe."

Her eyes widened. Did he take those fan letters that seriously? Did Jessica? "Really, there's nothing to worry about. I'll use an escort to the parking lot at night." That was standard procedure for nighttime on-air personalities. "And my condo is secure."

"Nothing is secure enough to suit me," he said solemnly, glancing at Alex's back on the other side of the glass. "Although he looks a little scary."

Jazz laughed. "Isn't that the idea?"

But Kimball narrowed his gaze at Alex again. "His job is to protect you. Not . . . anything else."

Of course he'd be jealous. What man didn't want Jessica all for himself? She smiled innocently. "You have nothing to worry about."

"Oh, but I do," he said, standing and reaching out to hold her hand. "I worry about you." His voice was tender and kind.

Could it be the top dog had a soft spot? Maybe that was what Jessica saw in him. Despite his movie star smile and elegant salt-and-pepper hair, Jazz wasn't remotely attracted to this man.

"Have the bodyguard bring you to Licorice after the six o'clock broadcast," he said, giving her hand a squeeze. "And don't worry about me watching this interview. You are the very best in the business, Jessie, and I love nothing more than observing you while you work."

As he opened the door and stepped out of the office, Jazz saw him lock gazes with Alex.

"If anything happens to her, Romero, I'll kill you myself." All the tenderness and kindness had evaporated.

Alex was in her office within the next instant. "What did he say?" he asked.

She dipped down behind the desk to pick her hand-bag up from the floor; she was due in hair and makeup five minutes ago. "He wants to go out on a date tonight."

"At least."

She looked up. "Jessica will be home by then, I'm sure. She'll handle it. But you are expected to go, too."

"Of course," he agreed. "So they are dating."

Jessica shrugged. "I sense that there might be some-thing more than an employee-boss relationship there."

"No doubt all that raw power and money would be the ultimate aphrodisiac for a television ladder-climber. The man is a walking ticket to New York."

She narrowed her eyes at him as she stood. "My sister doesn't sleep her way to the top."

"That's not what the natives think." He opened the office door and held it for her.

"Screw the natives." She slipped by him and added, "Anyway, he's the one paying your bills, so don't knock him."

He leaned closer to her. "*He* is paying to protect your sister, not play dress up and fool the boss." His voice was cold and serious.

She flashed a smile to a couple of technician types who walked by. "I would know if something's wrong," she said through her teeth. *Wouldn't she?*

"I don't believe in gut instinct," he said.

Neither did she—she believed in facts. And the fact was, she'd been in Miami for twelve hours and hadn't heard a word from Jessica.

"As soon as I'm done with this interview, I'll trace

that pay phone number. We'll spend the day trying to track her down."

"Not *trying*," he countered, then walked away.

"Where are we going?"

Alex maneuvered the Escalade onto Biscayne Boulevard, ignoring the horn from the van he cut off. "Sightseeing."

"Don't be a smart ass. I need to get on my computer, and Jessica's condo is that way." Jazz pointed, then sighed softly. "I wonder if she saw the interview."

"If she did, she'd have been very proud of . . . herself. You were good."

"Thanks," she replied. "But it was easy. The mayor was a piece of cake."

That wasn't true. Rodriguez was a skittish pain in the ass, but Jazz had handled him like a pro, even when he tried to make a political statement out of the event.

She reached forward and started playing with the GPS keypad. "How does this thing work?"

He eased her hand away. "Voice activated."

She leaned toward the device and recited the address of the pay phone she'd dug up.

"You really should be in the backseat," he said, half to himself.

The small screen flashed as quickly as her smile. "You lost that battle, pal. You're lucky I'm not driving."

"I'm used to it. I have four sisters exactly like you."

"Four? How so?"

"Pushy. Ballsy. Gutsy. *Not* docile."

"Are those their names?"

"Might as well be. Carmen is pushy, Maria is ballsy, Ileana is gutsy. And, oh God, Carina is not docile. My goal in life is to avoid women like them." He added a meaningful look. "If I can."

She laughed at the implication that he'd failed. "Older or younger?"

"All younger." He checked the rearview mirror and scanned the streets around them. "They're all safely married off, except for Carina."

"So you're free to protect the rest of the world now, is that right?"

He said nothing, listening to the female voice from the dashboard directing him to East Thirty-third Street and Eighth Avenue.

"*Calle Ocho,*" he corrected the machine.

"Excuse me?"

"Eighth Avenue is called *Calle Ocho* in Little Havana. Although that address is technically Hialeah."

"Guess the GPS lady isn't a local." She twisted to look in the backseat. "Where did you put all those papers? I want to go over all those names and addresses."

"We'll make some calls later."

"We're not going to start calling everyone on her Christmas list, looking for her. That undermines the whole reason I'm here."

Sudden brake lights prevented him from giving her the menacing look she deserved. "The only *undermining* in all this is your impersonation act."

She wiggled out of the yellow jacket and threw it over

the seat, then adjusted the air vent to blow directly on her face and the strappy silk top she'd worn underneath. He kept his attention straight ahead. "I'm doing what Jessica asked me to do."

"What you're doing is preventing me from finding her."

"How?"

"By pretending that she's at work, and playing cat and mouse with her boyfriend."

She released her seat belt and started rooting around the backseat, where he'd left the papers. "I am not—"

He took her arm and guided her face forward. "Don't you ever sit still?"

"No." Reluctantly, she relatched the seat belt and let out a slow sigh. "She'll call me. You'll see."

Reaching into the back, he slid the file folder from the seat pocket where he'd left it. "Here."

"She had last night blocked off from seven to eight," Jazz noted as she read the printout of a calendar page. "All it says is DR. A doctor's appointment at seven at night? Are there medical offices around here?"

"Hialeah Hospital." He closed his eyes at the thought of ever entering that vile institution again. "But your sister doesn't strike me as their usual clientele. What was the fund-raiser her boyfriend said he'd been at?"

"Economic Development," she answered. "That is, if Parrish really is her boyfriend."

He gave her a questioning look as he stopped at the I-95 entrance ramp. "You don't think he is?"

"She never said she was dating, or in love. She said she'd met someone amazing. Someone who could change her life. Someone . . . ," she paused, and added, "who was smart, connected, and had a heart of gold."

"Parrish qualifies for the smart and connected part." He was exactly the kind of man an ambitious woman would want by her side, a perfect accessory to her perfect apartment.

"He seems genuine," she said. "But I did sense he was doing a full-court press on Jess. Maybe she just hasn't committed yet. Or maybe . . ."

"Maybe what?"

"Maybe there is someone even smarter, more connected, and more golden of heart."

"Yeah, and she hooked up with him last night, got lost in the throes of passion and forgot to call you."

Jazz let out a snort of disbelief as she flipped through the printout. "Jessica doesn't forget. No matter what throes she's in."

"Then why aren't you worried?"

"Who says I'm not worried?" She blew out a breath. "I just prefer action to worry. Plus, she's very capable. And she'd warned me she'd be going away. I think she's left early, that's all."

Alex didn't push the point as he navigated bumper-to-bumper traffic. He got off at Seventy-ninth Street and headed west. The landscape was Hialeah's finest: run-down warehouses, low-end strip malls, abandoned buildings, and not a word of English anywhere.

"Look at this," Jazz said, tapping one of the papers. "Another DR note in her calendar, a week ago. With a Thirty-third Street address. Not the pay phone location, but it looks like it might be close."

"What is that address again?"

She repeated it, and he did a mental calculation of the number of blocks. "The Hialeah Park Racetrack?"

He slowed the car in front of Bright Park and Pool. "The phone is there, in that park. The racetrack is a block away." He zipped the SUV around and turned toward a pink monstrosity surrounded by flamingoes and flowering trees. "Maybe your sister went to the races last night. Is she a gambler?"

"Not in the least. Nor would she pal around with one." Jazz peered up at the landmark. "But this might have to do with the story she's working on."

"Illegal gambling. Bookmaking. Does that seem like a story that would interest her?"

"I guess it would depend on the angle."

Jazz's phone beeped and she immediately dug into her handbag to find it. "That's a text message," she said. She punched a button, then tapped his arm with the phone, letting out a little whoop of joy. "Yeah, baby! We got her. I told you my sister never forgets."

Alex took a left to circle around the track. "Well? What does she say?"

"Thanks. Sorry I missed you." She tapped another button. "See you soon, sis."

He glanced at her, noting a strange tone in her voice. "Is that it?"

She nodded slowly as she scrolled to reread the message. "That's all."

"I wonder why she didn't call you."

She closed the phone and looked out the window. "She's busy."

He stopped at a light and studied her. "What's the matter?"

"Nothing," she said, the sparkle gone from her eyes. "I feel much better. Don't you?"

No, he did not. He whipped into an empty parking space and took the phone from her hand. "Let me read it."

She didn't fight him. "Suit yourself."

The text box read: *tx. srry i mssed u. c u soon, sis.* "Does something about this not ring true to you?"

She shrugged. "I'm just disappointed she didn't call. I really wanted to talk to her." Then she looked up at him with a bright smile that reminded him more of Jessica than Jazz. "Are we done in Hialeah now? I prefer the bright lights and big city."

"All right. But don't erase that message."

"I won't." She slipped the phone back into her purse.

They didn't talk much on the way back to Brickell Key. Jazz continued to study the contents of Jessica's address book, occasionally mentioning a name she knew, but she seemed content to believe all was well.

Alex wasn't. A meaningless text message was not the assurance he needed.

He hated the idea of calling in backup on a job this lightweight. At least one of the Bullet Catchers was a missing person expert, and Alex had some lifelong contacts on the Miami-Dade police force. But surely he could find one wayward newscaster in Miami. Before he had to report in to Lucy.

As he cruised the road that ran along the north side of Jessica's condo, looking for parking, Jazz opened her bag and dug around again. "I think this card key I found upstairs will work for the parking garage. Why don't you take Jessica's spot? This thing is more of a target than my rental car."

He slid the card key into the electronic reader and rumbled over the metal grate.

"It looks like the slots are numbered for the apartments," she said. "Keep going until you get to 3701."

He maneuvered the vehicle around to the next level and slowed down as they approached the spot.

"Oh my God," Jazz whispered, yanking at her seat belt in a frenzy. "She's home!"

A silver BMW convertible sat in the slot. Jazz bolted out of the car.

In a flash, Alex was beside her. "Wait," he said sharply.

But she seized the door handle and jerked it open. "It's not locked," she said with shock.

The car was empty, immaculate, and still smelling like the factory. Jazz slid into the driver's seat and put her hands on the wheel, staring at the dash. Then she reached to the ignition and he heard the jangle of metal, mixed with Jazz's quick intake of breath. Turning to him, he saw the first glint of fear flash in her eyes.

"She forgot her keys."

By the time Kimball Parrish seated Jazz at one of the pink leather sofas and black concrete dining tables of Licorice, she'd had enough. She didn't want to be in some achingly hip restaurant on the arm of a handsome, rich, powerful man. She didn't want to be dressed in Jessica's slinky black cocktail dress, wearing three-inch heels and carrying a handbag so small it wouldn't have fit her gun. And she sure as hell didn't want to be under the watchful eye of Alex Romero.

All she wanted to do is was figure out where Jessica was.

Instead, Jazz had read the six o'clock news, then gone home to dress for a date she didn't want to have with a man she didn't particularly like at some high-end South Beach restaurant on Ocean Drive. Her only hope was that Kimball knew something about the story Jessica was following, and could give her some clues.

If she didn't figure out where her sister was by the end of the night, she would come clean with Parrish. She'd promised that to Alex in exchange for him agreeing to play along.

"Blackberry martini?" Kimball asked as though it were Jessica's one and only cocktail. Miami must have really changed her.

"That would be fine."

He slid closer and a whiff of peppery cologne reached her, but he didn't touch her. No possessive arm, nothing more than an air kiss hello. "Just remember what happened at Verve," he warned. "They're potent."

Good God, what had happened at Verve? Jazz had never seen her sister drunk in her life—and couldn't imagine it happening on anything as silly as a blackberry martini.

Kimball waved for the waitress, and while he ordered, Jazz glanced at Alex. He stood at the end of the bar about twenty feet away, with a direct view of their table. At the moment he was panning the restaurant with his intimidating gaze. He managed to blend in, with his Latin good looks, and still be a presence no one in their right mind would mess with.

She forced herself to concentrate on Kimball, a wholly different kind of handsome. His face was carved by strong, masculine lines, his body broad in the way of a man who'd once been in amazing shape but now waged a war with age. She'd done some quick research so she could converse intelligently, and she knew that he was fifty-two, widowed, the father of two teenage girls, and a staunch Catholic.

There was no shortage of press coverage about his conservative mindset. Just last week, he took some heat from liberal watchdogs for his crackdown on a shock jock on one of his Texas radio stations. Kimball Parrish "aired" on the side of the angels. That was his sound bite to the media—most of which he owned.

"So any news on the situation in Dallas?" she asked.

"Nothing's changed, including my decision," he said, an obstinate set to his cleanly shaved jaw. "You did a masterful job this morning, did I tell you that?"

She gave him Jessica's most photographed smile, and a point for deft subject change. "Several times. Thank you."

"The word from New York is very, very good." He shifted to get a little closer to her. "I'm meeting with the *American Sunrise* production staff tomorrow afternoon. The changes are imminent."

His tone implied she knew precisely what he meant, and that those changes would somehow involve her. If changes were imminent, why would Jessica stand on her head to get a big story to guarantee network notice?

He leaned a little closer, his elegant cologne wafting toward her again. "And did I tell you how beautiful you look tonight?"

"Thank you." Couldn't he see the differences between her and Jessica? Jessica's skin glowed, she was a tad thinner than Jazz since she was less muscular, and flawless porcelain laminates enhanced her million dollar smile. Jazz's teeth were real—orthodontically improved and perfectly straight, but not blindingly white like Jessica's. But attitude covered a lot of flaws, and she'd draped herself in Jessica's personality. So far, it worked.

The waitress delivered the drinks, and Kimball raised his highball to meet her amethyst-colored martini. "Aristotle said, 'Change in all things is sweet.' To changes," he said with a devilish twinkle in his eyes.

He could change my life.

She could practically hear the excitement in Jessica's e-mail. Smiling, Jazz touched his glass with hers, then took a tiny sip of the frothy liquid. When this was over, she would never let Jessica forget she had to endure a disgusting drink *and* a date with a man who quoted Aristotle. That was really pushing sisterly love.

"And you do know what changes I mean, Jessica."

His statement caught her off guard. "Why don't you elaborate, Kimball?" she asked in her best anchorwoman voice.

"I prefer when you call me Kim. I told you that."

Jazz covered the faux pas with a sip of her drink that included a long gaze. Kim. She'd have to remember that.

He placed his glass on the table, straightening the napkin under it to align with the place setting. Maybe that's what Jessica liked about him—a companion in neatness.

He surprised her by dropping his hand on the exposed skin of her thigh. "I also told you I don't like games."

She swallowed and her pulse kicked into a faster rhythm as she replayed Alex's solemn warning: *He's paying to save your sister's life, not play dress up and fool the boss.*

His fingers weren't groping, just . . . affectionate. "At least, not games I don't win," he added quietly.

"I'm sure you rarely lose, Kim."

His hand slid an inch higher. "You know how I feel. I'm ready to take this to the next level."

Tonight? She smiled sweetly. "I have so much on my mind these days." *Like where the hell my sister is . . . and how I can fend you off.*

One finger gently caressed her skin, as he glanced toward Alex. "You're not still mad at me about the bodyguard?"

"I know you only want to do the right thing." She stayed perfectly still, not wanting to brush him off, but definitely not digging being felt up by her sister's admirer.

He finally released her leg, taking a drink. "I worry about you."

She sipped her mix of sweet fruit and potent alcohol. "I'm fine."

He leaned closer as though he were going to kiss her, but instead pulled her into him in a tender embrace. Over his shoulder, she looked directly into Alex Romero's eyes.

He looked purely disgusted.

She felt the vibration of a phone between them, and Parrish pulled back and released a cell phone from his belt with an apologetic look.

Oh, God, what if Jessica was calling *him*? Then she'd have to come clean.

As he turned slightly away, she studied the polished patrons of Licorice.

The music drowned out Kimball's soft conversation. Closing her eyes, she took another sip of her drink, returning to the questions that had plagued her that afternoon. Nothing could cause Jessica Adams to leave her keys in the ignition and her car unlocked. And she hadn't called Jazz "sis" since they were ten years old. So why did she sign her text message that way?

Should she follow her gut, which said something was wrong? But what if nothing *was* wrong? What if Jessica was deep into this story and just couldn't call her? Then she'd blow Jessica's cover.

"I'm so sorry," Kimball said as he disconnected the call, looking right into her eyes. "I am really so, so sorry to do this to you. It appears I have to travel to Cincinnati before I can go to New York tomorrow. I'm going to leave tonight."

She managed to look suitably disappointed. "Why?"

"Some liberal assholes are rioting at a radio station I have there." He shook his head angrily and waved at the waitress for a check. "Sorry again. I know you hate profanity."

"Really?" Jess could swear with the best of 'em. "They're rioting? Seriously?"

"I believe the left wingers call it 'protesting,' but

whatever it is, I have to control the coverage. This will be all over the leftist media. Those bastards are out to get me." He squeezed her hand. "I have to defend my position. I hope you understand."

She worked not to look relieved. "Oh, I do. I completely understand."

"They're getting my plane ready now." He chucked her chin as if she were a little girl. "Unfortunately, this is not what I'd hoped for tonight." She backed out of his touch, but he leaned closer and brushed her lips with a soft kiss. No tongue, closed mouth.

"I'll be back next week," he promised. "You think about . . . changes."

"I'll be here," she said lightly.

"You'd better be." She couldn't tell if that was a tease, a hope, or a threat. "I'll have the bodyguard take you home now," he added, giving her shoulder a possessive squeeze.

As he left, he paused to speak to Alex, who nodded and immediately headed toward her, his ebony eyes trained on her.

Jazz took one more swallow of the martini, reminding herself that she despised men who insisted on control. They grated on every independent cell in her body. Yet Kimball Parrish's gentle suggestion that they get to "the next level" certainly didn't leave her in a pool of lust, either.

She drank again as Alex moved toward her like an animal. A hungry, predatory beast who brought out the most primal instincts in her. That man could throw her down and take her about *six* more levels in one easy move, and leave her begging for the next one.

Desire hit her as hard as the vodka, at precisely the same instant. The raw and sudden need for him took her breath away.

Alex held out his hand to help her up from the sofa, but she refused the assistance.

"Let's do it," he said, tipping his head toward the door.

"Oh, yeah. Let's."

CHAPTER
Five

Alex Romero knew women, and he could read this one's mind as clearly as if she'd just stripped naked and handed him a condom.

"Let's get something to eat," he said as they hit the steamy sidewalk. He hustled her toward the car, his gaze darting up and down the streets teeming with revelers, tourists, and drunks. Dangerous dark alleys separated the art deco buildings outlined in neon pink and bathed electric blue, and the streets overflowed with a population as colorful and hungry for attention as the architecture.

South Beach was a bodyguard's nightmare. But he didn't dare take her home to a secluded condo—not with that look in her eyes.

"I'm not hungry," she announced.

Oh, yes you are. "You haven't eaten all day. And in case you didn't notice, your date dumped you before you had time to open a menu."

"I don't need food." Her voice was tight.

"I think you do. I watched the bartender make that drink."

Jazz managed a scathing look. That was good; he could handle pissed off. But not hot and bothered. Well, he could handle hot and bothered. He glanced down at the V-neck of her form-fitting dress, his gaze lingering in her generous cleavage. But not tonight.

He rapidly reviewed his options to keep her in public but secure. There were a few restaurants with ideal floor plans nearby, if they could get a seat with no one at his back.

"I could go for something . . . spicy," she said with a sly smile. "Cuban?"

Great. This was *just* what he needed on a job that already bent the rules big-time. A brazen woman with a killer body, a martini buzz, and sex on the brain.

A group of partiers turned a corner in front of them. He automatically molded her into his body as the pack cruised by with an eruption of laughter and some Spanish he was glad she didn't understand.

The side of her breast rested against his rib cage and she made no attempt to move away.

You know the rules, Alex. Of course, Lucy didn't specify if *pretend* principals fell under her regulations.

Hell, pretend or real, Jazz was under his protection.

"I wouldn't mind stopping somewhere for another drink," she suggested.

"Food. You get only food." At the car, he pressed the keyless entry and opened the back door.

She stepped in front of him and opened the front passenger door. "I don't do backseats." She grinned. "Unless we're parked."

The slit in her dress parted as she climbed up, revealing a long, lean thigh. When she reached for the seat belt, he saw right down the halter top of her dress.

Carajo. He closed the back door and hustled to the driver's side, then muscled the SUV into the standstill of Ocean Drive traffic.

"I take it you conveniently forgot to mention to him that you aren't the real Jessica Adams."

She let out a long sigh. "He left so abruptly, I really didn't get a chance. But they haven't slept together."

"You sure? He seemed pretty at home with your legs."

"You noticed that, did you?" He heard the tease in her voice, but didn't take his eyes off the road.

"I don't miss anything, Jazz. That's my job. What did you two talk about?"

"Aristotle." She laughed, a throaty sound as pleasant as the delicate fragrance she wore. Unable to resist, he stole a look. Her head was back, her eyes half closed.

Just the way she might look if he kissed her. "You really want Cuban?"

"That's all I can think about." Her eyes opened slowly, and she turned toward him. No smile, no doubt. No playfulness. Just pure lust. "What's good?"

"Media noche. Arroz con frijoles. Café cubano."

"You make it all sound so . . . sensual."

"Sensual? A sandwich, rice and beans, and coffee? You're imagining things."

Her gaze darkened to a smoky gray. "No, I'm not."

He couldn't look away from her. A sudden smack on the hood of the car yanked him back to reality, and he jammed on the brakes to keep from hitting two young men jaywalking across Ocean Drive.

He swore softly. "Let's go to Versailles." The popular, kitschy, late-night spot would be perfect if he could convince the hostess to give them a booth along the back wall. Plus, it was too crowded and noisy to get flirtatious and intimate. He could easily monitor the crowd for her safety, and she'd sober up with some of the best espresso outside of Havana.

The famous Cuban diner on *Calle Ocho* was already wall-to-wall with hungry barhoppers shouting in as many different dialects of Spanish and English as there were items on the mammoth menu. Safely situated in the back, Alex scanned the crowd.

"Oh my God, this is so good," she said after her first bite of a *media noche*. "This is heaven."

He took a bite of his own sandwich, enjoying watching her eat.

"So how Cuban are you?" she asked. "Were you born in the United States?"

"I'm as American as you are. My parents came over shortly after Castro took over the government, in 1961. They spent about eight years waiting to go home before they started a family, but they never did get home. I was born in sixty-nine, followed in rapid succession by the girls."

She smiled. "Yes. Four of them. I remember."

He swallowed the bite, then washed it down with water. "Five, actually."

"Five sisters?"

"We lost Vivi as a baby."

"Oh." She studied his expression. "How sad. What happened?"

"She was born with a heart defect. She had to have emergency surgery, and died on the operating table when she was two years old."

"How awful for your parents. How did they handle something like that?"

He set his sandwich down and looked at her, thinking of the dank halls in the very hospital they'd passed that afternoon in Hialeah. "My father never found out. He was in Cuba at the time. And he died there."

Her eyes widened. "How?"

"He went back to San Tomás, his family's village. He had hatched a plan to smuggle his only brother, Roberto, and his wife and children to the United States."

Jazz waited, her sympathetic look telling him she'd figured out the rest of the story.

"He was killed trying to get them out. At least he didn't have to live through the pain of losing Vivi."

Or the pain of a son who couldn't keep a simple promise to look after the women. He took a deep breath, filling his nose with the familiar scents of cumin and coffee.

"I'm so sorry," she said, her eyes as soft as her voice. "Did Roberto and his family ever make it here?"

He shook his head. "That was in the early eighties, right after the Mariel boatlift, when Castro dumped hundreds of thousands of refugees on Miami. Getting out was—and still is—difficult, if not impossible."

"Do you ever go there, to Cuba?"

"Not once in all my thirty-six years." That would certainly be pushing Lucy's CIA-trained tolerance. "But I still hope that someday my cousins and relatives can find a way out." In the meantime, he exceeded the limit of donations to family members by thousands and thousands of dollars every year.

"So you were how old when your father died?" she asked. "Twelve?"

He nodded. "With four younger sisters, who all grew up to be beautiful and wild. Not easy for me to take care of, I'll tell you."

"What about your mother?" Jazz looked almost fearful that he would tell her his *Mami* died of a broken heart. "Didn't she take care of them?"

He felt the tug of a half smile. "In the Latin culture, *querida,* the man is in charge. No matter how young he is." He ignored her raised eyebrows. "Of course my mother cared for us and made sure we were fed and clothed, but Cubans are patriarchal." He took a sip of coffee. "Men make the final decisions."

She dropped both elbows on the table and stared at him. "You really think you can still live that way? It's the twenty-first century, for God's sake."

He shrugged. "I recognize the realities of our society, and I doubt anyone outside of our culture would understand. Anyway, it wasn't like I asked for the job. My father died and my sisters, all younger, turned to me for protection."

"And how did you handle that?"

"None of them had a date until I left for college."

She smiled at his deadpan, and he didn't tell her it was only partially true. "Is that why you became a bodyguard? A passion for protection?"

He imagined if he'd examined it closely enough, she'd be right. "Maybe," he agreed. "Somehow my path brought me here."

"Where did you go to school?" she asked, sipping the espresso.

"Notre Dame on an ROTC scholarship. Then I was in the army for six years. A Ranger."

"The perfect job for an alpha dog." She studied him over the rim of her cup.

He wanted the conversation off him. "So tell me more about Parrish."

"Not much to tell, really." She raised a shoulder in disdain. "He quotes dead philosphers and votes Republican. He has his hands full with a bunch of protesters in Cincinnati right now."

He'd *had* his hands full of her leg about an hour ago. "You kissed him."

She looked up from her plate, a teasing glimmer in her eye. "He kissed me. Big difference."

A foreign sensation of envy pulled at his insides. "So how was that?"

"Dry." A sneaky little smile lifted her lips, that smoky invitation back in her look. "I bet you don't kiss like that, Romero."

He leaned forward just enough to whisper, "If I kissed you, *querida,* nothing would be dry."

Her lips parted as she sucked in a tiny breath, moving infinitesimally closer to him. "Is that a promise or a threat?"

His gaze drifted down to her mouth, her glossy, full mouth looking way tastier than the food in front of them.

She bit her lower lip enough to whiten the flesh, then let it slide free.

"Neither." He couldn't resist touching that lip with the tip of his index finger. "It is just a fact."

A dish clanged and a howl of laughter erupted from the bar. The waitress zipped by with a sizzling platter of sweet fried plantains. But the only sense that functioned in Alex was concentrated on the tip of his finger. On the silky wetness of her lower lip.

She opened her mouth and flicked her tongue against his skin, the sensation shooting a hot rush of blood to his loins. He slid his finger one centimeter farther. Inside. Inside.

His whole being focused on the need to be *inside* of her.

From his peripheral vision, Alex sensed a man approaching their table. In one move, he tensed, stood, and trained his steely glare to the intruder.

"Miss Adams?" The man asked, setting a paper napkin and pen in front of her.

"Yes?" Even in one syllable, she nailed the anchor voice.

"My friend over there is a big fan." He pointed to the other side of the room, where Alex saw only a sea of faces.

Alex cleared his throat. "Miss Adams is in the middle of dinner."

The man gave him a wary glance, but pushed the napkin closer to Jazz. "Chill out, man. My girlfriend wants Jessica's autograph."

"It's okay," Jazz said, picking up the pen and scribbling a great big J. "Here you go."

He thanked her, shot Alex a dirty look and disappeared. They finished dinner without any more discussions of how he kissed.

But the damage had been done—now he couldn't think of anything else but how wet he could make her, and the crushing need to be inside of her.

As soon as the elevator door opened on the thirty-seventh floor, Alex froze and Jazz knew something was wrong. Seriously, majorly wrong.

He looked at the floor in front of Jessica's door, and held up one hand to silence Jazz and keep her back.

"What's the matter?"'

Dark eyes flashed in warning, sending her pulse flying. "Don't move," he whispered, then he took a few slow steps toward the door.

It looked utterly normal. Exactly as they'd left it. "What's—"

He silenced her again with a look, and produced a nine-millimeter Glock from under his jacket. What in God's name did he see that she didn't?

With his toe, he lifted the corner of the green mat at the foot of the condo door. "Someone has been in there."

"Really?" She peered at the lock for signs of entry. "Maybe it's Jessica. Maybe she's home."

"Give me the key," he ordered, holding his hand to her. "Wait here."

"Don't you dare shoot her," she hissed at him, right on his heels.

He seared her with a warning look. "Shhh." Unlocking the door, he eased it open, revealing a condo as dark as it had been the night she'd slipped in. But they'd left lights on.

Had Jessica come home, and gone to sleep?

He stepped into the apartment and moved his free hand to the wall for the alarm pad, his attention directed straight ahead, along with the gun. Jazz stayed right behind him, every fiber in her being focused on the firm belief that Jessica was inside. She *had* to be.

"The alarm's still set," he said softly, disarming it with four soft beeps.

Of course it was set. Jessica set it. She was in the back, in her bedroom.

Please God, let Jessica be here.

"I'll check the bedroom," he said, putting his free hand out toward her. "Stay right here."

She started toward the kitchen.

"Jazz." His fingers closed around her shoulder. "You're unarmed. Don't move for one minute, okay?"

She nodded in silent agreement, then he disappeared into the back bedroom. As her eyes adjusted, she scanned the room. Had she left that pillow leaning against the sofa? The armoire doors open?

In a moment, she saw light spill from the hallway to the bedroom. "It's clear in here," Alex said, coming back out toward her.

"She's not back there?" She couldn't help asking the question, hating that her hopes were dashed.

"No. But someone's been here."

Jazz looked around as he checked out the second bedroom and bath. Something was different, but she couldn't pinpoint what it was. She tiptoed toward the galley kitchen, then stopped dead in her tracks. "What's that noise?" she asked.

Alex appeared from the second bedroom. "What—"

"Listen. The dishwasher's running." A wave of sheer relief made her place both hands on her chest to laugh. "The dishwasher! Oh God, that's my sister for you. She couldn't stand that I left dishes in the sink."

He flicked on the kitchen light and they both stared at the pristine kitchen counters, and the red light on the dishwasher. Jazz gave him a victorious look as she bounded toward the humming machine. "This—" She flipped a handle and the door popped into her hand, a little burst of steam shooting up at her. "—is Jessica's calling card."

She pulled the door open. Sure enough, the dishes they'd used that day were stacked inside, along with the two wineglasses that Alex had said were on the counter the night they'd arrived.

Jazz sailed into the bedroom. It looked exactly as she'd left it—the bed a bit rumpled, some makeup strewn across the vanity of the bathroom. Wouldn't Jessica have neatened the comforter, and put away the makeup?

And God, why wouldn't she leave a note?

Alex walked to the dresser, opening a black and mother of pearl box. "Jewelry's still here."

Glancing around, she searched for some definitive clue. She walked toward the closet door, which she'd left open, and flipped on the light as she strode in. Her foot hit something on the floor.

A cell phone slid next to the laundry basket. She

practically pounced on it. "That's not my phone. Is it yours?"

He touched his jacket pocket, the gun, she noticed, still in his right hand. "No. I have mine."

On her knees, Jazz opened the phone. Stabbing the on button, her heart thumped.

"Maybe it's Jessica's." She glanced into the closet, but didn't know her sister's wardrobe well enough to know if anything was missing. "She came home to get clothes or something, and dropped her phone."

The device vibrated and a beep told her she had service. She thumbed down the menu to a phone book. Alex crouched next to her to see the screen.

"I'm accessing the call history to figure out the number to this phone and trace it to find the owner." A bright screen flashed with a web ID, and the readout blinked. *Welcome jadams0418. You have no new messages.*

"J Adams oh four one eight?" Alex said. "Is that you or her?"

She looked up at him. "That's our birthday and her e-mail." Jessica had been here . . . and *left*. Why wouldn't she wait or at least leave her a note? "This is Jessica's phone. She was definitely here."

He looked around the room, and at the phone. "Not like her to drop something, is it?"

No, it wasn't. "But what other explanation is there?"

"That the phone was there all along and you didn't see it?" he suggested.

She jerked as the phone screamed a digital melody. "Oh my God," she exclaimed. "Someone's calling her."

She tried to hit talk but then realized it was a text

message that had been sent while the phone had been turned off. She pressed a series of buttons to retrieve the message.

jazz don't stop cvr 4 me pls pls pls so impt J

They always signed e-mails to each other "J".

"She's fine," Jazz announced as the pieces fell into place. "She realized that she left her phone here and is letting me know."

"Where did the call come from?" Alex asked.

She thumbed through the calling history, but the message had been generated by a blocked phone number. "I can't figure that out."

"So why wouldn't she just call you on your cell? And how is she getting around? Her keys were in her car, remember?"

"She didn't call me because she didn't have her phone, and this was turned off until one second ago," she said, holding it out as though it were evidence. "She left this message over an hour ago. She has another set of keys—you said yourself the alarm had been reset. And we discussed switching cars a few days ago. She said hers would be too noticeable for what she was doing."

"Which was what?"

"I don't know, Alex." Frustration made her voice crack. "But that's why I rented that Taurus. She must have rented her own car." This had to be the explanation. "She was here tonight; no one else could get past the guard. You're being overprotective. I understand that's your job, but you have to understand how important this is."

"Sorry, but I don't. I can't believe you would risk your sister's life."

She blew out a ragged breath. How could she explain this to someone who didn't know her? After a lifetime of being one step behind Jessica, of being the one who always needed a little rescuing, a little reminder, a little cover for a big mistake . . . Jessica needed *her.*

"If I buckle and come clean to her boss, I blow this story for her." She shook her head and looked at him. "For once, I don't want to be the twin who takes the easy way out." The one who slept in, missed deadlines, forgot Mom's birthday, and couldn't be depended upon. "For once, I want to be the capable twin."

"What if she's in some kind of danger? Then you'll be the stupid twin."

She narrowed her eyes at him. "The evidence isn't compelling. All you have is a couple of cheesy letters from a fan, and a horny boyfriend who hired a bodyguard to impress Jessica. And she's sent me two messages now."

"I see it differently." He stood slowly, his gaze unwavering. "She asks you to fly to Miami, arranges to meet you here for dinner and never shows, never calls you and never leaves a voice message. We find her keys in the car and her cell phone on the floor. A woman who all but has her underwear alphabetized. I think the evidence is extremely compelling that she could be in trouble."

Jazz shook her head. "Jessica doesn't get in trouble. You just have an overactive imagination."

"There's a security camera in the hall." He reached for her hand. "First thing tomorrow, I'm looking at the tapes."

"Okay." She stood without assistance. "And if Jessica did come in here, will you back off then? Please?"

"I'll have to alert Lucy."

Lucy? *I hate you, Lucy.* She could still hear the tone of his voice, the resignation and dry humor. "Who's that?"

"My boss, Lucy Sharpe."

He'd said it, she remembered with a morsel of shame, when she'd sleepily presented him her body that morning. Well, lucky Lucy. "Okay. You tell your boss and then you'll leave, right?"

"Wrong."

She slammed her hands on her hips. "Why *not*? Jessica's not here, and you're not here to watch me. I'm not your principal."

"Unfortunately, at the moment, you are."

"Unfortunately?" She choked. "What's that supposed to mean?"

His lips tilted upward just enough to soften the dark warning in his eyes. He placed a single finger on her mouth and skimmed her lower lip with a feather touch, sending a flash of heat lightning through her as he had in the restaurant. "If you weren't my principal, *querida,* I would take you up on your offer."

She swallowed and leaned out of his touch. "I haven't offered anything."

His half-grin was slow and teasing. "Must be my overactive imagination."

He turned and left her standing with his touch still on her lips.

Something snapped.

Alex was out of bed and at the doorway to the living room within a second. The light of the television flickered, revealing a female form standing in front of the armoire pointing a remote control.

"What are you doing?" he asked.

He heard Jazz's exasperated sigh. "Watching television. Is that okay? I'm a night owl." As the picture came on, he could see she wore some kind of thin cotton T-shirt and dark underwear. And nothing else.

Turning toward him, she caught him staring at her bare legs. "All that diesel fuel you call coffee didn't help, either."

He moved into the room. "What are you watching?"

She pulled out a drawer below the TV. "I was hoping to find a movie in Jessica's collection."

"I'll watch with you."

Her glare raked his bare chest and sleep pants. "That's okay. I feel pretty safe out here."

"Sorry. Those are the rules. I can't sleep if you don't." He approached the open drawer. "What are you looking for? Romance? Comedy?"

"I prefer some dead bodies and action—Bruce Willis or Denzel Washington. How about you?"

He lifted out *Independence Day.*

"Nah."

He moved down the alphabet. "*Lethal Weapon?*" he asked.

"Getting better."

On top of the DVD player, he noticed a blank disk. Unlike everything else, it wasn't protected in a case nor was it filed neatly. "Not like our girl Jess to leave a DVD out to get dusty."

"No, it's not," she agreed, pressing the button to open the changer. "Let's see what she was watching."

He slid the disk in. The screen lit up with high-gloss lips being licked by their own tongue and the words *Climax Distribution Presents.*

"Oh my God." Jazz coughed back an awkward laugh. "Is this porn?"

Red letters filled the screen. *Wet Kiss.*

Alex chuckled softly. "So the perfect twin has a seamier side."

She sliced him with steely glare. "I'm sure it's research for a story. Or a joke."

"A joke?" On the screen, he saw a closeup of a woman's breast, her nipples engorged, and pierced. "Yeah, this is a riot."

He reached toward the DVD player, but she grabbed his wrist. "Wait. I want to see what this is."

The camera pulled away, and the actress's blond head dropped as she lifted one large breast to her own mouth. Her pink tongue extended to lick the swollen nipple.

Alex gave Jazz a disbelieving look. "Have you ever seen hard-core porn?"

"A little." She shrugged, then flashed him a guilty smile. "Once. At a bachelorette party."

The woman on the TV screen slid her hands down her flat abdomen and spread her long, tanned legs. His lower half tightened and he realized he stood right in front of Jazz in nothing but thin drawstring pants. He blew out a disgusted breath at himself.

"Go to bed if you can't handle it, Romero." She stepped back to lean against the armrest of the sofa, and tapped his shoulder impatiently with the remote. "You're blocking my view."

On the TV, white-tipped fingernails caressed golden skin, dipping into the classic Brazilian wax job on a glistening female body part. Feeling the stirring of an involuntary hard-on, Alex closed his eyes.

What would be more agonizing? Watching the movie, or watching Jazz *experience* the movie?

"Oh, would you look at that?"

He did. The white-tipped fingernail disappeared into the woman's body as she whispered a sexy plea to the camera.

"You wanted action," he said with a shake of his head. "You should get plenty with this one."

She settled onto the sofa, draping her long, bare legs along the length of it. "Jessica was watching this for a reason. I want to know what it was."

"I'm sure her reasons were the same as everyone else who watches this stuff," he said dryly. "Maybe Jessica wasn't getting any from Mr. Heart of Gold."

She lifted her arms to tuck a pillow under her head. "Jessica Adams would not watch porn for stimulation. Believe me, she has to fend off men."

He watched her get comfortable on the sofa, the outline of her bare breasts clearly visible as she moved, a whisper of her underwear peeking out from the T-shirt. No way. He couldn't do this.

"You have yourself a nice little porn party, *querida*." He tapped his forehead in a casual salute. "I've had enough stimulation for one day."

He left the door to his room open, the sounds of a whining sax and the murmurs of excruciatingly bad dialogue drifting into his room for the next forty-five minutes. Hard and sweaty, he lay with his hands locked under his head, staring at the ceiling and forcing himself to concentrate on the mystery of where Jessica Adams, anchorwoman superstar and closet porn watcher, could be.

Had she come home tonight? To run the dishwasher? He replayed every detail over and over, blocking out the sounds from the next room.

Until the gasps and moans of a female orgasm drowned out his thoughts. The music intensified to a driving beat that matched the frantic breathing, and his cock thickened uncomfortably.

Although it went against all his training, he got up to close the door. As he glanced in the living room, he couldn't resist a look at Jazz. She lay on her stomach, the pillow fallen to the floor, one arm hanging limply over the edge, the remote dropped from her fingertips.

Wasn't this how he'd started this day . . . watching her lost in slumber, while he nursed an uninvited hardon? He grabbed a blanket from the closet and covered her, easing her deeper onto the sofa so she didn't fall off. Exhaling softly, she turned toward him, but showed no signs of awakening.

She slept with the same intensity she lived, as though her entire soul was invested in the process. Smiling, he repositioned the pillow under her head, admiring the narrow column of her neck, the sleek, toned muscles of her shoulder.

At another time, in another place, he'd enjoy nothing more than discovering if she made love with the same power and passion she gave everything else. But not here, and not now.

Taking the remote, he pointed it toward the TV—and

froze at the face on the screen. He blinked at it, certain his eyes were playing tricks on him.

Jazz?

The camera zoomed in and she laughed, her head tipping back to reveal the long, lean neck he'd just been admiring. Then it cut to her body from the neck down, her breasts being thoroughly licked by some model-type actor.

The camera cut back to her face, showing her shaking her head with her eyes closed. As it zoomed closer, his gaze locked on a small beauty mark under her left jaw.

He looked at Jazz and leaned close enough to feel her steady, peaceful breaths. There was no beauty mark; not even a freckle marred her skin in that spot. Back on the TV, the camera had moved to the place where the couple joined, the apex of their fused sex organs filling the screen.

So the *good* twin did more for the camera than promise film at eleven.

He almost hated to wake Jazz up. Did she need to know that the sister she so obviously admired had a dirty little sideline? It would shatter a lifetime of illusions and ruin a classic case of hero worship.

Then again, maybe that's where Miss Jessica was all this time—making bad movies. Was it possible?

"*Querida,*" he whispered into her ear. "Wake up. I've found Jessica."

Her eyes popped wide open immediately.

The slow, rhythmic sound had become almost musical to her. *Swoosh* and *thump, swoosh and thump,* every few seconds. It was the only thing she could sense. Everything else was dark and still.

But there was an odor, too. A salty, wet smell that tickled her nostrils.

It had been dark for so long, she couldn't remember the light. Couldn't remember colors or tastes or . . .

Jessica Adams.

That was her name. The sound of it in her head sent a funny sensation through her body. A sense of accomplishment, of victory.

She remembered her name.

But why couldn't she see? She blinked. Her eyes were open, weren't they? She couldn't tell. She lifted her hand to touch her eyelids, to see if she was really blinking or imagining it, but her arm didn't move. Nothing moved. Not a single muscle. Oh, Lord, she was paralyzed!

Had she been in an accident?

Was she in a coma?

Terrified, she opened her mouth to call for help. But her jaw didn't budge. Her muscles contracted, her teeth separated slightly—but her mouth remained closed.

She was paralyzed. Or worse . . .

"Oh, you're awake. We'll have to do something about that."

It was a man's voice. A familiar, friendly voice she trusted. Who was he?

A sharp sting pinched the flesh of her upper thigh, then she felt heavy and tired and lost again. *Who was she?*

She heard the *swoosh* and *thump,* but couldn't remember her name.

CHAPTER
Six

Jazz jumped at the first chirp of her travel alarm. She'd never really slept again after Alex had awakened her on the sofa, her mind replaying vivid, repulsive images that she prayed would someday disappear from her memory.

She closed her eyes and curled into the pillow, the metallic taste of sleeplessness filling her mouth. Nothing, absolutely nothing, would let her believe that those filmed images of Jessica having sex were real.

Alex had reluctantly agreed the whole thing didn't seem right on many levels. There was never a shot of Jessica's face and body at the same time. And while that body was similar in type, it seemed unfamiliar. Plus, the scene had nothing to do with the rest of the movie—as uncomfortable as it had been to watch the whole damn thing with him to confirm that. Because of the DVD format, they were forced to watch the beginning of every scene until they got to the segment where Jessica appeared.

Had her face been dropped in as a hoax? Was it some kind of sick joke? Was that man in the movie her lover? An actor?

What really made her mad was Alex's assumption that Jessica had some underground dark side to her. And that Jazz had wrongly placed her sister on a pedestal. Jessica had her faults—plenty of them. But they didn't include making dirty movies.

Unless she'd done it . . . for fun? With a boyfriend? And he made a video they liked to watch alone together.

Was that *possible*?

Jazz flipped off the comforter, heading to the shower to wash the sleepless night out of her. As she waited for the water temperature to rise, her gaze flitted over Jessica's things: aloe and cucumber body wash, a fluffy lavender loofa, shampoo and conditioner, a pale purple razor. All lined up in military precision on a sparkling marble shelf. Her own toiletries were a jumble in the opposite corner, lids off, of course.

Pain pulled at her heart. She missed her twin. Everything in this high-end doll house made her long for her sister, to hear her confident voice, to see that radiant smile. She ached to soak up all the stability and security that Jessica effortlessly oozed. To once again fall into the human safety net that had ensnared and protected Jazz so many, many times in thirty years.

She stepped into the hot spray and dropped her head back to let the steam and water sluice over her. *She* was the safety net this time, and the responsibility suddenly felt heavier than she could bear.

A short time later she stood in Jessica's closet, clad in

underwear. She'd applied some makeup and did her best to style her hair as Jessica would, and now had to choose another convincing outfit. The yellow suit had been fine yesterday, but today she wanted something a little less conspicuous.

Hmm . . . she thought she'd hung that unworn sheath with the other daytime dresses. She could visualize the tag dangling from the sleeve when she'd hung it back up. *Neiman Marcus. Café au lait. Size six.*

She slid clothes from one side to the other, dug in the back of the closet, searched the floor, and opened the hamper. The dress was gone. Could Jessica have taken it last night? Was it possible she stopped in for a change of clothes?

Yeah, right. And dropped her phone on the floor and forgot to leave a note. Instead, she just left her home sex movies on the DVD for them to watch.

The dishwasher, though—starting the dishwasher was as good as Jessica's signature on a note.

Wasn't it?

A tap at her bedroom door pulled her from the depths of doubt.

"Hey, Sleeping Beauty," Alex called through the closed door. "Up and at 'em."

No sultry Spanish wake-up call today. "I'll be right there."

She picked a silk blouse and a conservative skirt, along with shoes designed by a sadist, then opened the door to find him not one foot away, waiting. A solid wall of shoulders and chest and that long, glossy hair that smelled clean and woodsy.

"Security is waiting for us," he told her. "We're going down to see the videotapes of the hall camera."

She slid by him in the narrow hallway. "What did you tell them? About me?"

"I informed them that Miss Jessica Adams has retained the services of a personal protection specialist because of an overzealous fan. And that she has requested to see the security tapes to be sure no one is lurking near her apartment when she is gone."

Reasonable enough. She glanced at the living room, noticing that he'd straightened up, thrown her empty water bottle away, and folded the blanket. Slipping her handbag over her shoulder, she asked, "How did they react to your request to see the tapes?"

He handed her a small cup of espresso. When had he gone out for this? "Indignant. The Del Mar Towers has impeccable security measures, according to management."

"Maybe they do," she countered, tossing back the potent liquid as she'd seen him do, then cringing as it burned her throat. "And maybe the only person who got by them last night was the owner of 3701."

He punched the alarm pad, then unbolted the door. "I really want to change this code but I can't find the alarm handbook."

"Don't change it yet," Jazz said. "Then Jessica won't know it."

"So when she comes to visit—which conveniently only happens when you're not here—she can't get in?" Skepticism was all over his face. "Only someone lazy would use their social security number for an alarm code, by the way."

"Jessica's not lazy," she said defensively. "Those genes were stored up for the younger twin."

"You're selling yourself short," he said, stepping into the hallway before indicating for her to join him. "So you're the younger one, huh?"

"Yep, by twenty-six minutes."

"That's a long time between twin births, isn't it?"

"And I've been late ever since." She punched the elevator button. "Where are the security offices?"

"Near the lobby." With the gentlest touch on her arm, he held her back when the car arrived. "I'm first, remember."

"Have you called Lucy?" she asked when the doors closed behind her.

He regarded her for a moment. "You didn't sleep well." He feathered the delicate skin under her eye with his fingertip.

Her skin burned under his touch and the intensity of his midnight-black gaze. "I didn't sleep at all," she admitted. "Which is not good for my disposition."

"Thanks for the warning."

She gave him a tight smile. "Thanks for the coffee. You didn't answer my question. Did you call your girlfriend?"

"I don't have a girlfriend," he said as the elevator doors opened and he walked out.

"You're not sleeping with your boss?"

That earned a sharp, heartfelt laugh. "I'd sooner have sex with a black widow spider and die when it was over. Same general experience."

Before she could pursue that, they arrived at the security offices and Alex swept in with a quiet air of confidence and authority. The security manager spoke Spanish to him, and she noticed that Alex answered in English for her benefit.

Even in the mixed languages, Jazz could tell they had a problem.

"You mean there's no video?" Alex demanded after the other man had spewed a breathless explanation in rapid-fire Spanish.

"We don't know what happened." It clearly pained the manager to admit the security at Del Mar Towers was subpar. He shook his head and pointed to a blank monitor, part of a bank of video screens that lined one wall of the office. "The thirty-seventh floor camera was not working yesterday."

"Let me see what you've got," Alex said, barely hiding the disdain from his voice. "Take it back to the last recorded image."

A young man at the control panel punched a few buttons, keeping a cautious eye on Alex. "There is video up to yesterday afternoon," he said, pointing to one of the screens that showed a still image of the hallway. The digital print read 3:40 P.M. and yesterday's date.

They'd been inside the apartment then, Jazz recalled. Tracing e-mails, making phone calls, and doing background checks on names she didn't recognize in Jessica's address books. Looking for someone with the initials DR who might have had a meeting scheduled with Jessica.

And at that same time, out in the hall, a man walked off the elevator wearing a baseball cap pulled very low, and a jean jacket.

A jean jacket? It had to have been eighty degrees yesterday. Sunglasses and a slight build completed a totally unremarkable, forgettable man. He'd managed to keep his face from the camera, walking toward Jessica's neighbor's door, rapping only once, then backing out of the camera's range.

Then the picture went blank. It had stayed that way until someone on the night shift noticed.

"No one was watching the video feed from the thirty-seventh floor for almost twelve hours?" Irritation was thick in Alex's question.

The more senior of the two men shrugged and said something in Spanish.

Alex closed his eyes, his jaw tight. "The seven o'clock shift never showed," he explained to Jazz. "The security cameras back here weren't watched all evening."

"What about the guard at the desk? Doesn't he watch monitors?"

"He only sees the outside entrances on those monitors, and they are not on videotape," the man at the panel explained. "The feeds from each floor are only shown back here and taped in case we missed something."

"Let me see that video again," Jazz requested.

The two men stepped out of the room, arguing in Spanish as Jazz and Alex watched the replay. She leaned over the control board to study the visitor's body language. This guy was good. He must have known where the camera was, because he deliberately kept his head turned at an angle so the camera couldn't quite capture his face. He was not a big man, maybe five foot nine. No hair visible under the cap or over the collar of the jean jacket. Big glasses, no special designer frames. The ball-cap was plain navy blue.

Behind her, Alex placed his hands on either side of her and leaned over her shoulder, his body a breath away from hers. "He slipped out of the camera's view, slithered back down the hall and disabled the camera," he said softly.

"We don't know that," Jazz replied. "He could have been let into 3702 after the camera went out."

He put his mouth against her ear. "You're fooling yourself, Jazz. This guy dodged the camera, then disabled it so he could break into the apartment while you were out at night."

She turned her head, bringing them face to face, nose to nose, lip to lip. "He broke in to start the dish-washer?"

"Or he's a sicko fan and broke in to leave her his little home movies." His voice was low and steady and patient.

"Let's talk to the guy in 3702," she finally said. "And if you want, you can call your black widow."

"Good girl," he said, backing away.

She seized a handful of his hair and pulled him even closer to her face. "But not a word to anyone at the station. Not yet."

She had to cover every base. Wasn't that what her sister would do?

God help her, she had no idea what her sister would do anymore.

The level of noise and activity in the newsroom was exponentially greater at three thirty in the afternoon than it had been at dawn the day before. Police radios blared from the assignment desk, and on each of the walls, long banks of monitors played all the major networks and cable stations. Phones jangled constantly and no one dreamed of using an intercom when yelling over heads would work just as effectively.

Jazz itched to get out there and into the thick of it. She missed a lively newsroom, having given it all up to work in the silent, dreary office of Sandusky Investigations and then, after breaking up with Elliott, in her own quiet apartment in San Francisco.

But she couldn't take the risk of conversations with strangers. Alex stood sentry outside her glass door, eliciting a few interested looks—especially from women—but no one seemed that surprised that he was there.

That led Jazz to believe that the threats against Jessica must be public knowledge and considered legitimate. There were so many more questions than answers. Even the visitor to the thirty-seventh floor remained a mystery, since Jessica's neighbor hadn't answered the door when they'd tried earlier.

Glancing through the glass at the newsroom, Jazz searched the faces of her sister's colleagues. Didn't she have one good friend here? Why didn't any women come in to shoot the breeze? Jazz longed to confide in someone, to identify the one person whom Jessica completely trusted, and tell that person the truth. Or ask questions of someone who might have an inkling of the story Jess was pursuing. Jonathan Walden had stopped by to make small talk, but a sixth sense told her he was no one to trust. His smile never made it anywhere near his eyes and he just smelled like a phony.

She read her copy for the live update and then the newscast as it was forwarded to her computer, and made a few changes. Then she rifled through the files in Jessica's desk drawers, looking for clues, and dug again through all of Jessica's recent e-mails, and even the database of local news stories. But whatever Jessica was doing, she hadn't left a trail to follow.

When the floor director knocked on her door to announce it was time to get ready for the live update, she almost leaped out of her chair.

Alex fell into step with her as they crossed the newsroom and headed down the hallway toward hair and makeup.

"Jessie!" She turned to see Oliver Jergen hustling toward them. Alex immediately stepped forward and created a human barrier as the man rushed closer.

Oliver halted midstep as he realized what Alex was doing. "I'm a friend, not a foe," he said, pulling his hands out of his pockets to show he was unarmed, adding a look of dismay to Jazz. "Can I talk to you for a minute?"

"Of course."

"Alone? It's, uh, personal."

Jazz put her hand on Alex's arm. "Please. He'll walk with me to makeup."

Alex shook his head.

"Never mind," Oliver spat out. "I'll catch you in your office after the update, Jess." He gave Alex a disgusted look and walked away.

"What the hell is the matter with you?" she demanded. "What if he had something important to tell me?" She lowered her voice and narrowed her eyes at him.

"Listen, I have to talk to some of these people to figure out where Jessica is."

"So talk," he said as they continued toward the dressing area. "I'm not stopping you."

"In case you haven't noticed, you're a little intimidating."

A smile tipped his lips. "That should get me a bonus."

She snorted and left him in the hall while a makeup artist dabbed concealer under her eyes and did her hair.

The update took less than five minutes, with Jazz seated at the main anchor desk, reading from a TelePrompTer above a robotic camera. The evening news promised to cover a murder in South Miami, a fire in Fort Lauderdale, the resignation of a local judge, and the next day's opening game for the Miami Heat.

Oliver Jergen was waiting in her office when she finished.

"Your thug let me in," he said with a quick smile when she greeted him.

"So, what's up?" she asked as she dropped into her chair and casually clicked her mouse to the e-mail screen. Just in case.

"You tell me."

His solemn tone grabbed her attention. She turned from her computer to see his hazel gaze on her, noticing that his beard had grown even shaggier since yesterday. An ancient "Dave Matthews Live" T-shirt hung loosely over narrow shoulders.

"What does that mean?" she asked.

He leaned forward and dropped both elbows on the desk, no smile evident. "How long have I known you?"

Her chest tightened. How long had Jessica been in Miami? "Two years."

"And in all that time, have I ever jerked your chain about anything?"

"Only if I deserved it," she said with what she hoped was an honest smile.

"So why the hell are you acting like this?"

She tamped down a flash of panic. Was she doing something wildly out of character? "Like what?" she asked, innocently and with the perfect anchor voice.

"Like a goddamn bitch."

Her jaw dropped. "What?"

"Jessie." He threw a look toward the glass wall where Alex's back was plainly visible. "You said it didn't matter."

Damn. *What* didn't matter? "Talk to me, Ollie."

She saw color rise on his cheeks. "We talked enough. And you promised me, you promised me—" He punctuated his words with a finger pointed toward her, "—that you would treat me exactly the same. And now you don't even say good goddamn morning."

"Calm down, Ollie," she said softly. "You don't understand."

He dropped back into his chair and crossed his arms. "Oh, I understand plenty."

"No," she said quickly, "You don't. There's more to this than meets the eye."

He just shook his head. The hurt in his eyes was evident and Jazz whirled through the possibilities. Had he been jilted? Not for one moment would he be someone Jessica would be involved with, but . . .

Could *he* be Mr. Amazing? Or could he be one of the very cutthroat colleagues Jessica wanted to keep in the dark about her story?

"Ollie." She reached out a hand across her desk. "Can you just give me a few days? I'm having a really hard time with this whole bodyguard thing and the . . ." The *what*? "This story I've been working on."

She watched his face for any possible clue or reaction, but he pushed the chair back and stood. "I don't know who the hell you think you are, but you're not fooling me," he said with a scathing look. "You're a complete phony and it's only a matter of time until he finds out."

He? Who?

He bolted out of the room, leaving Jazz to stare at his back and replay his words.

Did that mean he knew she wasn't Jessica? If so, wouldn't he come right out and accuse her? However she had inadvertently hurt the guy, she could only hope the relationship would be mended by Jessica when she came back. Surely she'd tell her closest friends what she'd done to get her story.

If Ollie was indeed a friend.

Denise Rutledge managed to slip through the sliding gate into the Channel Five parking lot behind someone with a key code pass. Gripping the Reliant's wheel, she pulled into a spot far away from any other cars, but where she could still see anyone entering or leaving the TV station.

Her whole body hurt from work today. That jerk-off director made her swallow every drop those guys could eke out of their balls, and then he eighty-sixed the one condom Dirk Pierce bothered to wear. "No rubbers!" the asshole had insisted, stopping the shoot and ripping the thing off poor Dirk's flagging cock himself. "Viewers hate rubbers!"

Viewers. Puhlease. Like they had freakin' fans.

Pathetic losers too stupid to get their porn from the Internet, more like. Morons who had to buy videotapes so they could get their rocks off the old-fashioned way.

She had to try one more time with Jessica Adams. Because, face it, no one else gave a rip about the lousy working conditions of a porn actor. Denise would have continued doing them without any real hope, but then that pretty red-headed woman walked up to her outside the studio, waving a Metro-Net business card.

They both worked in front of the camera, Jessica had said in her smooth voice to get Denise to talk. Yeah, sure, Jessi-belle. How many orgasms did you fake during the eleven o'clock news?

But now Denise was in too deep. She'd committed a crime by stealing paperwork and all those DVDs from the studio. The thought made her temples throb. Even worse, she'd made the biggest mistake of all—imagining she could live a different life, could realize her dream of returning to Minnesota, and Grady.

If she got caught having these "conversations" with a TV person, she'd be blackballed so fast, she'd never get the money she needed. She'd already lost plenty of work to packs of silicone-enhanced eighteen-year-olds who thought screwing for the camera was a ticket to Hollywood. Or worse, the girls doing it on the Internet for free.

Denise had no such illusions. She fucked for money. She might not like doing it in a cold studio and having to service a few crew members for extra cash, but it was not against the law. At thirty-three, she wasn't really stripper material anymore. Plus, she got professional hair and makeup, pretty clothes that she could some-times keep—or forget to return—and the money was decent, especially if she was willing to do some of the more kinky shit.

Then came Jessica Adams and her empty promises.

No, maybe not empty. If she could get what Jessica promised—and what they all deserved—she could go up to Minnesota and get a legitimate job, like working at a makeup counter in a department store. Those girls must make enough money to live. Enough money to pay for school and clothes and health insurance. She was good with makeup and hair. She'd love that job.

She had to give Jessica Adams one more chance.

Out of the corner of her eye, she saw a security truck cross the parking lot. She dropped down on the passenger seat until he passed.

Slowly, she sat up and watched the main door every time it opened, praying she hadn't missed her. What would Jessica say when she saw her? She might not be too pleased that Denise had tracked her down at work, but what else was she going to do?

The guy caught Denise's attention first—he was really tall and great looking in that steamy Latin way. His hair was so long and straight it fell over the collar of his shirt, black as night. Right behind him strolled Jessica Adams. Dressed, of course, in clothes that cost more than Denise made in a month.

Grabbing her backpack, Denise opened the car door. Heels tapping on the asphalt, she started for the steps leading up to the TV station lobby.

She felt the dark eyes on her like daggers immediately. If looks could say "don't take one more step," that man's piercing black stare did the trick. She instinctively slowed down as his gaze raked her.

Jessica's attention was on her own feet, then she looked up. First, straight ahead of her, then, as if following the man's gaze, directly at Denise.

Denise's heart leaped to her throat and she swallowed a nervous hello. Jessica's gaze flitted over her, then beyond her, then back down to her feet. Denise almost tripped. She couldn't believe it. The bitch was completely ignoring her!

The guy still stared hard at her. She averted her eyes and then took one more look at Jessica, just as they passed each other. Her cool grayish eyes stared straight ahead. No flicker of acknowledgment, not even a casual nod.

Anger and shame roiled through Denise. Not knowing what else to do, she climbed the three stairs to the front doors, hearing the click of Jessica's high heels on the pavement of the parking lot.

She opened the door, stared for a moment at the security guard behind the desk, and then snapped her fingers as though she'd forgotten something. "Be right back," she said with a fake smile, turning to face the parking lot just in time to see the ice princess climb into the passenger seat of a big black SUV. She memorized the license plate, swearing viciously.

Who the hell did she think she was, that she could snub someone who risked her whole career just to get her the fucking information she needed?

You're going to be sorry, bitch. Payback sucks. And she knew just who to call to settle the score.

CHAPTER
Seven

Alex would have preferred to interview the neighbor alone, but he didn't bother to suggest that to Jazz. True to form, she stood in front of him, knocked on the door of 3702, and stuck her face right in the peephole of Christopher Norton's condo.

"Mr. Norton? Can we talk to you for a moment?" she called out. "We need to ask you a few questions."

"Is that you, Jessica?" The question was muffled through the door, but the note of surprise was evident.

Jazz threw Alex a quick look of warning over her shoulder before answering. "It's me, Christopher," she called.

The door opened a crack and a diminutive man in his late twenties poked his face through the space just above the chain. "What are you doing here?" he asked, openly surprised.

"I live here," she responded without missing a beat

"Why aren't you at the studio?" Norton's confused gaze slid up to Alex. "What's going on?"

"Ms. Adams has reason to believe her apartment was broken into, and the security tapes are malfunctioning," Alex announced. "We'd like to talk to you about a visitor to the thirty-seventh floor yesterday."

Bottle green eyes raked him with a mix of interest and disdain. "Are you a cop?"

"I'm a personal protection specialist."

A broad grin broke across his face. "Jessica, you hot ticket, you got a bodyguard." He closed the door, slid the chain, and opened it just enough for them to get the message that they weren't invited in. He propped a hand on his hip and looked skyward. "Somebody was bitching about this at the condo association meeting last week. That's the sixth time since I've moved in that the camera malfunctioned." He looked sympathetically at Jessica. "Did they take anything valuable? Are you all creeped out, honey?"

Christopher Norton couldn't have been five foot six, wearing a Hugh Hefneresque silk bathrobe with bare feet. The aroma of cinnamon and sugary spice drifted from inside the apartment.

"I'm fine." Jazz gave him a noncommittal smile. "We're trying to identify a person who knocked on your door around three thirty yesterday afternoon."

Norton lost some color. "Are you serious, Jessica?"

"We're trying to identify the last person recorded on the hallway security video tapes," Alex corrected. "And if you don't know him, then we know he simply used knocking on your door as a cover for the few seconds he had to be on camera. He may have disengaged the system to break into Jessica's apartment last night."

"He's really not a cop?" Norton asked Jazz.

She shot a warning look at Alex before answering. "No, he's not."

"All right," Norton said, holding up fingers to make air quotations. "Official statement here: Nobody was here yesterday at three thirty."

As much as Alex wanted to believe him—it supported his theory that the person on tape broke into Jessica's home—he knew Christopher Norton was lying.

"Would you be willing to look at the tapes with us?" Jazz asked. "Just to be sure you don't know the person who knocked on your door?"

"It's not necessary." He gave an exaggerated eye roll, then examined the fingernails of his outstretched hand. "I was *alone,* okay?"

"All day?" she prodded.

He looked hurt. "Are you really going to do this to me?"

Do what? Alex wondered. "Could it have been a delivery person?" he asked. "Do you work from home, Mr. Norton?"

"Yes."

"Were you working yesterday?" Jazz asked.

"Couldn't you smell it? I had a big fat chipotle fest."

Jazz gave him that genuine look of concern Alex had seen her use when she read about a crime victim on the TelePrompTer. "If you insist that no one was here, then I'll have to let the police run their checks on the man they have in the security photo."

His Adam's apple moved up and down. "Can they do that?"

"Absolutely," she assured him.

Alex managed not to give her a look of complete disbelief. Who was she kidding? They couldn't get an ID with that picture.

But Mr. Norton's interest had clearly ratcheted up to concern. "Really?"

"Or we could avoid that," Jazz said gently. "If you can verify that the man . . . was with you."

"There was no guest," Norton said quickly.

Why was he lying? "What do you do for a living, Mr. Norton?" Alex asked.

Norton *tsked*, as though it were common knowledge. "I'm a writer."

"What kind of writer?"

Norton gave Jessica an imploring look. "You didn't tell him?"

She paused for just a second. "No. Not yet."

"I write cookbooks," Norton said with a proud grin. "And she's so modest. Jessica is going to be one of the featured celebrities in my next book. Wait till you taste her chilled papaya soup." He kissed his fingers like a classic French chef. "Award-winning."

She gave them both a self-effacing smile. "Christopher, could you help me, please? Just come with us to the security office and tell me if you've seen this guy. I hate to get the police involved—we don't want this place crawling with reporters from the *Herald*." She lowered her voice and leaned closer to him. "You know how much we need our privacy and security in this building."

He raised a clefted chin. "Come on, Jessie. Don't do this to me. You know."

"I know. But, please?" She put a warm hand on Norton's arm.

He swallowed visibly. "Okay. New official statement: Someone delivered some galleys from my publisher yesterday. It could have been around three thirty. Will that keep the police away?"

"Did you see the courier?" Alex asked.

Jazz burned him with a look, then turned her charm back on Christopher. "This won't go public, I promise. It's just for my peace of mind."

"Okay, okay." His cheeks darkened slightly. "I was . . . I needed some creative stimulation yesterday."

"And you had a visitor," she gently urged him on. "Didn't you?"

"A very reputable escort service, Jessica. I assure you."

She whipped her head around to give Alex a look of sheer victory before flashing a smile to Christopher Norton. "Thank you. You are a good neighbor, Christopher."

He reached out and touched her arm. "Only for you, Jessica."

"Could you identify him?" Alex interrupted.

Norton looked up at Alex with pure irritation. "Well, yeah."

"Will you come downstairs to security with us?" she asked.

"With *you*, Jessica," he responded, firing Alex another withering glance.

"I go where she goes," he said darkly.

"Lucky you," Norton said in a stage whisper to Jazz. "Wait while I get dressed."

The door closed and Jazz turned to him. "So. Mr. Avoid the Camera was a gay male escort."

"Possibly."

"I just knew it," she said. "I knew he was hiding something immediately."

"Maybe he is." At her confused look, he added, "Maybe the little twerp has your sister bound and gagged in there and is doing all sorts of unmentionable things to her."

She choked back a disbelieving laugh. "He's a gay chef, Alex. What could he do to hurt her? Force feed her chocolate chip cookies?"

"Then why didn't he let us in?" Alex countered.

"Because you are just way too intimidating."

The door whipped open and Norton had changed into jeans and a button-down shirt. Jazz gracefully got him to talk about his latest project all the way down the elevator and into the security offices. She managed to guide the guards out of the room after they cued up the tape. And then she proceeded to make mincemeat out of Alex's intruder theory by getting Norton to admit that the man on the camera was his "escort" the day before.

When they were back in the SUV, headed toward the studio for the evening broadcast, they were no closer to knowing who'd entered Jessica's apartment than they had been the night before. Alex had procrastinated calling Lucy all day. Meanwhile, Jazz was cloaking herself in her belief that her sister was fine—except for her tawdry sexual activities on the side.

The whole situation infuriated him.

He pulled off Brickell Avenue onto a side street through the heart of downtown Miami. Despite the glitzy location right near the white-collar, high-end financial district, the Miami River section of downtown gave the local DEA plenty of work.

The streets were nearly deserted, but he noticed headlights of a car about a block behind him that had taken the last two turns he did.

"After this broadcast," he said, his gaze shifting between the rearview mirror and the road, "you don't have to be at the studio for two days or pretend to be Jessica for forty-eight hours."

She turned in her seat to look at him. "Does that mean you're leaving?"

"No. We're going to find your sister. No matter what it takes."

As the lights approached his back end, he purposely dropped his speed. A sedan with blacked out windows passed slowly.

"She'll call by then, believe me."

The passing car picked up speed quickly and turned off at the next crossroad. Alex eyed the darkness of Brickell Park as they approached a two-lane drawbridge over the Miami River.

"Do you have that kind of identical twin experience where you feel what she feels?"

"Empathy? Nah, we never had a 'shared language' or any of those twin weirdnesses. We are night and day."

"Rivalry?"

She shifted in her seat. "I'm not the jealous type."

"And Jessica?"

"Jealous of me?" She laughed as though it were preposterous. "Jessica's got it all going on and then some.

Trust me, this is the first time I ever got called in to get her out of a jam. On the other hand—what is that guy doing?"

The sedan sped out of the cross street and turned into their lane.

Her gasp matched Alex's curse. Blinding bright beams bore down on them as both cars approached the opposite sides of the short bridge.

The sedan picked up speed, heading straight for them.

"Alex!" Jazz called out, gripping the dashboard. "Watch out!"

He swerved into the left lane to avoid a head-on collision. The sedan slowed down and whipped into the same lane as Alex threw the Escalade into reverse and cut backward. The rear end smashed into the side of the drawbridge with a deafening clunk.

The sedan bore down harder, directly at the passenger seat. A ninety-degree hit would shove the SUV right over the bridge. Alex slammed on the accelerator and fired forward, swerving again, narrowly avoiding the sedan before it screamed across the bridge.

"Go get him!" Jazz ordered, turning to watch the taillights disappear into the next side street.

Alex just glared at her.

"What are you waiting for?" she demanded. "He's getting away!"

"You don't get it, do you, Jazz?" he asked.

She slammed her hand against the seat. "How could you sit here after someone just—"

"I protect, not provoke," he said simply. "There's a

huge difference. My job is not to stand and fight; it's to anticipate risks them and avoid them. My job is to keep you alive."

"Very noble, Mr. Bodyguard," she said, glowering at him. "But you just let some idiot get away who tried to run us off the road."

He narrowed his eyes at her as he stopped at a red light. "Let me ask you something."

She looked at him silently.

"You love your sister, right? You want her to have her great career and fancy apartment and legions of adoring fans."

"Where are you going with this?"

He floored the accelerator, channeling his frustration into his right foot, keeping his voice calm. "Pull out your phone, cancel your newscast, then step aside and let me call in some experts so we can find Jessica. Before it's too late."

He heard the quick intake of her breath. Then she slowly reached for her bag and pulled out her cell phone. "On one condition," she said.

He barked a laugh. "I don't do conditions."

"I'm in charge of the investigation, Alex. I am an equal here, not a tag-along."

He tried to think of one Bullet Catcher who could come into this job and match her investigation skills, but he didn't know any who could hack and cajole information out computers or people better than Jazz.

"Fine. You be in charge of the investigation. Just stop pretending to *be* her so we can *find* her. If you don't show up for a few newscasts, she might call to find out why you're jeopardizing her job."

Jazz's heart was still smacking against her ribs as she dialed the newsroom number. He was right, damn it.

"This is Jessica Adams," she said slowly. "I need to talk to . . ." She looked up at Alex for a moment. ". . . whoever's on the desk right now."

In a moment, the line clicked. "Assignment. Jergen."

Did Ollie ever go home? Jazz could have sworn he spent every waking minute at the station. And she wasn't thrilled that he'd answered her call; their parting had been too uncomfortable.

"I'm not able to do the eleven o'clock newscast," she said quickly.

For a long moment, there was dead silence.

"Ollie?"

"I heard you. You're being really, really dumb."

Guilt swirled through her gut. "I know, but I'm sick, Ollie. That stomach virus is totally—"

"Jess!" He hissed into the phone. "This is me, for Christ's sake. Cut the crap. I know what's going on, remember? I know exactly what you're doing on your off hours."

He did? "Well . . ." She glanced at Alex, whose impassive expression didn't change as he'd turned the SUV around and headed back to Del Mar Towers. "What do you think I should do?"

Ollie snorted. "Sweetheart, what I think isn't important. The only person who matters is Yoder. At least to you."

Yoder? Her mental computer called up the Y's in Jessica's address book. Had there been a Yoder? "Why do you say that?" she asked.

"Why the hell do you think? You've made your decision and you've made your commitment. Forget me." He laughed sharply. "Well, you did that, already."

"Ollie, stop it." How had Jessica forgotten him? "What about Yoder?"

"What about him? He came after you, baby, and you bit the hook. Now you have to live with that decision. But this? Calling in sick at ten o'clock? It's unprofessional, unethical, and stupid. What's gotten into you?"

She had no idea what to say, but he sighed softly.

"I don't know, Jessie." Some of the anger had gone from his voice. "This whole thing came at you hard and fast, and I understand the allure. I mean, I obviously do. I guess even you are entitled to be weird. Especially after you got those wacko letters, and now you've got Guardzilla dogging you every time you go to the bathroom. "

The allure? Of what? "It's been difficult," she said, going over his words in her mind. "But what's the allure, exactly?"

He chuckled. "You kill me, Jessie. You really do. Go do what you have to do. I'll get Jon Boy Walden to cover for you. But on Monday, you gotta tell loverboy the truth. And don't expect him to write you up a flattering *au revoir* press release. He'll do everything possible to make your name mud when he finds out you went behind his back on this one."

Mud? An *au revoir* press release? Jazz clenched her teeth in frustration. Did she dare trust Ollie with the truth?

Before she did anything rash, she'd follow the lead on

Yoder. "I'm having a hard time reaching Yoder. I can't find his number here. Do you have it?"

He was quiet and she heard an alert from the police scanner in the background. "I gotta go, Jess," he said quickly. "Anyway, I threw that number away." He clicked off the line without another word.

His phone number must be somewhere in Jessica's cell or home phone. She'd find him. She could find anyone.

Except her sister.

As soon as they got back, Jazz locked herself in Jessica's room to launch a skip trace on someone named Yoder. There was no mention of the name in Jessica's computer, or on her caller ID on either her home phone or the cell Jazz had found in the closet.

She tried every directory on the Web, and found a few Yoders in Miami, two in Miami Beach. Were they worth a try?

She replayed the conversation with Ollie. Perhaps Jessica was about to break up with Kimball Parrish for this Yoder guy. Would Parrish fire her for that? No. He'd been talking to her about network opportunities.

And where did Ollie fit in? Why was he so hurt? Did he love Jessica and feel jilted?

Could Yoder be a source? Could the story she was working on risk getting her fired? Or be something she would quit over?

Jazz trolled through her own computer files and reread all of Jessica's messages over the past few weeks. There was a rushed quality to everything, but Jess had indicated that she was working on a big story and the station management frowned on that for some reason.

Right there, that didn't make much sense. They liked their anchors to have some ownership of breaking stories—at least they had at the TV stations where Jazz had worked. But Jessica gave the impression they were not keen on her doing any investigative reporting.

She said she'd need to be off-site for a while—whatever that meant—and she was sure if Jazz could step in for her, she'd never be missed. And there was that one e-mail, sent a few days before Jazz left.

I've met someone amazing, Jazz. He could change my life. He's smart, connected, and, best of all, he has a heart of gold.

Connected. There was something distinctly unromantic about that description. What kinds of connections were important to Jessica?

She cared about the breast cancer foundation she'd been involved with for years. But a scan through all the computer files on the subject revealed no one named Yoder. She'd never bothered much with social connections; work was always more important than her personal life.

She'd never hid her ambition; in fact, she wore it as well as any of her gorgeous clothes. With unabashed determination, she'd always had her eyes on the prize and had eschewed romance, fun, and travel since they'd gotten out of journalism school. Jazz, on the other hand, had pretty much embraced fun, managed to find romance—albeit mediocre—and loved to travel. Which was why Jazz didn't make it in cutthroat TV land and Jessica was on top of her game.

So what business connections would matter to Jessica?

She started Googling the local television stations, then the major networks, easily hacking into the intracompany telephone databases. There was a Yoder at ABC, a female production assistant on a syndicated talk show, but Ollie had definitely said *he*. There were no other Yoders at the major television networks, including Metro-Net.

All the networks were owned by larger conglomerates, so she started checking those corporate Web sites. Metro-Net was owned by Yellowstone, Inc., a megalith with fingers in more pies than she could imagine. But none of those pies was baked by someone named Yoder.

Who was higher than the executives at these corporations . . . the boards? Her fingers flying, she quickly found the board of directors for Yellowstone.

Bingo! She stared at the name highlighted on her screen, then scanned his bio.

Miles Yoder, a former investment banker who'd made billions on the Internet bubble, had been on the board of Yellowstone since 1999. That was *connected*. A surge of excitement burst in her as she clicked madly until she found the phone number of his office. She grabbed Jessica's cell phone and resumed a search for incoming and outgoing calls.

She almost called out with joy when she matched the number. Since it had no corresponding ID, she'd skipped over it before. He'd called her five days ago from his office! A thrilling rush of adrenaline burst in her veins.

Smart, connected, and a heart of gold.

Jazz leaped off the bed to tear into the hall and tell

Alex, then froze. Would he help? Or would he *avoid risks* at all costs? She hated how he'd refused to finish the job on the bridge, demanding that she play the game his way, on top of it. The macho man who had to call the shots. Sorry, Alex, but not this time.

In a few moments, she had her computer logged onto every different name-search capability she could unearth. No home phone number was listed for Miles Yoder in the metro New York area. She tapped into the private sites for name search information, and finally unearthed what looked like the exchange for a cell phone number for Miles H. Yoder in Manhattan.

Cross-checking it with Jessica's phone, she found the same number there, again with blocked name on the ID screen. Giving herself a mental pat on the back for investigative brilliance, she pressed dial without taking a moment to think about what she was doing.

It didn't even ring one full time. "Jessica? Is that you?"

She almost fell backward in relief. "Yes."

"Why aren't you doing the newscast? I'm watching it right now."

A member of the Yellowstone board of directors was watching a Miami local newscast? "Where are you?"

"Exactly where we left off," he said with a hint of a soft laugh. "Hung out to dry and waiting for you."

Somehow, she just knew he had the answer to where Jessica was. But she couldn't ask him, "Where am I?" while she was playing Jessica on the phone. "Are you . . . here?"

"Of course. I told you I'd stay until you were finished."

With what?

"Are you?" he prodded.

"Almost. I need to see you."

"Now?" he asked, surprised.

Every minute mattered. "Yes, if that's possible."

He was quiet for a second. "Have you made any progress?"

"A little." *Come on, Miles. Give me something to go on here.*

"You haven't gotten yourself in too deep, have you?"

Something twisted in her stomach. What was Jessica up to? She had to know, and Miles Yoder had the answers.

"I need to talk to you," she said. She had to see him in person and assess his trustworthiness. Possibly confide the truth. "It can't wait."

"My wife is asleep." A little aftershock rippled through her. This was definitely business, then. Jessica would never be involved with a married man. Of course, she'd have made the same claim about Jessica's owning, watching, or *participating* in sex videos. "Why don't we meet in the bar or at the pool?" he suggested.

"Okay. Where are you?"

"Still at the Biltmore. I'll meet you in the lobby in an hour."

Guardzilla would love her traipsing around the Biltmore at this hour. "I'll be there."

She popped off the bed and dropped Jessica's cell phone, a buzz of exhilaration making her head light. She had to ditch Alex. He'd ruin everything with those piercing, inquisitive eyes and that supersize body, demanding she sidestep danger even if it led her directly to Jessica.

Miles Yoder could be hard to crack, and, with Alex there, he might be totally unwilling to tell her anything.

But how could she lose Alex? He never slept. She'd bet any amount of money he'd be standing outside her door when she opened it. She blew a hair out of her eyes and went to the bathroom to touch up her makeup.

He had to have a weakness. Cuban coffee? Would he go out for some now? Probably not.

Well, he did have another weakness. Absently, she ran her hands over her chest. Yes, he had a weakness. She'd caught him indulging it more than once.

But how could she use that to distract him? She could hardly steal off to the Biltmore if he was on top of her. Unless . . . unless . . . she made him utterly weak, panting, and then sent him off . . . in search of a condom.

Yeah. It could work.

Her brain skimmed a bunch of scenarios until she landed on one. As plans went, it didn't merit much more than a C, maybe C-plus. But it could work. And it sure wouldn't hurt to try.

On the contrary, it might feel . . . really good.

CHAPTER
Eight

Alex closed his eyes and rubbed his temples, resting his elbows on the dining room table. Something was bothering him—a detail so minute, so faint, that he couldn't quite pull it into focus. He went through every moment of the day, from the trip to the security offices, to the studio, to the interrogation of the next-door neighbor, to the not-so-subtle message sent by a dark sedan. What was it? A missing piece teased him like a word he could practically taste in his mouth, but couldn't give voice to.

"I'm going to work out."

Jazz's announcement yanked him out of his concentration, and when he opened his eyes, he had to struggle to keep his jaw from dropping.

She was wearing ass-hugging biker shorts and a white mesh contraption that did exactly what he wanted to do with his hands: gift wrap her breasts with just a few choice inches left exposed.

"Aren't you going to put more clothes on?" he blurted.

She laughed. "I'm not your little sister, Alex. And I'm perfectly decent—this is a sports bra."

Is that what they called it? He'd call it . . . the afterlife.

"I'm just surprised you're going to exercise at midnight," he said casually.

She threw a bulging bag over her shoulder. She was clearly staying in character: she'd put some makeup on to work out. "The condo health club is open twenty-four seven, you know I'm a night owl. I'll be back in an hour."

He shook back the hair that had fallen into his eyes, taking another slow trip over her outfit. Lucy had promised him an easy client, yet he got stuck babysitting a plucky PI with a rack that belonged on the cover of *Maxim.* "All right," he said. "Let's go."

"You don't have to go," she insisted. "I'll be fine. I just need to lift weights for a while."

He scooped up the cell phone in case Lucy returned his call. And wouldn't *that* be a great time? Watching a near-naked Jazz pump iron while Lucy chewed his ass out for total incompetence. She'd have Gallagher or Roper down here by dawn.

On the bright side, once Jazz wasn't his principal, he could apply for a job as her personal sports bra.

"This is overkill," she argued. "The gym is locked and no one else will be there at this hour." She strode to the front door. "Plus, I'll be surrounded by hundreds of pounds of iron for personal safety."

He was next to her in less than two seconds. "You'll be surrounded by *me* for your personal safety."

Her gray eyes morphed to pure silver indignation. "I

need some time alone, Alex. Don't you give any privacy to the people you guard?"

"That's contrary to the point." He grabbed the house key from the table. "Privacy is exactly what your stalker wants you to have."

She rolled her eyes but waited while he set the alarm, then marched toward the elevator, leaving him to lock the door and watch her gluteus max flex under the shiny shorts.

The health club was a multistory affair, as luxurious as the rest of the place. Alex insisted on walking through the whole facility first, including the dressing rooms, with her two steps behind him. Then he gave her a nod.

"You can work out now."

She glanced around the empty gym. "I have to go to the bathroom," she said quickly. Too quickly. Why hadn't she gone before they left?

"I'll go with you."

She dumped her overstuffed bag next to the treadmill with an exaggerated puff of disgust. "Never mind."

Confident that the place was secure, he leaned against the wall by the entrance. If someone came in, he'd see them first, and he still had a direct view of his principal.

Who was already in a light jog on the treadmill, her gaze on the computerized readout in front of her. Unable to resist, he watched the sexy, rhythmic bounce of her breasts, rising and falling with every step she took. And it wasn't only her impressive chest that held his attention. His gaze moved to the mirror, which reflected a just-as-distracting rear view. She was slim but muscular, the shorts revealing every cut of her quadriceps and the sexy little dips in her buttocks.

As she picked up speed, the tip of her tongue peeked out from between her lips and a gloss of perspiration shimmered over the V-neck above her cleavage. She glanced up at him and their gazes locked.

He didn't look away. Neither did she.

On the contrary, she smiled. Slow. Sweet. Sexy.

She tilted her head, just enough to make him think he'd been invited on the treadmill with her. Instantly, he turned to the second floor balcony. Scanned the training machines. Studied the glass door to the pool.

But his gaze meandered back to the treadmill.

She was slowing down a bit, her attention still locked on him. Oh, Jesus. His belly tightened. She had that look again. The one she had in the restaurant the other night.

She stopped the machine and grabbed a hand towel, dabbing at her throat, the nape of her neck, and her exposed midriff. She never took her eyes off him. She sauntered over to the dumbbells, choosing two fifteen pounders before laying her towel on a narrow bench. Now what torture did she have in mind?

She eased onto her back on the bench and placed a leg on either side, knees to the mirror. The position offered him a clear shot of the shiny material between her legs, dark from sweat.

His pulse raged, his body reacted. But whatever game she was playing, she was outmatched—he could do his job with a hard-on. He already had been, for a couple of days.

Taking a dumbbell in each hand, she spread her arms. Blowing out a breath, she brought the weights together in a chest fly, causing her breasts to firm up and rise into insanely sexy peaks.

The first drop of sweat broke out on his forehead.

Five, six, seven. He lost track of her set, counting backward from one hundred in a dismal effort to get blood flowing back to his brain.

Finally, she stood up. She turned and gave him a quick smile, her gaze raking him.

"You okay over there?"

He lifted his chin in assent. "What's next?"

"Kickbacks." She placed one knee on the bench and balanced on the other leg. Bending over, she looked up into the mirror and he looked straight down her bra. The curves of her breasts were completely visible.

His mouth went desert dry and his whole lower half hummed with heat. What the hell was she trying to prove?

She went through two fairly fast kickback sets, working her upper arms. Her triceps constricted with each push, along with the heart shape of her backside. In the mirror, he could see her breasts firm and relax with each movement.

The image burned his brain. That's how they'd look if she were on top of him. And he could close his mouth over each nipple.

Arousal pumped through him in the same rhythm as her exercise, and he clenched his jaw.

"I need a spotter," she said as she hoisted a weight onto a barbell. "Can you help me, Alex?"

Just what he needed. *"Chiflada,"* he mumbled, pushing himself off the wall.

"I'm sorry, I didn't get that?"

He walked toward her. "I think in Spanish." At the most awkward times.

"Come on, Alex," she said, a laughing tease in her eyes as she swiped a damp lock of hair from her brow. "You know I don't speak Spanish. What did you say?"

"I said of course I can spot you." She didn't need to know he'd called her a prick tease. Hell, she'd probably take it as a compliment right now.

As he stood behind her and the bar, she held his gaze in the mirror. "And what are you thinking . . . when you think in Spanish?"

He dropped his gaze over her white top, drinking in the sheen of sweat, the obvious points of her nipples.

"I'm thinking about you. That's my job."

"You can quit anytime," she said flippantly. "You really don't have to stay down here in this gym if it's a drag for you."

"I'm used to it. My job tends to get tedious."

She drew her tongue against her lower lip again. "I'm sure you find ways to eliminate tedium."

He almost laughed at her lack of subtlety. "I watch for security breaches. That generally alleviates boredom."

She spun on her backside, then lay down on the bench, looking straight up at him. Even upside down she was sexy. Especially upside down. "I told you this place would be completely empty."

"But not secure." He placed his hands on the bar and stared down at her.

"It is secure." She flattened her back and closed her eyes, smiling. "And it's secluded."

"Lift," he commanded, rattling the bar gently against its brackets.

She curled her fingers over the metal. "I'm ready," she told him, inhaling a slow breath that pushed her chest higher.

He touched the thirty-five-pound weights on either side of the bar. "Can you handle this much?" he asked.

She looked into his eyes. "Can you?"

He smiled at that, but simply lifted the bar and helped her ease it down over her chest.

"Let go now," she requested as she took over the bench press. Her color started to heighten on the fifth press, so he took the barbell and placed it back on the rack.

"Not bad, Jazz. No wonder you damn near knocked the wind out of me the other night."

With a grin, she sat up and pivoted to face him, inches from his visible erection.

She leaned back on her hands, the fabric of her thin top straining. "You're being kind. I barely surprised you."

He laughed honestly. "You surprised the hell out of me."

She took the towel and wiped her neck again, this time sliding the terry cloth slowly over her chest. "Would you be a darling and hold my feet and count my crunches?"

A *darling*? She was definitely up to something. "Of course."

She dropped to a floor mat, a clear summons in her

eyes. Her lips parted as she lay back. She eased her knees up, then crossed her hands under her head.

"I need you now, Alex."

She was making that pretty damn obvious.

He slowly walked to the mat, and placed one foot on either side of her and looked down into her eyes. If she did one upward crunch, her mouth would be level with his crotch.

A rush of blood screamed in his ears.

"You can't do it standing," she said, pointing toward her feet with one elbow. "Hold my feet. Wait." She reached down and slipped her sneakers off, leaving just ankle-high socks. "Better yet, sit on them."

No one in her shape needed that kind of help for a sit-up. She could hang upside down and touch her knees with her nose. She was definitely up to something.

She moistened her lips. "Please, Alex. I want you . . . to."

He dropped to a crouch and encircled her ankles with his fingers. She tucked her feet under him and wiggled her toes. The sensation against his hard balls shot straight up his back.

He kept his face impassive. "How many can you do?" he asked.

"How many can you take?" she shot back.

"What are you trying to prove, Jazz?"

She eased one foot out from under him and slid it between his legs. Her eyes widened as her foot pressed against his erection. "I'm not trying prove anything. I'm trying to see . . ." She slid her foot up and down the length of him. ". . . If you're human." His shaft pulsed against her arch.

"Why don't you just ask me?"

Her lips curved up. "What's the fun in that?"

"Is this fun?"

She curled her foot over his hard-on, her toes caressing the sensitive tip, her heel prodding his balls. "You tell me."

He didn't move.

She sat up and threaded her hands at the nape of his neck, pulling him to her. "Kiss me, Alex." Before he could, she did. Crushing his mouth with hers and sucking at his tongue, nearly unbalancing him.

Damn it all, he was cursed. With a quick moan of desire, she took his hand and placed it over her breast.

He closed his fingers around the soft mound and heard the groan torn from his throat.

Nothing about Jazz had signaled that she'd be so brazen. Once again, something wasn't *right.*

But her breast filled his hand and her tongue filled his mouth and blood filled his cock so effectively that there was none left for his brain. Purring and moving like a cat, she slithered out of the sports bra in a quick, graceful move, and tossed it next to her shoes. Pulling him with her, she dropped back to the mat, arching toward him to offer two lush, womanly breasts.

"Just taste me, Alex," she crooned in his ear, combing her fingers into his hair and pushing his head to her nipple. "Taste me."

He flicked the tip with his tongue and she fisted her hand and ground her hips against him. His brain short-circuited with a flash of white light as he gave into the desire to suck her. He opened his mouth and took her in, pulling the nipple between his teeth, tasting the salt of her sweat and the cream of her flesh.

She wrapped her legs around him and rode harder, guiding his head to her other breast and pushing her pelvis against his erection.

"Me estás matando," he murmured. And she *was* killing him. He couldn't even think.

She laughed softly as her fingers dipped into the waistband of his pants. "What you said." Her hand closed around him and he jerked forward, lost in the pleasure of her first, mind-boggling stroke against his skin. She moaned appreciatively and brushed her tongue over his jaw, his lips. Heat surged through him, and he grew even bigger in her fingers.

"Wow," she whispered. "You hum."

The vibration of his cell phone ripped him back to reality.

"That's my phone."

"You'd better get it."

His gaze dropped to her breasts, the tips dark and wet and swollen. The phone vibrated again.

Jazz pulled her hand from the nest between his legs and raised one eyebrow.

He pulled the phone from his pocket and looked at the readout, confirming his suspicion. Lucy had flawless timing. Jazz reached up and suckled his lower lip. "Take your call. I need to run to the bathroom."

Lucy vibrated again, and he could just imagine one long red fingernail tapping in frustration with each ring.

Jazz slid out from between his legs and scooped up her shoes and the sports bra. "I'll be right back."

He opened his mouth to stop her and she leaned over, pressing one finger on his lips, trailing it down over his jaw, down his chest. Her breasts were inches from his face. "I'll be quick. I don't want to stop."

Before he could answer her, she pressed her lips against his, giving him a long, openmouthed kiss. "I'll be right back."

If Lucy hadn't been on the phone, he'd have followed her right into the women's locker room, which he imagined would be the scene of his undoing. And hers. He watched her backside as she bent to retrieve her bag. Running a shaky hand through his hair, he answered the phone. "Yeah, Luce. I'm here."

"I got your message." The fact that there was no ice in her tone pulled him out of his sexual haze and forced him to focus.

"And?"

"It's fine, Alex. Just continue to do what you're doing."

She didn't want to hang him by the balls for losing the principal and guarding the wrong woman? No—she really didn't mean that. "What do you mean?"

"I mean that this is an unusual and interesting turn of events, but not the end of the world."

He couldn't comprehend what Lucy was saying. "You listened to my whole message, didn't you? I don't know where Jessica Adams is. She's being replaced by her identical twin. There are threats against her." He hadn't even had a chance to go into the mysterious sex tape.

"Alex, just go along with it."

What the hell did that mean? "What about the client? Does he know?"

She was silent for what seemed like forever. "Don't get involved in that. Just protect her, and, as I told you, stay in front of him enough to make a positive impression."

Alex dropped on a workout bench, noting the rapid disappearance of his hard-on. "Lucy, listen to me. I have no idea where the woman he's paying us to protect is."

"She's on a story investigation."

"Are you sure? Does Kimball Parrish know that for sure?"

"Have you heard anything at all from her?" Lucy's voice was sharp, and she'd purposely avoided his question.

"Some bogus text messages."

"All right. Until further notice, this is your assignment: provide personal security to the woman that you have. And get as much face time with Mr. Parrish as you can."

Nothing made sense. "He's left Miami, do you know that?"

"He'll be back. You just do what I've asked you to do. Do you understand, Alex?"

No. He did not. He glanced toward the locker room door, pushing himself off the bench and heading in that direction.

"Do you understand, Alex?" The bite was back when she had to repeat her question.

"Yeah, I got it covered, Lucy." He opened the door and listened. Silence. "But let me ask you a question."

"Of course."

He walked past the lockers, a long vanity, mirrors and sinks. Nothing. "Is this sister still technically the principal?"

Lucy laughed softly. "So the twin is as attractive as the real thing?"

"She has a certain appeal." He checked the stalls. Every damn one was empty.

"Yes, Alex, my rules still hold."

"*Carajo,*" he mumbled as the truth of what Jazz had done hit him.

"This is important. Stay on the course you're on and don't complicate things with sex."

Alex spun around and stared at an emergency exit door that locked from the inside. Grabbing the handle, he swung it open to the hallway of the second floor.

"Your job is to keep everything under control, Alex."

He managed to mute the blackest curse he could think of, but punched the wall as frustration and fury careened through him. "Everything is under control," he lied.

"Even your libido?"

"Trust me, Luce." He leaned into the hall and could have sworn he heard the ding of an elevator around the corner. The little witch had escaped. "With this one, that's the least of my problems."

Once Miles Yoder got the call and learned that Jessica was being "replaced" by a twin sister, he pulled himself from the bed and slipped down to the Palme d'Or. This he had to see. Otherwise he would have remained in his suite, snuggled peacefully with the woman he loved.

From the far end of the bar, Miles sipped his Highland Park single malt and remained in the shadows. Fortunately, he wasn't the only man alone in the hotel bar that night. Would the imposter have the nerve to walk up to every one of them and ask his name?

If she was anything like Jessica, she just might. And he'd take it from there.

If she didn't approach him, he wouldn't approach her. As a twin sister, she may or may not be trustworthy. He couldn't know from one quick meeting in a bar. Either way, she was doing him a huge favor, and he preferred to keep it that way. She was obviously good enough to fool some very discerning audiences.

When he saw her pause at the entrance and scan the bar, he tried to be objective. Would he know she was an imposter if he hadn't been warned?

He'd spent quite a bit of time with Jessica over the past few weeks; they'd had several meals and long conversations. He had to admit, at first, he would think that woman was Jessica. Not just because of the face—which was eerily identical—but her posture, the tilt of her head, the body language as she nodded to the bartender and took a seat.

But Jessica would have known him on sight. And she never would have arrived twenty minutes late.

As she settled onto her stool, he decided he *would* have been suspicious because of her wardrobe. He'd never seen Jessica in anything but high-quality, elegant clothes. He couldn't imagine her wearing army pants, or going out with her hair looking like she'd combed it with a rake.

Intrigued, he sipped his scotch and observed her. Everything in him wanted to talk to her, test her. But he hadn't made it to the top of his game by gambling. He couldn't take the chance that she'd tell the wrong person, the wrong "friend" at work.

He felt her gaze fall directly on him and he ignored her.

As the bartender brought her bottled water, she leaned forward and asked him something. He shook his head.

He saw her shoulders sag a bit. As the bartender walked away, she added, "Could you bring me a Cuban coffee?"

Miles took a bill from his wallet and slipped it under his cocktail napkin. *Yes, Miss Jasmine Adams. You drink some coffee. You'll be sitting here for a long time waiting for a rendezvous that will never take place.*

He left the bar and strode through the historic lobby of the Biltmore, his curiosity satisfied. Now he was eager to get back upstairs to his soul mate.

The last thing Jazz expected when she opened the condo door at two in the morning was to find Alex watching porn. As she entered, he burned her with a look that matched precisely how she felt.

"Did you have a good time?" he asked, his voice low and humorless.

She shrugged off her bag and took a few steps into the living room, looking at the TV.

"I got stood up." She shoved her hands into the pockets of her pants and indicated the screen with her chin. On it, two women writhed around in a huge bathtub with a heavily tattooed man. "Hope I didn't drive you to that level of desperation."

"Not even close." He leaned forward with his elbows on his knees and stared at the soundless TV.

She slowly approached his chair, wired from espresso and frustration. His gaze remained riveted on the TV, expressionless. He didn't look like a sexually frustrated man reduced to watching porn to get his rocks off. His face didn't have that raw lusty look she'd seen a few hours ago.

Her body instantly responded to the memory of the moment he'd lost control, the second that she saw him give into the power of passion. She'd never seen anything so flat-out erotic in her life. When Alex Romero lost control, she'd almost come right on the health club floor under him.

Then some guardian angel had intervened before her pitiable plan backfired in the most glorious way.

"So DR didn't show, huh?" he asked.

DR? The question wrenched her back to the moment. "I didn't go to meet with DR. I have no idea who that is."

"Really?" He shifted in the chair, the colors of the screen casting an eerie glow on his jet black hair. A thick lock had fallen over one eyebrow, and another grazed his square jaw. Her fingers tingled to touch the strands.

"Allow me to introduce her," he said, pointing the remote toward the TV. "As soon as she finishes that blow job, you can meet Desirée Royalle."

Stunned, she turned toward the screen where a blond woman was indeed up to her neck performing bubble bath fellatio. "This isn't the same movie we watched last night."

"Nope. I hit the all-night video store."

She dropped to her knees, and glanced at the bizarre scene on TV, then back to Alex. "How'd you figure out she's DR?"

He froze the frame, then changed disks with a click of the remote. The machine droned and whirred, breaking the silence. Alex still didn't spare her a single glance.

Sighing softly, she placed her hand on the armrest, as close to him as she dared. "I'm sorry about . . . how I did that."

He barely raised one shoulder. "Forget about it."

Like that would happen in this lifetime. If she hadn't been hell-bent on a mission, she'd have spent the last two hours . . . She looked at the frozen image on TV.

Like *that*. Upside down and inside out, underneath and on top. If he'd gone looking for a condom, she'd have run after him naked—instead of running to the Biltmore, only to get blown off by some mystery TV executive who wasn't even a registered guest and never answered his cell phone again.

"Look," he instructed.

The screen suddenly flashed to something more familiar. *Wet Kiss*. As the opening credits rolled over a woman's face and pierced nipples, she slid her finger in her mouth and gave it a long, sensuous lick.

Jazz was in no mood to watch this trash again. "What am I looking for, Alex?"

"Her."

"What about her?" The actress dipped her wet finger

between her legs and said something to the camera before it cut away to the first scene.

"You didn't recognize her?"

Jazz squinted at the screen. "Not a lot of face time in that last shot."

"Come on, Jazz," he prodded. "You're the PI. Don't you remember where you've seen that woman?"

He skipped back to the opening again and froze the screen on the actress's face.

"Sorry, Alex. I've never seen her before."

"You saw her today. She walked right past you in the parking lot of Channel Five."

"No way!"

"And look at her here." He switched to the other disk, skipped a few scenes and froze the screen on the same blonde, this time with waist-length hair, wet from her bathtub frolicking. "That's your sister's source. Or maybe it's her good friend and coworker."

Slack-jawed, she looked from him to the TV screen. "How did you figure that out?"

"I kept thinking about it, and finally decided that it was during that moment in the parking lot that the sense that I'd missed something started to bother me."

She knew that feeling, but she hadn't experienced it today. Was she so wrapped up in pretending to be Jessica that she overlooked obvious clues?

Alex continued his explanation. "I saw that woman walking toward us and I knew I'd seen her before. And it wasn't in the newsroom or anywhere else we'd been. After you disappeared tonight, I remembered the video last night."

Jazz inched closer to the TV, sitting on the floor in front of him. "Hit play again. I want to get a better look."

The action started up again. "The closing credits list a woman named Desirée Royalle—DR on your sister's calendar. To be sure, I stopped by the triple-X video store and found two more of her movies. Both produced in Miami, by the way."

The actress in the tub pulled back from her lover for a close-up.

"That's the woman we saw in the parking lot," he stated. "No doubt about it."

"I hardly noticed her." She remembered the moment, however. She'd been trying to navigate the steps in Jessica's high heels.

"She was carrying a backpack and smelled like cigarettes," he said. "She also glared at you for a long time."

Realization rocked her. "She probably thought I was Jessica—and that I ignored her."

Alex turned off the TV, leaving the room lit only by a golden sheen from the nightscape reflecting off Biscayne Bay. "But that's not our problem, is it? Just go about your life as your sister, and when she comes back, she can explain everything to us."

Jazz looked at him, dumbfounded. "What? You don't want to go find this woman? What if she knows where Jessica is?"

"Jessica is working on a story," he said quietly. He reached over to the end table and picked up a bottle of water. He took a long pull and then let his head drop back, black hair falling against polished white cotton. "We'll just wait for her."

"Like hell we will." She rose to her knees and suddenly realized she was in front of his lap, on her knees, in the dark, not two feet from his body. The vivid memory of his throbbing erection against the sole of her foot knocked her right back down. "I'm going to find this Desirée and talk to her, with or without you."

"How are you going to do that, Jazz? Blind me with lust again?"

Without the TV, the only sound was the soft hum of the air conditioner. He stared at her from under half-closed lids, his long eyelashes making black circles under his dark eyes. "What exactly did you have in mind, Jazz? Did you think you could fuck me unconscious?"

The raw language cut through her. "I thought . . . you might have to come back up here for a condom. And then I could . . . leave."

He shook his head with a caustic laugh. "Do you seriously think I'd make a mistake like that?" He held up a hand as if to correct himself. "Though I admit I've been a little off my game since you first walked in that door."

God, she'd hate to see him *on* his game. "I knew it was a lousy plan."

"Lousy? Nah. I liked it." His smile was forced. "But you knew that."

"I really needed to get out on my own tonight." The explanation sounded as pathetic as she felt.

"Your technique was creative, I'll give you that. But reckless."

"How so?"

"I could have skipped the condom," he said. "I could have just taken you."

It was more like the other way around, and they both knew it. "But that would go against your training."

Slowly, he leaned toward her. Without a word, he reached under her hair, taking her neck in his hands and pulling her so close that his breath warmed her face as her heart skidded around her chest. "Everything about this assignment goes against my training." There was no disguising the loathing in his voice.

With one strong hand, he eased her head to the side and pressed his mouth to her ear. "I've never lost a power struggle in my life, *querida*." His husky voice sent shivers to every nerve ending. "And I assure you I won't lose this one."

He released her, picked up the water bottle, and walked toward his room. The next sound she heard was the latch of his door.

Jazz sat on the floor and stared at the empty chair. Instead of indignation, or even a healthy dose of repugnance at his macho threats and cold dismissal of her, she ached. In the most physical way. In the most private places.

Not that he was about to ease that ache. No, that would be tantamount to waving the white flag in their *power struggle.*

There was nothing for her to do but figure out how to find Jessica. Tomorrow she would start a skip trace on the porn actress and find her.

Tonight she'd study her target, and lick her wounds. She settled into the club chair, soaking up the warmth that his body had left behind. She picked up the remote, prepared to watch Desirée Royalle do all the things she wanted to do with Alex.

But a sharp, unfamiliar sense of despair settled over her. She dropped the remote on the floor and pushed herself out of the chair, her eyes and throat suddenly stinging. What could cause that?

She shook it off and glared at Alex's closed door. It must have been all that Cuban coffee—or all that Cuban man.

CHAPTER
Nine

Consciousness hit Jessica like a physical punch. One second, she was as deeply asleep as she'd ever been, the next moment she was fully awake. She opened her eyes, but squeezed them shut just as quickly.

Confusion gushed through her, hot and scary in her stomach.

Where was she?

She frowned and squinted, slowly letting her pupils contract enough to be able to stand having her eyes open. She turned her head, seeing only a blank wall. The movement brought a sense of relief, and she scoured her brain to remember why.

Of course—she'd been paralyzed. But now she could move her head.

She wiggled her toes. Her fingers. Bent her right knee. Glorious muscles—they worked!

Holding her breath, she turned her head in the opposite direction. Skinny bands of light danced in her hazy vision, filtered through window blinds. She frowned as her gaze traveled to the foot of the bed where she lay. Everything was pale and gauzy and neat.

She liked that.

She tried to swallow, but her throat was painfully dry. She lifted her head and propped herself up on the pillow. Lifting the heavy comforter, she looked down at her body, sucking in a little breath when she realized she was completely naked.

She closed her eyes as a forbidding shudder trembled through her.

She remembered sleeping. And waking up paralyzed. And . . . forgetting her name. The terror of that particular memory caused the hot rush in her stomach again.

Jessica Lynn Adams. *I am Jessica Lynn Adams.* Born April 18, 1976. She recited it as though it were her name, rank, and serial number. A comforting, safe piece of knowledge that she could cling to.

Jessica Adams. A reporter. An anchor. In Miami.

Miami . . . She scooted higher on her elbows and looked around. Was she in Miami now? Was she a guest somewhere? Overnight? With a man?

A quick glance at the pillow next to her assured her she'd slept alone. Yet she was naked and in a strange bed. Instinctively, she reached between her legs. Her flesh was dry, and not the least bit tender. She hadn't been engaged in anything sexual.

But why was she undressed and in a bed? And how had she gotten there?

Had she driven there? Yes. Yes, she had been in her car. Her brand new beautiful car. She could still smell the fresh leather, hear the opening notes of a Mozart CD right after she'd turned on the ignition . . . and headed for . . . work. *Had* she been going to work?

She'd been going somewhere. At night. She squeezed her eyes shut, but her memory was totally blank.

Was this a hospital? Had she been in a wreck? Attacked in the parking lot?

And, Lord, why did her brain feel so utterly empty?

She tried to sit up, but nausea coiled through her. She clutched her stomach, certain she would throw up. Her tongue swelled and she couldn't stop the gag, but nothing came out of her. Two more dry heaves followed, and her limbs started to quiver. God, she couldn't remember being this sick.

She inched to the side of the bed, scanning the empty nightstand, the lone chair across the small room. A door with a brass knob. Absolutely nothing looked familiar. She stood on wobbly legs, glancing down at her body. Her stomach looked concave, and an angry purple-green, days-old bruise marred her left thigh. How long had she been there?

Cold, clammy fear wrapped around her heart.

"Where am I?" she whispered in a raspy voice. She managed one step to the window, using two fingers to lift a blind and peer out.

Crisp white moonlight reflected off black water. A rippling wave curled up and the translucent foam sparkled in the moonlight, just before it broke against a long stretch of sand. She could make out the faint *swoosh-thump* of the ocean.

She knew that sound; she'd been hearing it in her sleep. And the view looked vaguely familiar. It wasn't home, because her view was thirty-seven stories in the air. That little memory warmed her.

Just as the next breaker rose, a wave of pain and sickness crested in her stomach, so sharp that she doubled over, falling back on the bed and gagging. This time, tears came, and her body exploded with chills.

She needed help. She really, really needed help.

Jazz.

The name echoed in her head, and if she'd had the strength she would have called it out loud. Jazz! Jazz was on her way to help her. She'd promised.

Fighting the pain in her stomach, Jessica forced herself off the bed. She had to find clothes. A phone. *Answers.*

The burn of resolve felt as comfortable as knowing her name. She had to do something—and nothing stopped Jessica Adams when she had to do something. Stumbling to the door, she tried to twist the handle, but the knob jammed against her hand. She managed to get back to the window, yank open the blinds, and push at the metal casing. Locked.

All she could see was that long stretch of desolate beach. She banged a weak fist against the glass and whimpered in frustration.

A sense of panic rose but she forced it down. Dropping to her knees, she pulled open the drawer of the nightstand. There, she saw the most beautiful sight in her life: a pink suede handbag. With sudden clarity, she remembered buying the Chanel bag at Bloomingdale's, remembered the sensation of making the frivolous purchase.

She grabbed the purse like a starving woman who'd

found food. Her phone was in here. She could call 911. Or Jazz. Or . . . work. Yes, she could call Ollie. Ollie would always be there for her.

As she stared into the satin lining, disappointment stabbed her. She thrust her hand inside, flipping out a makeup bag, a plastic tampon case, and a comb and mirror. Where was her wallet?

Where was her phone?

Shaking, she curled on the floor and did the only thing her tired, aching, sick body would allow.

She wept.

Until a gentle touch on her shoulder jolted her up. Just as the gasp of recognition replaced her next sob, she saw the glint of metal catch the moonlight.

"It's not time yet, Jessie." Oh, that voice. She'd never noticed it was actually . . . menacing.

She tried to jerk away, but the sting in her leg stopped her cold. She looked down to see a needle buried into the ugly bruise. For one crystal clear moment, she understood everything.

And then she remembered Jazz. Oh, God. Was she pretending to be Jessica right this minute? If he found out the truth . . . if he knew who she was . . .

Then the world went dark and silent again.

Alex smelled the American coffee as soon as he approached 3701. After a six-mile run on the beach, the last thing he wanted was a cup of Chock Full O' Nuts, but he hadn't stopped for a *colada* and *pastelitos* because he wanted to shower and be ready for Jazz when she decided to get up. With her, he had no idea what to expect next.

And there she was, at seven A.M., dressed and sitting at the kitchen counter with her laptop open, a phone book next to her, and the coffee aroma wafting from a Krupps countertop percolator.

If it weren't for the fact that she wore no makeup and the same skimpy white tank top she'd arrived in, he'd have thought Jessica had mysteriously returned.

"You should use the chain lock when I'm gone," he said as he entered.

She didn't look away from the screen, tapping the keyboard ferociously. "I didn't do a bed check. I thought you were still asleep."

"I figured I could run and get breakfast before you stirred."

"You figured wrong."

"What are you working on?" He stood behind her and glanced at a database on the screen, inhaling the smell of her citrusy shampoo. "The Yellowstone intracompany phone book?"

Tipping the screen to dim it, she spun around on the barstool and came face to bare chest with him. She was so close he could see her individual eyelashes and the cream of her just-washed complexion. She was much prettier as Jazz than as Jessica. She didn't need stage makeup. She oozed an undercurrent of sexuality that was far more attractive to him than high gloss TV polish.

He forced those thoughts away. He would not be brought down by an audacious woman with a bodacious body. He would not risk everything because of his libido or his temper. He was his own man, with a job to do, a responsibility to meet, and lives—many lives—to protect.

She lifted her gaze, having studied his chest with the precise intensity he'd just given her face. "I'd like to make a deal with you," she said.

"No deals," he responded without stepping back. "I don't do deals, concessions, bargains, or special arrangements."

She narrowed her eyes at him. "What *do* you do, Alex Romero?"

"Don't start," he warned softly. "You'll lose."

She spun back around and flipped up the laptop. "I was simply going to suggest a compromise so we could help each other."

With a sigh of resignation, he found a cup. American coffee was enough of a compromise for him. "How can you help me?"

"I can . . . cooperate."

He couldn't resist a smile at the way just saying the word pained her. "Meaning?"

"I will let you . . . protect me." More pain.

"You really cling to that independence, don't you?" He leaned against the counter, bracing himself for the first sip.

She shrugged, her focus moving from the computer to his bare torso and back to the computer again. Another nice thing about no makeup; he could see the color rise in her cheeks.

"I don't like to be so needy."

"Needy?" He almost spat out the dishwater coffee. "You?"

"Maybe needy isn't the right word." She shifted on the barstool. "But I've always seemed to need . . . assistance."

Were they talking about the same woman? "How so?"

"It doesn't matter. I always—"

"It does matter," he interrupted. "I want to know what I'm dealing with here. And to be honest, you don't strike me as a woman who's ever needed anyone to do anything but get out of her way."

She flashed a smile. "I take that as a compliment."

"Take it any way you want. It's true."

"It hasn't always been."

He set the mug down. "I find that hard to believe."

She sighed briefly. "About a year ago, I quit newscasting. I told you, I sucked at the politics and games. Then I . . . got into my new business. Sort of."

"Sort of?"

"Well, I helped my boyfriend start his own PI firm."

For some insane reason, his heart rate kicked up. She had a boyfriend. He waited for her to continue.

"In fact, it all goes back further than Elliott. I should tell you, so you can understand why finding Jessica, helping her, is so important."

"Go on." He attempted another sip of the muddy brew.

"Jessica has always been—well, just look at her life." She waved a hand at the showplace around her. "She's a bona fide success story. Nothing challenges her, nothing trips her up, nothing gets in her way. She doesn't know what failure feels like."

"And you're jealous of that."

"God, no." The vehemence in her voice told him it was the truth. "I admire her for all that she's achieved. It's what makes her *her,* and, believe me, she's . . . amazing." She shook her head. "I mean, really amazing."

"So you've said."

"I grew up depending on her. She would always come through for me. She'd taken the notes for class, she had the money in her pocket, she made sure we got home by curfew, she got our applications for college and grad school and jobs in on time, she . . . did whatever needed to be done. I took. She gave."

"I'm sure you brought something to the party."

"Precisely." She laughed softly. "I brought the party. I provided the comic relief, the occasional adventure, the fun. Jessica is very conservative, in control at all times. It was a nice balance when we were young. I'd get a little action going, and she'd be sure it didn't go too far. But . . ." Her smile faded. "Then we grew up. And found out that our visions of life were as different as our personalities."

"Did that cause a big falling out or something?" He could imagine a woman as accomplished as Jessica not liking her lifelong plans being shaken up by her less ambitious sister.

"Not really," she replied. "She just wasn't thrilled at my decision. She didn't understand choosing a low-paying PI job over the glamour of TV. And when I moved in with Elliott . . ."

She lived with the guy? He dumped the rest of the coffee in the sink to hide his reaction.

"She thought he was all wrong for me. Too much of a power monger, too determined to tell me what to do. But I learned how to be a PI from him, and even though I didn't get my license or a paycheck for the first year, I liked the work."

Past tense. All past tense. "So what happened?"

"I hit my personal wall."

At her serious tone, he turned to look at her.

"I realized that I had spent my life depending on my parents, on Jessica, and then when I floundered in Fresno, all alone, I hooked up with Elliott Sandusky, who was another caretaker. I hadn't done anything autonomous in twenty-nine years." She crossed her arms. "I had to change that. I decided to stop depending on anyone except me. So having Jessica actually depend on me, instead of the other way around—well, this is really important to me."

"What happened to Elliott the caretaker?" Not that it mattered.

She shrugged. "He liked the old me better."

He loathed the relief that swept him. Why should it matter if she had a boyfriend or not? Lucy's rules were enough to keep him out of her bed. And he *was* staying out of her bed, regardless of his physical response to her. Once he'd acknowledged that response—which he had during the mostly sleepless night—he could conquer it. "And then?"

"I moved to San Francisco, got my PI license, found one runaway teen, caught a woman cheating on her husband, and came to Miami because Jessica said she needed me."

"And impersonating her as a favor is part of your grand scheme for self-actualization?" He failed to see the life-changing aspect of the stunt. It still struck him as stupid and childish.

"It's more than a favor. It's . . . it's proof."

"Proof of what, Jazz?" He couldn't resist pushing what he suspected was a hot button. "Proof that you're as good as she is?"

Resentment darkened her eyes to pewter gray as she spun off the barstool and headed for the coffeepot. "No. It's proof that I'm good *enough* to be her twin sister. Not *as* good—that'll never happen."

While she poured, he drank in the sight of her backside sheathed in hip-hugging jeans while familiar heat started low in his gut.

"Taking foolish chances is no way to prove anything. I don't believe in risks." Which was why he forced his attention away from those jeans.

"Well, I do. And that's the deal I'm offering."

He gave her a deliberately confused look. "I forgot we were discussing a deal. I thought we were confessing inner conflicts to Oprah, here."

"Very funny. That's what I get for being honest."

"Sorry to make light of your *issues,* Jazz." He gave her a lazy grin. "But why don't you tell me your deal and I'll think about it while I'm in the shower." Because one more minute in the tiny kitchen with her and her skin-tight clothes and lemon-flavored scent, and his own issues would be straight up and obvious.

"I'll let you protect me and be my bodyguard, if you'll let me go where I need to go to try to find her. But I go as her, not me."

"I've been the one wanting to find Jessica from the beginning. I'm willing to do whatever I have to—"

"*We* have to."

"—do to find her." He spoke right over her correction. "But I don't think your pretending to be her is helping."

"How is it hurting?"

"If she's in hiding or undercover for some reason, then you're not giving her any reason to contact you. And if she's not, if she's hurt, or worse, then there's no missing person, no crime, no body."

Her jaw dropped. "Body? You think some horny fan *killed* her?"

"That's the worst case scenario. But that's just how I think."

"Lovely."

"Reality rarely is," he said, placing his hands on her shoulders to make his point. And touch her bare skin again. "Here's *my* deal, Jazz. We spend the next forty-eight hours looking for her. We're truthful about who you are. If we haven't found her by Monday morning, we go to the authorities and you come clean."

The plan was completely counter to what Lucy wanted, but too bad. His boss was so blinded by her need to impress this client that she didn't realize how much danger Jessica Adams could be in. He had to do what he could to help Jessica; *that* would impress the client. Not playing games with the stand-in while his gut told him something was wrong with the woman he'd been hired to protect.

"Fine. We start with a studio in Hialeah where they produce porn movies." She backed away. "But we agree now: we don't tell anyone at the TV station. No one who works with Jessica." He started to shake his head. "Just say yes or no. Stay or go. You'll agree, or you'll leave."

He chuckled. "You really want control of me one way or another, don't you?" And they both knew how effective the *other* way was. "No way."

He turned toward the bathroom, but she stopped him by grabbing his arm. "I mean it, Alex. No one from the station."

God, ultimatums and negotiating *and* risk. The woman was making him nuts. It didn't matter anyway; they wouldn't see anyone from the station for two days. He pulled out of her grasp and shook back his hair. "Okay, fine."

Her shoulders relaxed in relief. "Thank you. And, in return, I'll promise not to . . . not to . . ."

"What?" He let his gaze linger over her curves, his mouth suddenly dry. "No more foot massages?"

A soft flush spread from her cleavage up her throat, where a tiny pulse jumped in a rapid rhythm. "I'm sorry. That was unfair and sneaky and not nice."

"Unfair and sneaky, yes." He couldn't fight the smile. "But it was real nice."

She grimaced at his tone. "I won't do that again."

"You can do it anytime you want," he said, leaning into the warmth that quivered between them. "But next time, I'll know precisely what you're up to."

"And what will you do?"

"The last thing you expect, *querida*."

He could have sworn a little glimmer of anticipation sparkled in her eyes, and her lips parted just enough to prepare for a kiss. He took another visual slide down to the taut buttons of her nipples.

One more inch, and those points would touch his bare

skin. All he had to do was ease forward, and her breasts would graze his chest and that paltry piece of cotton would be history. His hands and mouth could feast on her again.

"What will you do, Alex?" Her breath was tight with the repeated question.

Every muscle in his body tightened with one single need: to find a way inside of her.

"Absolutely nothing," he said flatly.

The light went out of her eyes, and he left to take an ice cold shower.

CHAPTER
Ten

Lucy Sharpe crossed her long legs, her bare calves rubbing against the warm leather of the custom-designed recliner. She accepted a glass of champagne as the Gulfstream IV hit cruising altitude of thirty thousand feet on its way to Florida. She never apologized for her love of luxury; instead, she shared it. The result was a happier work force—even if they weren't always thrilled with what she asked them to do.

Holding the crystal flute toward two of her most favored employees, she looked from one to the other and raised her glass in genuine gratitude.

"Thank you both for rearranging your schedules."

A rare, ironic smile lifted Max Roper's lips.

Dan Gallagher's quick hoot matched the twinkle in eyes the color of an Irish hillside. "Yeah, Luce." Dan's grin revealed the tiniest imperfection in an otherwise heart-stopping smile. But there was something about his slightly crooked front teeth that was as endearing as the man himself. "Like we had a choice."

"You always have a choice," Lucy reminded him, and sipped a few sweet bubbles. "You may say no to any assignment, at any time, for any reason."

Not that they would. Her salaries were quadruple what any other security firm paid its top bodyguards, which was why she had the best in her force. And two of the best of the best were in front of her.

Max's expression returned to unreadable. "I'd rather be enjoying my seats on the fifty yard line of the Steeler game on Sunday than saving Alex Romero's ass."

"I realize you haven't even unpacked from Cannes yet, Max." She gave him a sympathetic smile. "With luck, you'll get to the next game."

They sat around a cocktail table in the center of the plane, the crew appearing only when summoned by a call button under Lucy's armrest. She preferred to conduct her business dealings in complete privacy.

Dan stretched out his solid six-foot-three frame across from her, locking his hands behind his dark blond head. "Seriously, Luce. How bad is the situation in Miami?"

"Not dire yet," she said, thinking of her phone call with the client that morning. "But I want to cover every base, and Alex needs to stay with the principal."

"The fake one," Max put in. "Not the real newscaster."

She nodded. "He's protecting Jasmine Adams and I don't want that to change. I prefer Kimball Parrish to think all is copacetic with his soon-to-be network star. In the meantime, I need more eyes down there to be sure we're on top of the entire situation."

Max's background in sniffing out drug runners for the

DEA in the Caribbean and Dan's undercover experience with the FBI were ideal for what she had in mind. "It's important that Alex stays close to her and in front of the client, who will be back in Miami shortly."

She reviewed the facts for them. True to form, Max rarely exhibited any emotion or response, his sharp mind simply sucking up the details. Only the flecks of gold in his chocolate eyes revealed his interest. His jaw was clenched tight, his thick, muscular body always spare in its movements. She would trust this bear of a man with her life, and she did trust him with those of her clients every day. Their only complaint was they never had any idea what he was thinking. Which was exactly how Max liked it.

Dan Gallagher couldn't have been more opposite. When Max had suggested Dan as a Bullet Catcher a few years earlier, Lucy's first reaction was amazement that the two were friends. They had, in fact, grown up together, gone to the same elementary school in Pennsylvania, and remained close friends, choosing to work together as often as they could. Unlike the indecipherable Max, she never doubted where Dan stood on any issue. He wore his emotions and values on his sleeve, and all over the ever-changing expressions of his handsome face. He was a man in constant motion; clients appreciated his easy sense of humor. Even more, they appreciated his ability to kill with either a gun or his bare hands if necessary.

Neither of these men had ever lost a client. No Bullet Catcher ever had, in the five-year history of their existence.

That record was safe as long as Jessica Adams was alive. If she was, these two men would find her and protect her; Alex could continue to do the real job she'd sent him to do.

"We proceed with the usual caution," she told Max and Dan. "And Alex will continue to keep Jasmine Adams out of any precarious situations."

Dan chuckled dryly. "Then she should stay away from him."

"He's on his best behavior," Lucy assured them.

Max raised one eyebrow. "I heard he gave new meaning to tea and crumpets over in Geneva."

Lucy fought a smile. "As though you two have never had to fend off a principal's admiration."

"A principal, sure," Dan said with a laugh. "Not a principal's *wife.*"

Max shook his head, disgusted. "Romero's a hothead, and too damn pretty for his own good."

Dan punched him lightly. "Good thing you don't have to worry about that, Mad Max."

"He's keeping the situation under control," Lucy said. "And he knows the consequences of a mistake."

Dan sliced his throat with his index finger and let his tongue hang out. "*Adiós,* Señor Romero."

"Or worse," Max said quietly. "*Adiós* to the client."

Lucy wasn't being entirely honest with them, which left an unwelcome weight in her chest. She'd agreed to handle this intriguing assignment a particular way for what seemed a very good reason. She hoped to God it didn't cost any jobs or lives in the process.

"He knows you're coming in as backup," she told

them. "Call him on his cell phone when you get to Miami and he'll brief you in full."

"Are you heading back to New York after we land?" Dan asked as one of the attendants approached with appetizers.

She raised one eyebrow in the direction of the crew member. "I have some business in Miami."

Dan and Max were far too well trained to ask what it was, and Lucy was relieved they didn't. She hated to lie to her employees.

In all of the years Alex spent growing up in Miami, he never knew there was a thriving porn industry tucked into the run-down commercial neighborhoods of Hialeah. If not for Jazz Adams and her relentless pursuit of information, he never would have discovered the studio sets and distribution warehouses that produced, edited, and exported sizeable amounts of USA-made porn to South American countries. Evidently they paid extremely good money to see the American girl next door perform.

Ever since they had struck their "deal" that morning, Jazz seemed to hum with energy. She'd talked him into taking the little BMW, saying that if she needed to convince someone she was Jessica in order to get to Denise, it would be easier if she drove Jessica's car. Plus, the Z4 had a GPS system installed.

So Alex found himself in the passenger seat of a convertible two-seat sports car being driven by a bold and beautiful woman who not only resisted his efforts to protect her, but embraced every risk he tried to avoid.

At a nearly deserted studio, Jazz charmed her way past

a bored security guard who seemed to recognize her. Inside, they meandered through vacant offices, then found an editing suite where a large man with a mane of black curly hair worked on a computer.

He looked up from his desk, color draining from his face at the sight of Jazz.

"What do you want?" he asked as he clicked the screen blank. "What are you doing here?"

She took a step into the office and Alex gripped her elbow lightly to keep her from going any farther. "I'm looking for Desirée Royalle."

He pushed his chair back and turned the monitor away from them, his gaze moving toward Alex, then back to Jazz. "I thought you were done with her."

"I need to ask her a few more questions. Do you know where I can find her?"

Alex turned at the sound of footsteps behind them, bracing himself to protect Jazz and take down two men if he had to.

"Find who?" The voice, and footsteps, belonged to a petite dark-haired woman, wearing a bright orange University of Miami football jersey. "Oh . . ." She swept Jazz with a gaze. "You want Denise Rutledge."

"She's not here," the man offered quickly. "She's gone for a few weeks, maybe longer."

The woman gave him a look of disbelief. "She's shooting next week, Howie. She might even be in today to pick up this script." She waved papers she was holding at him and then let out an exasperated sigh. "You fired her, didn't you?"

Howie glared at her. "She quit."

"Jesus," the woman muttered, shaking her head. "She was just trying to help."

Without another word, she marched down the hallway. Jazz watched her for a moment, then turned back to Howie. "I have to speak with Denise. It's urgent."

He stood, his sheer bulk menacing in a clumsy way, and Alex moved his hand toward the gun in his waistband.

"She's done with you," Howie said to Jazz. "She's done with this studio. I don't have a number, an address, or any other way to reach her. And no one else is going to help you with your story." He cocked his head toward the hall. "Leave now."

Alex nudged Jazz. "Let's go."

She stood just long enough for him to believe she was going to put up a fight and demand information, but she didn't. She looked at Howie, glanced at his computer, then turned and left.

The minute they were out of the building, Jazz pulled at his arm. "Let's go find her."

"Denise Rutledge?"

"No, the woman we just talked to. She knows something." Jazz responded, looking left and right. "I saw her dig into her pocket and pull out a pack of cigarettes. We just need to find the place the smokers hang out."

They followed the warehouse-style building around to the north side, and sure enough, under an overhang blocking the sun, the woman stood puffing on a cigarette and looking furious.

Jazz marched toward her. "Can I talk to you a minute?"

The woman squinted through her stream of blue smoke and nodded. "Sure. But I can't really help you."

Of course not, Alex thought, she's probably afraid she'll get fired, too. But why?

"I'm not who you think I am," Jazz said, pausing at a foot-high metal ashtray overflowing with butts. "My name is Jazz Adams and Denise has been talking to my sister."

The woman's eyes widened in sheer disbelief and she stepped back. "No shit. You look exactly alike."

Jazz stuffed her hands in her jeans pocket and her whole demeanor changed to one of a trusted friend. "I know. We're twins. What's your name?"

"Carla. I'm the script supervisor."

Jazz extended her hand, and the other woman shook it. "Hi Carla. Look, I really, really need to find Denise. Do you have any idea how I could do that? Today? Now?"

Carla shrugged. "I don't think she has a phone, but I know she lives somewhere out in West Kendall. But she might be gone now. Off to Wisconsin or Minnesota."

"Why would she go there?"

"She has a son there. I don't remember exactly where. Somewhere up north and freezin' ass cold. But that's why she did all this, why she talked to you—your sister."

"Because of her son?" Alex asked.

Carla stuffed her cigarette butt in with about a hundred others in the ashtray. "All the time we smoke together out here during breaks, she talks about that kid. He's living with his father's parents up there. She don't have a clue where the father is. Anyway, she wants custody, but these grandparents won't let her have him."

"Why not?" Jazz asked.

"Insurance," she said as though it were perfectly obvious. "This kid has some weird heart condition and Denise doesn't have any health insurance. So they found some legal loophole and have custody."

Jazz looked at Alex, then back at Carla, clearly confused. "How could talking to my sister change that?"

"She thinks Channel Five is somehow going to get people upset about how these poor actors and actresses are paid and treated." Carla smirked. "As if that's happening."

"That's the story?" Jazz couldn't keep the surprise out of her voice. "An exposé on the mistreatment of porn stars?"

"Not *stars,* honey. This ain't Hollywood, and she sure as hell ain't Jenna Jameson. This is export trash, and Denise and those girls are more like naked laborers. And it's only getting tougher, with the Internet cutting into the business. Denise hoped that if the TV station made people aware . . ." Carla glanced at the building behind them. "But Howie . . ."

"What?" Jazz prodded. "What about him?"

She shook her head quickly. "Nothin'. I just want to keep my job like everybody else. Denise—she wasn't going to last much longer. She can't keep the extra weight off and, let's face it, this is a young girl's business."

Across the parking lot, a man emerged from the building and they all turned to see Howie's hulking frame walking toward the cars. He glanced over his shoulder and saw them talking. Then he turned the corner out of sight.

"Howie Carpenter," Carla said the name with obvious contempt. "He's got no heart at all."

"What does he do here?" Jazz asked.

"Makes a shitloada money." Carla stuck her Marlboros back in her pants pocket. "I gotta go. If you see Denise, tell her I said hey."

When she left, Jazz looked at Alex. "Do you think she's telling the truth?"

"I don't know." He put a hand on her back and headed back to the car. "Health insurance for porn actors doesn't strike me as a network-worthy story. And don't forget the first amendment, Jazz. Not much is illegal in this industry anymore, just pedophiles and animal acts."

She made a face as she clicked the keyless entry to the BMW. "The ick factor is too high for network TV. Jessica wouldn't waste her time on anything like that. She doesn't work for the *Enquirer*."

"You ever heard of snuff porn?"

"Killing people during sex on film?" She rolled her eyes and reached beneath the driver's seat to pull out her laptop. "Urban folklore. There has to be a more obvious angle."

"Maybe she just wanted to break open the story of Hialeah's secret porn industry."

Jazz considered that, but shook her head as she fired up the computer. "Too local a story for network."

Her fingers skimmed the keys, and he noticed she had a habit of slipping her tongue between her lips when she concentrated. Mesmerized, he watched her hands. Her tongue. And everything in between.

Man, he admired her.

The thought smacked him as hard as his Cuban grandmother had when he took the Lord's name in vain. *That's* what felt so disconnected and alien. Plenty of women had earned his attention and affection and protection, and he enjoyed nothing more than showering all of those on a worthy lover.

But no one had earned his *respect* until Jazz Adams. With her wickedly sharp memory and talented fingers and daring attitude . . . and a body that made him rock hard and starved for sex.

"She doesn't have a phone," Jazz confirmed, peering at the screen. "But I still might be able to get an address."

As she worked, his cell phone vibrated. Dan Gallagher's ID appeared on his screen and Alex bit back a curse. Not only had he found himself relegated to the passenger seat, now he had to contend with backup. His lips curled in a wry smile as he answered the phone. What a pair he and Jazz made: two people who hated help, but desperately needed it.

"Dan the Man," he said as he flipped open the phone. "Welcome to Miami, *amigo.*"

Jazz flashed him a quick look as Alex listened to Dan's quick laugh. "Hey Alex. We're at the Delano. Nice place."

"If you like topless supermodels," Alex said.

"Well, except for them." Dan chuckled again. "Where are you?"

"You don't want to know. I can meet you later tonight, but can you do me a favor right now and see if Raquel can get a home address for a Denise Rutledge, somewhere in west Dade County, probably Kendall?"

"Hang on."

Dan put him on hold as Jazz's look became more pointed. "Who's Raquel and how can she get the address?"

He grinned, enjoying the twinge of resentment that colored her voice. "Come on, Jazz. Surely you don't think you're the only one who can steer through cyberspace?"

"The only one in this car," she muttered.

"Raquel is Lucy Sharpe's assistant."

In a moment, Dan got back on the line. "I got it." As he read the street address, Alex leaned forward and punched it into the GPS.

Jazz's jaw dropped as she watched the screen transform into a map of the western suburbs of Miami, a star indicating the house where Denise Rutledge lived.

"Thanks, man," Alex said. "I'll call you back later." He pointed the phone at the screen. "She's good, Raquel. Well on her way to being a full-fledged Bullet Catcher."

Jazz swallowed an unwelcome rush of envy. "Good for her," she said, hitting the switch to flip the convertible roof down.

She drove fast, quietly thinking through her puzzle. Every thread brought her back to Miles Yoder, so when they stopped at a light on U.S. 1, Jazz shared the story of how the Yellowstone board member had missed their rendezvous the night before. Alex immediately jumped to the conclusion that Jessica was having an affair with Miles.

"Never. He's married. Not Jessica."

He looked up to the open sky. "You've gotta dismantle that pedestal, Jazz. I think we've established that the woman's human. Now you've got a powerful guy who

leaves his wife in a hotel room to meet a sexy, good looking chick who calls him for a late night rendezvous. This
wasn't a job interview, *querida*."

"You're wrong," she insisted. "Remember, he didn't
show."

"Two possibilities there," he said thoughtfully. "The
wife woke up, or he has Jessica bound and gagged in the
Biltmore with him and was playing with your head."

Damn, she hadn't considered that possibility. "He
may have recognized that I wasn't Jessica and left." She
closed her eyes and reviewed each of the faces she'd seen
in the bar that night. She hadn't been able to find a recent
photo of Miles Yoder on the Internet. After 1999, when
he unloaded a boatload of tech stocks and got ridicu-
lously rich, there were no more pictures.

She zipped the Beamer onto a side street, past identical houses distinguished only by the various piles of junk
in the yards and driveways. This was a thoroughly working class neighborhood, with early 1980s architecture
and few paint jobs since then.

Alex peered at the address and driveways. "I saw her
get out of a beat-up Plymouth Reliant in the studio parking lot," he said. "Gold. Maybe an eighty-three."

"Here's the number," she said, pulling into the driveway of a tiny, washed-out ranch with no landscaping . . .
and no Plymouth Reliant in sight. "God, I hope she's
home."

The doorbell didn't work, and no one answered their
knock. Blowing out a breath, Jazz walked to the front
window and peered in. Between the blinds, she could see
a ratty sofa with cushions pulled off and thrown on the

floor, a few overflowing ashtrays, and a *People* magazine with an open soda can on it.

Several kids rode by on bikes, calling in Spanish to each other. A few doors away, a heavyset man pushed an old lawn mower into his garage. Other than that, everyone seemed to be indoors escaping the heat.

"Come on," she said, marching toward the side of the house.

"Wait," Alex called. "Let me go first."

She paused and sighed. "Determined to take that bullet for me, aren't you?"

There were only two windows on the side, both covered with closed blinds. Alex opened a chain-link gate to a small, unkempt backyard, and jiggled the sliding glass door.

"It's unlocked," Alex said as it rumbled over a rusty metal track.

She stuck her head into the house and called, "Anybody home?" Then she looked up at Alex. "I'm sure you want to do the honors and scope the place out first."

"As if you'd wait out here." He stepped into the house and called out again. He walked into the kitchen with Jazz on his heels, his hand close to his gun.

"Denise?" she hollered. "Are you home?"

The place was tiny; it couldn't have been a thousand square feet. Off the kitchen was a short hallway with one bedroom, and a bathroom, all reeking like the ashtray at the studio. A double bed was unmade and women's clothes were strewn over the floor. On top of a bureau where all five drawers hung open, half a dozen photos of a blue-eyed boy were flattened as though the display had been wiped down by an angry hand.

Jazz returned to the living room, to an empty cardboard box that lay next to a pile of DVDs on the floor. Crouching down, she plucked through the jewel cases. Porn. Every single one.

She lifted up *Teenage Twats* and waved it at Alex. "A busman's holiday?"

He picked up another. "Maybe she's just studying her craft."

Jazz stood and glanced around, looking for clues to what made this woman tick. Except for her taste in movies, this could be the ordinary house of any single woman. A coffee mug in the sink had been rinsed clean, but not put away. There were no dishes in the drainer and the refrigerator was nearly empty. A few fast food containers were in the trash.

No drugs, except for tobacco and caffeine. No sign of the wild living of a porn actress. Sifting through the open drawers in the bedroom, Jazz found nothing damning, nothing incriminating. Nothing at all.

Including a suitcase. Could Denise have taken that trip to see her son?

"Look what I found in the trash." Alex held out a square tag. *Neiman Marcus. Color: café au lait. Size: six.*

Jazz gasped softly. "She was the person in Jessica's apartment? She took the dress?"

He shook his head slowly, still studying the tag while Jazz picked up one of the pictures of a golden-haired boy of about ten or eleven grinning in a classic grade school picture.

"This must be her son." Turning over the frame, Jazz tried to slide the cheap cardboard out of the back, but other pictures must have jammed it in place. "Maybe the school name is imprinted on the photo and they can give us some leads. Maybe she took off to find him and—" The cardboard suddenly popped out, along with several folded pieces of paper that fluttered to the ground.

Alex bent to get the papers while Jazz examined the back of the photo.

In childlike handwriting, someone had written, "Grady, age 8, Middlebrook Elementary."

"Jazz." Alex's voice had a decidedly ominous tone. She looked up from the picture to see him sitting on the bed, holding the papers. "You better look at these."

He handed her the packet. The top page was a print-out of an online daily planner. She recognized it immediately from Jessica's computer. The next six pages were copies of the e-mails from Jessica's stalker. Exactly as she'd seen in the print-outs Alex had shown her. She looked up at him.

"Did she take these from the apartment, too?"

He shook his head. "No. Our copies were in a case in my car, with us. These are her own copies."

The words danced before her eyes. *I love to watch you. I have to taste you. I'm going to fuck you while you scream at the camera.*

"Alex . . ." She frowned. "Could Denise be the stalker? Maybe she made that porn tape of Jessica by cutting together her face and someone else's body . . . maybe she was trying to scare her with it?"

"Or blackmail her. Keep reading."

The last sheet of paper looked like the others, but she hadn't seen this one before.

You went too far, Jessica and now I'm going to ruin your life and your job and your name. And won't that make great news? Poor Jessica Adams. She did bad things and got caught, and then she committed suicide.

Jazz's legs almost buckled. "Let's get out of here," she said, folding the letters in half and stuffing them in her purse.

Fighting down the ache in her chest and the itchy sensation that she had to *do* something, Jazz left the house and walked along the side yard. At the sound of laughter, she froze. Hiding behind a bush, she watched three teenaged boys on bicycles talking to someone in a dark four-door sedan in front of the house. The passenger side of the car faced her, and the blackened windows prevented her from seeing the driver.

One of the boys left the group, dropped his bike on the side of the road, and walked over to the BMW that sat in the driveway. They'd left the top down and the interior wide open. Jazz swore under her breath. What a target that car was in this neighborhood. She was about to march out and tell him to bug off when the car suddenly peeled away and the three boys huddled together, looking at each other and Jessica's car.

Spanish phrases floated in the air. As much as she wanted to confront them, she decided to get Alex. He could get rid of them in Spanish. She tiptoed to the backyard, and found Alex closing the sliding glass door.

"There are some kids messing around Jessica's car. Can you go scare them off?"

He nodded, shaking the handle of the door. "Think I should lock this?"

"What? As a personal favor to her? There's not much to steal in there anyway."

When they reached the front of the house, no one was there. The bikes were gone, the boys were gone, the car was untouched.

"That's funny," she said. "They sure looked interested in getting a better look at that BMW."

Alex frowned, glancing up and down the streets for the culprits. "Did you hear what they said?"

"It was Spanish," Jazz said. "They were talking to someone in a car, then he took off and they zeroed in on Jessica's car."

He held out his hand. "Let me drive."

She reached in her bag for the keys, glad to relinquish the wheel. She needed to search Jessica's files for any mention of Denise on her laptop.

Her *laptop*!

She yanked open the passenger door and hopped in, reaching under the driver's seat for the computer, but her hand hit something smooth and round. "Goddamn it. Did they take my freaking computer?"

Alex climbed in the car and started it. "Miami, man. Some thing's never change."

She felt again, reaching under Alex's legs. She moved the cylinder and her fingers touched the edge of the laptop. How did it get moved back? Trying to snag the edge of the computer without putting her face right in Alex's lap, she was suddenly aware of a powerful odor. She sat straight up. "Is that gasoline?"

Alex started to back out of the driveway, and sniffed. "Yeah. Maybe the car has a gas leak." He sniffed again. "You can't remember a word those kids said?"

The words had been fast bursts of conversation, all run together. *"Aparto?"*

He gave her a sharp look and sniffed hard. "What kind of car was it?"

"A dark four-door. Maybe a Lexus." The gasoline smell permeated everything, sending an unholy sense of apprehension through her. Or was that the look on Alex's face? *"Estallido,"* she said as the memory hit her. "They said *estallido.*"

He slammed on the brakes, knocking her forward. "Get out of the car!" he shouted, thrusting the shift into park and pushing her toward the door. "Get out!"

He flung his door open and she did the same. Before she could climb out, he raced around, pulling her toward him. "Move!" He pushed her away from the car. "Run!"

"My laptop!" she screamed, locking her legs in place and turning toward the car.

"Forget it!" He gave her a hard push toward the grass.

Spinning around, she tried to knock him out of her way. "I can't find Jessica without it! I can't lose all that information."

"Jazz, it's a bomb—run!"

Blood slammed through her head as she remembered the cylinder under the front seat, and the smell. A pipe bomb.

It would take ten seconds to get that computer. Without it, she didn't have a chance of tracking down Jessica. Tearing her arm from his grip, she lunged toward the car.

"Mierda!" He growled, grabbing the material of her shirt and flinging her backward. In a brain-blurring rush, he charged to the open driver's door and dropped to his knees. He grabbed something and tossed it into the backseat, then pulled out her laptop. Straightening, he ran toward her just as the bomb exploded with a deafening blast.

The impact knocked her right into the grass. Alex tumbled on top of her as sparks and shrapnel rained over them, a putrid wave of sulphur and smoke filling the air.

The pop and snap of fire and metal cracked in her ears, along with Alex's breath as he pinned her to the ground. "Don't you *ever* pull a stunt like that again," he warned.

He jerked up as brakes screeched out on the road. "Run!" He pushed her toward the backyard without looking behind him.

"Hey, Romero!"

The shout from the street froze them. Over Alex's shoulder, Jazz expected to see the black sedan again, with menacing black windows and a gun pointed at them. The same one that tried to run them off a bridge.

Instead, a small SUV had pulled behind Jessica's car and two men jumped out. One ran toward them; the other, a mountain of a man, rushed toward the blackened car.

Jazz blinked into the smoke, the smell of gasoline and fried leather making her dizzy. Why was Alex standing there? Why didn't he run, or shoot the tall, blond man approaching them?

"I knew I'd find you here," the man said, flashing a quick, crooked smile.

Alex sighed. "Damn. I hate it when you outsmart me."

The other man looked up from the car and snorted. "Yeah, like that's tough to do."

Alex gave him a look as fiery as the remnants of Jessica's BMW. "Fuck you, Roper. Just get us outta here. Fast."

CHAPTER
Eleven

Nothing had ever looked quite as out of place as big, bad Mad Max Roper on a Delano Hotel signature white settee. The delicate piece of furniture was obviously built to hold one of the hotel's ubiquitous Brazilian supermodel guests, and not a former DEA hunting dog who'd allegedly crushed the skull of a Cali drug lord with one bare hand.

Alex pulled himself back into the lively debate Dan Gallagher currently waged with Jazz, not at all surprised that the two of them had bonded like long-lost siblings. They both had inquisitive minds, rapier wit, and that bulldog quality that wouldn't let them drop a bone until it was chewed down to nothing.

"But it doesn't make sense," Jazz insisted, tucking bare feet under her. "Who blew up her car?"

"Somebody who knew how to make your basic potassium permanganate and gasoline pipe bomb," Dan said, "and paid cash to those kids to plant and detonate it."

"I want to know who and why," Jazz said. "And what it has to do with my sister."

"We all do," Alex assured her. Energy vibrated off her in waves; he could have sworn that a day of crime fighting and death defying just made her more radiant. One look at Dan and Max confirmed that; they hadn't taken their eyes off her for two hours.

And he didn't like it one bit.

"Maybe it's as simple as this," Dan suggested. "This Desirée character really is Jessica's source for a story, and someone knows it and doesn't want her talking to the media. The pipe bomb in Jessica's car was a warning."

Jazz looked at Alex. "Some warning. We would have been killed."

Alex levered himself from his relaxed position against the wall. They'd spent enough time talking. And *staring* at her. "We need a plan: Let's divide and conquer. You two go after every person listed in Jessica's address book who has no relation to the TV station. Jazz and I will handle the television station colleagues."

Max held up a hand. "Wait a second, Romero. Lucy was perfectly clear on your assignment; you are the body-guard to the stars."

Alex's fist tensed in response.

Dan leaned forward. "What he means, Alex, is that you are the exec protection expert. Jazz needs you more than ever. We'll handle the investigation. You lay low in the safe house you've arranged, keeping Jazz away from any threats to her personal security." He warmed Jazz with that boyish smile he had milked for most of his life.

"You stay in that house in Coral Gables, Jazz," Max

added. "Jessica is a obviously a target and you look exactly like her. You need to be very careful." His usual Rottweiler scowl was now a puppy dog face that Alex wanted to smash.

Jazz shot up from the sofa and glared at Max. "Not a chance, bucko." *Bucko?* Alex and Dan shared a lightning fast look of disbelief. "I am not staying in hiding while my sister is missing. I can get a lot of information from people. And I'll go crazy if we just wait in seclusion." She looked at Alex.

He'd go crazy, too. For an entirely different reason. But he had no intention of returning to Jessica's condo, or advertising themselves all over Miami while someone planned the next ambush.

"You need to find this Yoder guy," Alex told Dan. "Dig around the Biltmore. Go to New York, if you have to. Find the guy and figure out what his connection to Jessica is."

Max rose to his feet and the settee squeaked in relief. "We'll handle Yoder *and* the people at the TV station."

"What about Parrish?" Jazz asked. "I have to talk to him. Maybe I can track him down tomorrow."

"No, Jazz," Max said with a shake of his head. "He's the Bullet Catcher client. Ms. Sharpe will discuss the situation with him."

"Bullshit," she shot back, the vehemence practically knocking Max back onto the fragile seat. He opened his mouth to speak, but nothing came out.

Jazz slapped her hands on her hips and looked up at the big man. "I don't give a good goddamn whose client he is. My sister is missing and I'm going to do everything I can to find her." Her jaw set and Alex recognized the glint in her cinder gray eyes.

"We're calling the shots on this," Dan said gently. "Believe me, we know how to do this."

Her fire shifted to Dan. "I didn't hire you, and neither did my sister. Don't get me wrong, I appreciate the help—but Kimball Parrish has a powerful interest in Jessica, both personal and professional. No one will keep me away from someone who might know where she is." She turned back to Max, and Alex relished seeing that testosterone-laden square jaw slacken in the face of Jazz's pointed index finger. "Don't even *try* to set those limits on me."

Alex stepped forward and put his hand on her shoulder. "We'll talk to Parrish, Jazz."

She started to jerk out of his hold, but he held her tighter. "Together," he added. "You and I will talk to him."

He felt the taut muscle under his hand relax a tiny bit, but the spark still lit her eyes as she fixed her gaze on him. "You and I," she repeated.

"Yes," he promised. "All we need to do is make sure Lucy calls him first to grease the skids."

She eased out of his grasp, but didn't take her eyes off him. "I won't let you force me out of this, Alex. I won't be buried in some house in Coral Gables while my sister is missing."

"I promise, Jazz. You'll be involved in everything, but—"

"But *nothing*." She notched one eyebrow. "I don't do deals, concessions, bargains, or special arrangements."

He heard the echo of his own words. "Fine. But don't do anything stupid, either. It might make things worse for your sister."

"All right," she said with a hint of surrender in her voice. "That's fair enough. Now if one of you has a computer, I can probably download my sister's address book for you."

Dan took her into the back bedroom, where his laptop was connected to the Internet. When he returned, he closed the door to the bedroom behind him.

"Got your hands full with this job, big guy." Dan gave Alex's arm a friendly punch. "Even Mad Max can't scare that woman into submission."

Alex threw a dark look at Max. "Evidently she's not scared of monsters."

Max thumped back onto the settee, his hard glare locked on Alex. "You're so deep into her you can't see straight. Haven't you screwed up enough jobs because of that?"

Irritation skittered down his spine. "You don't know what the hell you're talking about, Roper."

"Hey." Dan cut the air between them with his hand. "Chill. You two are wasting your pissing contest on this girl."

Alex gave him a questioning look.

"She's too smart for either one of you," Dan said with a wide, dangerous grin. "But when this is all over, I may be taking a trip to San Francisco."

"Give it up, Gallagher," Alex said. "She'd eat you up for breakfast and spit you out for fun."

"I don't know." Dan rubbed his day-old beard

growth and looked toward the bedroom door. "I think she likes me."

Max let out a disdainful grunt. "Yeah, I thought so, too. Until the 'don't set limits on me' speech."

Dan laughed, but Alex crossed his arms and leaned against the bedroom doorjamb. "Forget it, both of you. She's mine." Where did that come from?

Dan raised an eyebrow. "Lucy'll love that."

"I don't give a shit what Lucy loves," Alex said. And this time, he meant it.

"Your sister lives here?" Jazz peered through the massive wrought iron gate tucked into the foliage along picturesque Old Cutler Road. Alex punched a code into a keypad on a stucco column, and the gates opened like welcoming arms.

"She works here," Alex corrected. "The owners are wealthy globetrotters who live here about five weeks of the year. Ileana keeps the house. I filled her in about what's going on, and she agreed we could stay here."

A canopy of banyan trees shadowed the winding drive toward a sprawling mansion that mixed old-world architecture with tropical chic to jaw-dropping effect. A woman in her early thirties, with flawless skin, chiseled features, and long black hair pulled off her face, waited near the house.

Alex climbed out of the car and leaned over to kiss his sister, who immediately started speaking Spanish. He shook his head and laughed, then held up a hand. "Ileana, this is Jazz Adams. Please speak English for her."

Ileana turned her attention to Jazz, a wary look in eyes the same inky color as her brother's. "Hello, Jazz." She held out her hand. "I'm a fan of your sister's."

With a stream of Spanish-flavored chatter, Ileana led Jazz into the side entrance of the house, and Alex followed with two bags they'd hastily packed that afternoon. They settled into a kitchen the size of Jazz's whole apartment, and filled with the scents of coffee, baked goods, and lemony cleaning solutions.

Ileana told them about the Sastre family, the homeowners. "Señor Sastre is a doctor, a very highly regarded plastic surgeon, and his wife is a world-class flute player. Very famous. But they travel constantly." Ileana set out a plate of guava pastries and poured tiny cups of Cuban coffee. "I come every day to take care of the house and supervise the landscapers and pool cleaners, but no one is scheduled for several days. And the Sastres are not coming home until Christmas."

"Thank you," Jazz said automatically, taking the coffee, her mind far away in Kendall, visualizing the exploding BMW, the damning e-mails, the piles of porn. Clues that were everywhere, but not yet understood.

"Do you know the city very well?" Ileana asked politely.

Jazz looked at her for a moment, processing the question, and tamping down her growing frustration. She burned with the need to take action, to get answers, to do *something,* but was instead eating sticky buns and chatting about *nothing.*

The sudden power of Alex's strong hands on her

shoulders transported her directly into the here and now. "We've hardly slept in days, Ileana," he said, his body warming her back.

"You can relax here," Ileana assured them. "Use anything you want or need. I'll take care of everything when you leave. In the meantime, you'll have complete privacy."

Was that her imagination or did Alex's hands tighten on her shoulders?

"Gracias, cariña." Alex's voice was so close to her ear that it made the tiny hairs on her neck dance. "I know we're safe, but I'm going to look over the property and secure the entrances so we can sleep tonight."

He left them alone with the words *we* and *sleep* hanging awkwardly in the air. Why did that make her stomach free-fall? She'd been sleeping with him in the next room for several nights. But somehow, she felt different now. Charged. Stimulated. *Needy.*

Ileana's hand closed over Jazz's. "Don't worry. He'll find your sister," she said softly. "Alex can do anything."

Evidently Alex lived on a pedestal himself.

"Why don't you get on the six o'clock news and make a pleaa for her to come home?" Ileana asked. "That's what I'd do."

"She's not technically missing," Jazz explained. "She's sent me some text messages, and I don't want to put her in a precarious situation. I'll go to the TV station tomorrow morning and start talking to people."

She wasn't sure who'd be there on a Sunday, but at least she had a plan. If Alex didn't try to stop her.

She remembered the impact of hitting the ground with his full-body coverage to protect her. "It's certainly a perfect job for him," Jazz mused out loud. "He was born to be a bodyguard."

"They are a very rare breed, the Bullet Catchers," Ileana said. "They work for some mysterious lady who used to be in the CIA, and all of their clients are powerful, wealthy, and important. I know his job is very dangerous, but it is a blessing to us."

Something in the wistful way she spoke got Jazz's attention. "Why's that?"

"Because Alex is keeping our entire Cuban family alive and safe."

Jazz gave her a quizzical look. "How so?"

She rubbed her thumb and fingers together in the universal body language for "cash." "He sends a hundred thousand dollars, maybe more, a year to Cuba. Our cousins, many, many cousins, live in a tiny village called San Tomás. Because he has this wonderful job, they can travel to see doctors, they have books and clothes." She shook her head. "It is very, very difficult to live in Cuba."

A hundred thousand dollars to relatives living under a communist regime? That was admirable. And illegal.

"Whoever hired a Bullet Catcher to protect your sister must have real clout," Ileana continued. "I know for a fact that the king of Sweden is a client."

Kimball Parrish had arranged for Jessica's protection and he certainly qualified as powerful, wealthy, and important, if not royal. "What other clients has Alex had?" Jazz asked.

"Most of the time he's very secretive, but I know this: They're more than just bodyguards, the Bullet Catchers.

They are like small armies of highly trained men who would kill anyone or anything that would harm someone they are assigned to protect. And they are involved in other things, secret things for governments and private companies, too. Always the people involved are very rich, very important."

Jazz raised her eyebrows. "He must have been seriously demoted to get this job."

Ileana's eyes flashed. "His last assignment ended abruptly, but it wasn't his fault."

Curiosity pulled her forward. "Did he lose a client?"

"No. He saved a man's life." Ileana shook her head. "All I know was that it involved a woman."

Big surprise there. "Where did the woman fit into it?"

Ileana shrugged and gave an apologetic look. "I think it was the principal's wife."

He screwed his client's wife? No wonder he went from protecting the king of Sweden to a local TV personality.

"It's not what you think," Ileana assured her. "What happened was—"

Alex came back into the room, snapping his phone shut. "What are you two so deep in conversation about?"

"You," Ileana said.

"Women," Jazz said at the same time.

Alex looked from one to the other. "Really."

"Somehow those two subjects always end up in the same conversation," Ileana said with a teasing grin.

He glanced at Jazz, a whisper of denial in his eyes, then put his arm around Ileana and led her to the door, saying something soft in Spanish.

Alex and women.

The very last thing she wanted was to be one of his conquests.

But sometimes what she wanted and what she needed were two opposing forces. And sometimes, need won.

Jazz prowled through the beautifully decorated rooms, her blood pumping at the same rate as her whirlwind thoughts.

"It's almost one o'clock, Jazz. We can't do anything until tomorrow morning. Go to sleep." Alex sprawled on a dark leather couch, his arms locked behind his head.

The heat of his constant scrutiny didn't help, either. As the night progressed, they'd both gravitated to the richly paneled great room that overlooked the pool and patio. She leaned against the sliding glass door and looked out at the moonlight illuminating a navy blue–bottomed swimming pool.

"Tell me about your client's wife," she said suddenly. "The one you did in Geneva."

He let out a disgusted breath. "I didn't do anyone in Geneva."

"Really?" She turned and smiled sweetly, the way she always did when she wanted to charm someone into giving her information. "That's not what your sister says."

"Ileana talks too much."

Jazz crossed her arms. "I like people who talk a lot. You learn such interesting things."

He simply raised an eyebrow.

"Like . . . the fact that you send all that money to Cuba every year." She paused long enough to see his dark eyes narrow slightly. "Isn't there an embargo against sending financial aid to communist countries?"

"Like I said, my sister talks too much."

"Your secret's safe with me." Jazz wandered over to a massive antique side bar, touching a colorful Chinese vase. Probably Ming. "But Ileana told me this Lucy person is ex-CIA. Breaking a U.S. trade embargo can't go over big with her."

A smile lifted his lips. "As long as it doesn't impact my job, Lucy doesn't care what I do with my money."

She wasn't sure she believed that, but continued her examination of the art and furniture. "What exactly is the Bullet Catchers? Is it a company? Where's the headquarters? How do you get to be one?"

His gaze stayed with her as she moved, sliding up and down her body openly enough to ignite the chemistry that arced across the room. "The Bullet Catchers are a group of specialists trained in personal and corporate security, threat assessment and risk management, executive protection, competitive intelligence, explosive detonation, crowd control, corporate espionage, and——" He grinned. "——some other stuff. The membership changes, there are no company headquarters, and you have to be invited to join."

She grazed her fingertip over the polished ebony of a Steinway as she continued her tactile tour of the room. "And to be a client?"

"You have to be recommended and referred."

"I wonder who recommended Kimball Parrish," she asked, her hands settling on the side of the piano. "Do you know?"

"If Lucy wanted me to know, she'd tell me."

Jazz sat on the piano bench, facing him. "She intimidates you."

He let out a sharp laugh. "No, she doesn't."

"You don't like powerful women," she mused. "Do you?"

"I prefer quiet women." He shot her a meaningful look. "Remember that if you want me to like you."

"I don't want you to like me."

"I don't believe you." He stood slowly, rising from the leather sofa and crossing the room to loom over her. He liked to do that, she'd noticed. He liked to remind her of his physical strength and size. She looked up at him as he put his hands on her shoulders. "Too bad, because I do like you."

She swallowed and rode the dip in her stomach. "As much as you liked your client's wife in Geneva?"

He leaned over, and for a moment she thought he was going to kiss her. "Even more."

She slid across the piano bench to escape him. "I need some air." She needed more than that. "Can you watch TV or something while I swim? I don't have a suit."

His lips quirked up. "Don't let that stop you."

"Don't be a smart ass."

"I'm not," he assured her. "I'll turn all the lights out and open the sliders so I can hear if you need help."

Swimming in the dark. Naked. With Alex a few feet away. A rush of craving nearly buckled her legs.

"Okay." The indifference in her voice was in direct opposition to the sensations ricocheting through her body. "I'll take you up on that offer."

Five minutes later, she emerged from the cabana wrapped in a thick black towel. While she'd been undressing he'd turned out every light, and the whole house and patio were now completely dark. Warm, humid air had already started to seep into the great room through the open sliders. Jazz found her handbag on the coffee table and unclipped her cell phone, setting it on a patio table as she stepped outside. She hadn't given up on the fantasy that Jessica might call.

"I hope this is dark enough." Alex spoke from the far corner, on a sun chaise. "I can't turn off the moon."

"And here I thought you Bullet Catchers could do everything."

She heard the soft rumble of his laugh, but couldn't discern his face. There were no lights under water, none coming from the house. With the elegant dark blue pool surface, she really could swim in some privacy if he stayed back in the corner.

And if he didn't . . .

"My eyes are closed," he said. "You're free to dip, *querida*."

The sound of the Spanish word hung in the air as thick as the tropical humidity, and as sweet as the fragrance of mango trees surrounding the patio.

"Are you lying, Romero?"

"Are you teasing, Adams?"

"No." Fantasizing. Imagining. But definitely not teasing.

"Then I'm not lying. My eyes are closed. Swim."

She dropped the towel and dove in, the cool water skimming her body like a wet kiss. She glided to the bottom, opening her eyes, her hands in front of her. It was dark enough to get completely lost.

Dark. And wet and warm and sensual. Her nerve endings tingled as the water caressed her, but didn't cool her down. Not even close.

What would he say if she shot up to the surface and told him exactly what she was thinking, what she wanted? *Come swim with me.*

Her lungs started to ache and she thrust herself through the water, up into the evening air in one smooth move. She let out a soft sigh of bliss, and heard him laugh from the chaise. Sucking in a deep breath, she submerged herself and launched along the bottom surface of the pool, the water enveloping her legs, caressing her breasts.

Take your clothes off and join me, Romero.

She pictured him swimming to her. Wet and hard and ready to do what she dreamed he would do. She imagined him stroking across the length of the pool, his brawny arms and back slicing through the water, his tight, masculine buttocks pale in the moonlight. She popped to the surface again and gasped for air.

"How's the water?"

Damn. He was still in the chaise lounge. "Amazing. This was exactly what I needed." Well, not *exactly.*

She dove under again, her heart thudding at the thought of Alex dipping his fingers into her, gliding his rock hard shaft along her swollen flesh.

She could drown with need.

Make love to me, Alejandro.

Out of air and ready to explode, she imagined his

hand on her aching nub. His mouth on her breasts. His—

From behind her, powerful arms slid around her waist. His hands closed over her breasts and his erection stabbed against her bottom. With one forceful kick, he propelled them to the surface.

As they broke the water, she gasped for air and he spun her around, his kiss taking her tongue and her sanity.

Strong, hungry hands slid up her body to fondle her breasts and she wrapped her legs around his, pulling them both underwater. She scraped her nails down his back and over his back side, palming the steel muscles while pressing her breasts into the wet, coarse hairs of his chest. He dragged them both to the surface again, and she pulled in a desperate breath while scooping his wet hair into her hands.

"You lied," she panted, breathless. "You were watching."

He kissed her again, all the while moving them to the three steps at the shallow end.

"I'm always watching." He tugged her onto his lap, turning her to face him as he settled onto the middle step. "And you lied, too," he said, his voice husky and thick. "You don't want to swim alone."

The water slapped against their chests in rhythm with their ragged breaths. "I don't want to swim at all." She encircled his hips with her legs, allowing his erection between her legs. "I want you."

"I want you, too." He captured her again with a slow, hot kiss. His tongue flicked her teeth and lips, then filled her mouth.

He palmed her breast with a sure, insistent hand, leaning her back so that the moonlight bathed her naked chest. Rivulets of water rolled down her neck and shoulders as she closed her eyes.

He whispered something in Spanish, then lowered his head to close his lips over her nipple, sucking gently at first, then with more intensity. He licked her skin as he traveled to taste the other one, leaning her back so that her hair dipped into the water as he buried his face in her cleavage. *"Mi fantasía, belleza."* The soft words floated over her, as weightless as her body in the water. She opened her arms and let them drift at her sides, but tightened her lock around his hips.

"Mi sirena del agua." He circled one nipple and watched it pebble, his member growing harder against her. "My mermaid."

"You speak Spanish when you've got sex on your mind."

Moving his hips to slide his erection up and down between her legs, he scorched her with his dark gaze. "Not true. Or I would never have spoken a word of English since I met you."

That made her smile.

"Estás tan rica que . . ." He slid his hand into the wet curls between her legs. *"Te quiero comer."*

He'd said that to her before, waking her up in bed. "What does that mean?"

With an evil, teasing grin, he lowered himself one step, positioning her knees on either side of his face. "It means you look good enough to eat." Spreading her legs, he placed a leisurely kiss against the inside of one leg, then the other. "So don't be surprised when I do."

He nibbled the tender flesh of her thigh, and her breath caught. How could her blood feel like lava when cool water covered her body, lapping over her flesh, between her legs?

He raised her hips to meet his mouth. Gently, delicately, he spread her flesh to dip his tongue deeper, finding the spot that made her quiver and moan.

She writhed and almost went under, tightening her gut to hold herself afloat. "Oh, please, Alex."

"Shhh, *querida*." He nipped her thigh, sending a fever straight down her body. Her hips rocked involuntarily, and he met each rise with a stroke of his tongue. Over and over he tortured her, swirling her flesh with dizzying intensity. Thorough and sure, he circled her sex with bold licks, delving into her body, sucking her tender nub so that she could think of nothing, nothing, *nothing* but the need to spiral into a release.

She shuddered with a fast, hard orgasm. *More.* She wanted him more of him, deep inside her and on top of her and around her. It wasn't nearly enough and she managed to tell him in broken breaths.

She could hear him laugh as her body floated back to earth. "I'm not going to leave you here alone while I search for a condom."

She closed her hands over his erection, thick and corded with arousal. "You will go nowhere without me. Not into that house, not out of this pool." She leaned into him for a kiss, her arms purposely pushing her breasts together and against his chest. "I *want* you."

He lifted her out of the water and laid her on the

towel she'd left at the pool's edge. His eyes half closed, he kneeled over her and held a condom package.

She choked out a surprised laugh. "You brought that out here?"

He slid the latex on as he looked into her eyes. "I left it out here this afternoon." Searing her with his hands and gaze, he kissed her deeply. His hard-on sought the heat between her legs, already swollen and slick from an orgasm. "Are you angry?" he whispered, a hint of a laugh in his voice.

She lifted her hips. "Furious."

"I like it when you get mad. Your whole body vibrates." He dipped his tongue into her ear and lightly circled the sensitive flesh. She shuddered. "Like that."

She wanted to laugh, but her lower half just rocked into him. "Please, Alex," she demanded softly. "Now. *Now.*"

He pressed his lips to her ear. "*Despacio, querida. Tenemos todo eternidad.*"

She suddenly felt as weightless as she'd been in the water. "What are you saying, Alex?"

His tip entered her. "It's just an expression. The language of love."

Her heart clutched. She didn't want to speak the language of *love.* She wanted to speak the language of *sex.* Good old-fashioned no strings, no control, no commitments *sex.*

Anything else with this Latin lover would be the biggest mistake she'd ever made in her life. Still . . . *Tenemos todo eternidad.* Something about eternity?

He inched a little bit farther into her, groaning with the pleasure and pain of it.

She stretched to take him, rising up with a soft gasp at the size of him. He moved slowly, taking a lifetime to slide in all the way. Fully hilted, he held perfectly still, as though to torture her to the brink of insanity. Jazz thought she'd explode with need.

He closed his eyes and breathed. His hard-on pulsed, his heart hammered, his muscles tensed.

"Feel this," he whispered. He thickened inside her, but didn't pump. "Feel me in you."

Her inner walls clutched at him. "Alex." Her breath was ragged, torn from her chest. "Please. *Please.*"

Still he didn't move—except to kiss her tenderly as if it was the last gentle thing he was able to do. Then, he started to rock. Slowly, easily, rhythmically sliding in and out of her at a maddening, leisurely tempo.

With each stroke he murmured in Spanish and English, his lilting voice crooning her name. As control started to slip away, he began to pound into her. His arms grasped her in a vise grip that tightened with each pump. His hips ground against her as he plunged. Faster, harder, deeper, wilder.

"Más, más, más," he repeated.

She rose to him, also wanting more, more, more. She dug her fingers into his flesh as a shattering orgasm began to coil inside of her. The world blurred and every sense failed her as the need became an all-consuming burn.

Somewhere in the faraway world something beeped, but the blood pounding through her head deafened her. Blissful, unstoppable release clutched her and drowned out everything but how much she needed Alex.

"Come with me, *querida*," he demanded as he pounded into her. "Come with me."

He threw back his beautiful head of hair and cried out with the force of his release.

As he lost control, so did she, the sight and sounds and smell and feel of Alex colliding into one shattering surge of pleasure that wiped out any chance she'd ever had of not needing him.

CHAPTER
Twelve

A cool trickle of water slithered between her bare breasts and jolted Jazz into consciousness.

"Your phone rang." Alex lay next to her on the towel, his hand cupping pool water that he dribbled on her naked body. "Do you want to see if there's a message?"

Couldn't they just lie here under the stars and bask in the afterglow? Couldn't they sleep here, wrapped up in each other as they rested for the next round?

"I fell asleep." She turned toward him. He lay on his side, his head propped on one arm, his wet hair skimming the rise of his bicep. He looked like a Mayan god, carved from stone and master of all he surveyed.

"You love to sleep," he noted, dripping more water on her.

"I do. Sleep is divine. I crave hours and hours of uninterrupted sleep."

"I crave hours and hours of uninterrupted sex," he said with a laugh. "I see a problem in our future. You want sleep. I want . . ." He leaned over and flicked his tongue over her nipple, hardening it immediately. "You."

She closed her eyes, not sure if the thrill that fluttered through her was a result of his talented tongue or the very idea of *their future.* "Get my phone and stop torturing me."

"Torture?" His hand slipped between her thighs. "You want torture?"

"I want my phone." A complete lie. She wanted his hand. And his mouth. And him . . . again. "Maybe it was Jessica."

As though on cue, the digital melody of her phone sounded again. Without a word, he rose to get it. Jazz rolled on to her stomach to watch him walk across the patio in the moonlight. No, the Mayans never had such a god.

On the third ring he handed it to her and she flipped it open, too intent on him to even look at the caller ID. "Hello?"

"I know who you are."

The man's voice sent a shudder rippling through Jazz, and she rose to her knees, jerking the phone in front of her face and squinting at the number. Jessica's office. She pressed the phone to her ear. "Who is this?"

"Oliver Jergen."

That gave her a small measure of relief. *Ollie.* "I was planning to tell you tomorrow."

He snorted lightly, giving her the distinct impression he didn't believe her.

"I need to find my sister, Ollie. She's missing."

Alex watched her carefully, but she concentrated on

listening to Ollie. "You only need to talk to Miles Yoder," Ollie said. "He knows her every move."

Miles Yoder again. "I tried. I failed. How did you figure out who I am?"

"I found the picture you took off Jessica's desk and hid in the drawer." He sighed softly. "She talks about you all the time. I knew she'd never put that picture away. She's so proud of her identical twin."

Surprise and gratification and guilt scrambled in her chest. Jessica was proud of *her*? "I came here to help her out for a week or so," she told him as she made room on the towel for Alex to sit next to her. She mouthed "Ollie" to him, and he nodded, listening.

"Well, you've certainly helped her." She heard the hint of a threat in the subtext.

"I want to find her," she said simply.

"She never told me you were coming." The threat morphed into irritation. "But she's told me everything about Miles. I know everything."

"Well, I don't," she admitted quickly. "Including how I can talk to him."

"Miles Yoder is a billionaire philanthropist."

"Who's on the board of Yellowstone," she countered. "But why does he know so much about Jessica? What is their relationship to each other?"

His laugh was low and dirty. "Their relationship? Obviously your sister hasn't been completely honest with you, Jasmine. Or can I call you Jazz?"

Distaste rolled through her. "I don't think it was a matter of dishonesty. We just haven't had the time to talk. And she hasn't been around since I got here."

He laughed lightly. "I would guess that's the whole idea, right? That's why you're standing in for her?"

She hated his condescending, know-it-all tone. "Do you know where she is, Ollie?"

"I have a few ideas."

Damn him. "Do you know what her connection to Denise Rutledge is?"

He waited a few dramatic seconds before answering. "She's the source on the story. Jessie's met with her." *Jessie.* Her sister loathed being called Jessie.

"What story?" Jazz insisted. "A story about the rights of porn actors?"

"Good God, Jazz. You can't be that naïve."

At his words, she swallowed hard and looked at Alex. "Ollie, you obviously know a lot about this situation and this story. I really want to talk to you in person. I'll meet you anywhere, anytime."

She watched a frown darken Alex's face, but she reached over and threaded her fingers through his, shaking her head a little to tell him not to worry and, please God, not to try to stop her. He closed his hand over hers, lifted it to his mouth, and kissed her knuckles.

The gesture was so protective, so unifying, that it broke her heart.

"I can meet you tonight," Ollie countered.

"Tonight?"

Alex's frown deepened into a scowl and he gave his head one negative shake. Okay, maybe not so unifying. She pleaded with a look. *This is important,* she mouthed.

His expression softened ever so slightly. She lifted

their joined hands to brush her fingers against the coarse stubble of his beard.

"Yes, I can meet you now," she told Ollie, holding Alex's gaze. "But I'm bringing my bodyguard."

"I don't care who you bring, as long as you don't breathe a word of this to Jessica's boyfriend."

Her boyfriend?

"Meet me at Crandon Park in Key Biscayne in two hours," he demanded, before she could ask who he meant by her boyfriend. "I'll tell you everything."

Two hours? It had to be nearly three in the morning. Her gaze fell on Alex's bare chest, and slid down his stomach, to his clearly interested manhood. The very last thing she wanted to do was leave.

"Do you know where that is?" he asked when she didn't answer. "It's Jessie's favorite beach."

Jessie again. "I'll find it. Where at Crandon Park?"

Alex closed his eyes in disgust at the mention of Crandon Park.

"At the north end, two palm trees form the entrance to the beach parking lot," Ollie said. "I'll be waiting for you."

"Crandon Park, north end of the beach. Two hours." She looked up at Alex, who just watched her, their fingers still laced together. "I'll see you then."

He clicked off without saying good-bye.

"I'm not sure he knows where Jessica is, but he has a good idea," she said, steeling herself for the inevitable fight. "He can lead me to Yoder. He can lead me to Jessica."

He squeezed her hand. "I figured out that much from listening."

"How far is Key Biscayne?"

"Fifteen or twenty minutes from here."

She searched his face. "We have two hours. What would you like to do until then?"

"Teach you how to operate my other gun. Have you ever shot a Glock twenty-six?"

"Yes," she said. "I learned on one." Then her heart sank with a sickening sensation. "You *are* going with me, aren't you?"

He smiled."You're kidding, right?"

Relief nearly choked her. "Good. Let's get dressed and get your guns. I want to be there long before he is to check the place out."

He stood up and reached for her hand. "Spoken like a true Bullet Catcher."

She let him pull her into his chest. "Actually, it doesn't sound like a bad gig."

"It's not." Putting his arm around her waist, he kissed the top of her head and pressed their bare bodies together. "Except for the fact that we're not allowed to get involved with the principal."

She tipped back and gave him a disbelieving look. "No sex on the job?"

"Not with the person we're protecting. Ever."

But he'd just . . . "I thought you were the man who didn't take risks. What if Lucy finds out?"

"Then I'm finished."

"You are?" He had to be kidding. He'd risked his job to make love to her? "Why did you do it? Just to break rules? Just for the conquest? Why?"

His eyes bored through her, black and serious.

"Because I wanted you more than I wanted . . . job security."

Her heart turned over at the words. An image of poverty-stricken cousins in a Cuban fishing village flashed in her head. "That's a crock," she said. "You thought you could have both."

"I want both."

"Do you always get what you want?"

"Always." He tipped her chin with one finger, guiding her face closer to his. "But I'm not delusional, Jazz. I don't have you. I just had your body."

And that's all she would ever give a man like Alex Romero. A man who would never be satisfied unless he had all the power and control. "My body's all that's available. Take it or leave it."

"I'll take it." He lowered his head and kissed her mouth lazily, his erection stirring between them. "I'll take whatever you offer, any time, any place, and as often as possible."

The warmth and security of the fluffy comforter vanished as someone pulled it away from Jessica's bare body. With a cry she barely recognized as her own, she bolted upright and blinked into the unnatural light in her room.

A blond woman stood next to the bed, wearing jeans and a navy blue sweatshirt. "You gotta pee?" she asked Jessica, a grimace forming wrinkles on what would otherwise be a passably pretty face.

Jessica stared at her, inhaling a whiff of cloying perfume mixed with the lingering stench of cigarettes. "Who are you?"

She rolled her eyes. "Please." She threw a ball of tan-colored fabric on the bed. "You gotta get dressed, but I figure since there's no bathroom in here, you need to pee."

Jessica looked at the lump of material on the bed, then back to the unfamiliar woman. She squeezed her eyes shut and fought the terror.

Jessica Lynn Adams.

Every time she woke up, she recited her name. Because that was all she could remember. Just as things would start to crystallize in her mind, she'd sink back into sleep. And when she woke up, whatever she'd remembered was gone. Like a dream she knew she'd had, but couldn't recapture.

Maybe this time she could stay awake long enough to commit something to memory. "I could use the bathroom, yes." She reached out to touch the woman's arm. "Where am I?"

Her eyes widened. "Man, that stuff works. He said you wouldn't remember anything."

He? Who? Jessica shook her head. "I don't. Please tell me where I am. And who you are, and who he is."

"No can do, pussycat. You not remembering is the whole deal." She raked Jessica's naked body with an appraising glance. "I didn't realize you were so stacked. Are those puppies real?"

Jessica covered her breasts, a shiver of warning raising the hairs on the back of her neck. Were they real? "I guess so."

That earned a snort. "You guess so? Well, I *guess* I'm gonna find out, huh?" At Jessica's appalled look, she leaned in closer. "Don't worry, honey." Her tone was truly, genuinely kind. "It's so much easier with a girl. We don't hurt each other, and I'm totally disease-free. Promise."

Nausea turned her stomach. "What—what are you talking about?"

The woman's brown eyes softened even more. "You've never been with a chick, have you?"

Had she? A scream threatened to tear from her throat. Why couldn't she remember anything? "No." Nothing about the idea had any appeal for her.

The woman shrugged. "It's no biggie, honest. And man, chicks eating each other out, that sure sells movies. Guys just can't get enough of that shit." She reached over and gave Jessica a little push. "Get up. I'll show you where the bathroom is."

Bile rose in her throat and Jessica willed it away. She stood, glanced down at her naked body. "I need something to wear," she said, looking at the clothes dropped to the bed.

The woman scooped up a beige dress that looked vaguely familiar. "That's for you to wear in the movie. That's what you start the scene in, at the anchor desk. Then you get it on with the weather girl." She smiled. "Me." She handed the dress to Jessica. "I guess it won't hurt for you to put it on now. But you don't need it; there's no crew on this shoot."

Jessica slid into the coatdress, still shivering and as scared as she'd ever been in her life. In the hallway, she could see a soft light at the other end, but the woman steered her into the first door on the right.

Alone in a tiny powder room, Jessica closed the door then turned to stare in the mirror over the sink.

Jazz.

She frowned at the thought. Why would she look in the mirror and think *Jazz*?

She gripped the porcelain sink and leaned closer to her reflection. She knew that face, knew those gray eyes. She touched her cheek, grazing her fingers along her chin, touching the dark beauty mark under her jaw.

Jazz doesn't have a beauty mark.

Jessica closed her eyes. They were there, for her to find and remember. She just had to work hard.

She had a twin sister named Jazz who didn't have a beauty mark. She was Jessica Lynn Adams . . . an anchorwoman.

She almost laughed out loud with the joy of remembering. Opening her eyes, she stared intently at her reflection, ignoring the dark circles under her eyes, the sallow tint to her skin, and the moppy mess of hair. She concentrated on her eyes and tried to pull out a memory. *Any* memory. A recent memory.

Steak. She remembered handling a filet, stirring . . . marinade. For . . . someone.

"Is she in there?"

She startled at the sound of a male voice in the hall. It scared her, that voice.

She heard the woman answer with an affirmative. "I'll have her ready in a few minutes," she said. "She needs some makeup."

"We can't do it now. Something's come up."

"In the middle of the night?"

"It doesn't matter what time it is," he said sternly.

He was mean, this man. Jessica covered her face to listen without any visual distraction, trying desperately to pull a picture of him . . . or a name . . . into her crippled brain.

"I have to go meet someone," he told her. "Get her back to sleep for a while. Can you handle that?"

Oh God, no. Not sleep. Not that dreamless, frightening sleep. Whenever she woke up, she was so lost.

"I don't want to be here all goddamn week," the woman said. "I told you I'd do this job, then I want my money and I want to get the hell outa here."

"Put her back to sleep," the man said. His voice was low, demanding, and so frustratingly familiar. "Use this."

The image of a needle flashed in Jessica's mind and she instinctively looked down at the mud-colored bruise on her thigh. This time she couldn't stop the bile in her throat. Turning to the toilet, she vomited, the force of it bringing her to her knees. She gagged over and over again, with no idea how much time had passed.

Then she heard the door open.

She looked up to see the woman's face in the mirror over the sink. The sight tugged at a memory, but she couldn't pull it out.

"Please," Jessica choked, wiping spit from her chin. "Please. I'll do whatever you want. I'll pay you more than he's paying you. I'll give you anything, please." She sobbed, tears soaking her cheeks. "Please . . ."

The woman gave her head a slow, dubious shake. "I don't know, Jess. You promised me that once before."

She had? Jessica searched the face, digging deep into her very soul for a memory. "Who are you?"

"They call me Desirée."

Des— "Denise!" she almost screamed the name as the memory smacked into clarity. "I remember you!"

Denise laughed quickly. "Well it's about time, baby-cakes."

Then she remembered something else. The thing Denise wanted most in the whole world.

"If you help me," Jessica whispered, "I'll get you back your son."

All the harshness disappeared from Denise's face. "You can't do that," she said softly, lowering herself to her knees. "Can you?"

"I can." Jessica glanced to the open door, unsure of who could hear her. "I promise I can. Just, please, don't put me back to sleep."

"How can you?"

Jessica had no earthly idea. "Trust me. If you help me, I will get him for you. Today. Tomorrow. Now."

Denise leaned back and pulled the bathroom door closed. Then she whispered, "He'll kill us both if he finds out."

Then, with sickening clarity, Jessica remembered who *he* was. A man she'd trusted. A man she'd believed in. A man who was most definitely capable of murder.

"Then he can't find out."

As the SUV rumbled over the deserted Rickenbacker Causeway, Alex stole a glance at his passenger. She'd dressed in the camos, a tank top, and the boots that she'd

worn all day. Jazz-wear. She looked good in it. Better out
of it, though.

The weight of sexual satisfaction settled over his
whole body, but he knew it was temporary relief. He
hadn't even come close to having enough of her.

She'd gotten way too deep under his skin. The exact
opposite of what he intended when he gave in to his
burning desire to get inside of her.

He'd done what he wanted to do, he rationalized. He
defied Lucy, he appeased his sexual cravings, and he
reduced the chemical reaction between them to its most
basic elements: raw, gratifying physical release.

Proving that sex did not, as Lucy believed, ruin your
concentration, inhibit your response time, or wreck
your ability to think straight.

But *had* he proven that? He was driving to a late-
night rendezvous with a guy he'd pegged as a weirdo
from day one, taking the principal with him—armed,
no less—and thinking only about getting home and
getting naked.

Carajo! Lucy was right.

"What if Ollie is the stalker?" Jazz's question pulled
him back to the moment.

"I considered that," he agreed. "I think he knows
more about Denise Rutledge than he's letting on."

"He's focused on Miles Yoder," she said, leaning her
head back and closing her eyes. "He's mentioned his
name over and over. And that my sister hasn't been completely honest with me."

Alex shot her a sympathetic look. "She wouldn't be the
first woman in history to mess around with a married man."

"This from the man who slept with his client's wife."

He took a deep breath, and let it out slowly. "Until tonight," he said, "I have never had sex with anyone I was protecting or their wife."

"So what happened tonight?"

"What happened tonight . . ." Transcended even his expectations. ". . . will happen again."

She groaned under her breath. "You're so damn full of yourself."

"As if you're not." He grinned at her. "Let's not talk about it, okay?"

"Why not?"

He tapped the brakes. "'Cause we're on the Rickenbacker Causeway, headed straight into trouble. If we weren't, I'd pull over and show you exactly how full of me you can be." And he would. Proving everything Lucy ever said about *sex* and *distraction* was true.

They continued the ride in silence.

"Is this Key Biscayne?" she finally asked.

"This is Virginia Key. The next island is Key Biscayne."

They passed the darkened entrance to the Seaquarium, then picked up the causeway again to Key Biscayne. Thick foliage arched over the road and blocked the moonlight. Crandon Boulevard was completely deserted.

"I'm going to turn off the air conditioner and open the windows to hear everything. Stay low," he warned.

She tsked. "Alex, we're meeting a nerd who works in the newsroom with my sister. Not a mafia don."

"Then why does the nerd want to meet in the middle

of the night in a deserted park known for drug deals?" As they approached Crandon's parking lot, he scanned for cars. None there.

He pulled into the lot, his trained eye taking in the trouble spots, the lack of lighting, and the options for escape. There was another entrance farther south, but here, at the north end, there was only one way in and out of the parking lot. The rest was lined with hibiscus bushes so thick he couldn't drive the Escalade through them.

He positioned the vehicle on one side of the bushes in the shadows, so they could see anyone pulling into the lot before they could be spotted. He turned off the car and lights, leaving his window partially opened.

Humidity and salt air dampened his neck and filled his nostrils. He took out his gun and laid it on his lap.

For once, Jazz was utterly still. She actually sat with her hands folded, looking directly out the windshield. To their right, the moon reflected off the surf of Key Biscayne. Crickets and cicadas ticked; the only other sound was their breathing.

This single act went against every precept of personal protection: avoid confrontation, keep your principal out of the line of fire, and *never* knowingly place your principal in a precarious situation.

Oh, and don't get distracted.

"I wonder what kind of car Ollie drives," Jazz whispered.

"A white Saturn. I saw him leaving the TV station—" He stopped talking at the sight of headlights on the main road. "Wait to see if they pass."

But the vehicle slowed down at the entrance to the park, and pulled in. Alex immediately recognized the outline of a pearl gray Mercedes 600. "This isn't Ollie," he said.

Jazz got her gun out. "Not in his price range," she agreed.

He spared her a glance, noticing her features were taut, her eyes focused, her breathing steady. He turned back to the Mercedes, watching it slowly circle the lot.

A dealer, maybe? Looking to make a delivery or pickup?

Suddenly, the car turned as if it sensed them hiding in the dark, its bluish halogen beams spotlighting them like trapped animals. Alex swore and ducked, pushing Jazz down with him. The lights stayed locked on them, and the car rumbled toward them.

Alex sat up and squinted into the lights. Who the hell was coming at them?

Gripping his gun, he flipped on his own high beams but that had no effect on the Mercedes; it continued at exactly the same speed, headed directly for them.

In an instant, he twisted the key, slammed on the gas and wrenched the wheel to get out of the way. As he did, the Mercedes driver's window lowered.

"Stay down!" Alex yelled at Jazz, gunning it.

"Wait!" Jazz screamed, turning in her seat to watch the other car as they passed it. "Wait! He's waving at you."

"Jessica!" The man's voice from the other car broke over the engine noise. "Is that you?"

Alex slammed on the brakes and threw it into reverse,

exactly at the same time the Mercedes did. In one second, they were window to window. Eye to eye.

Client to bodyguard.

"What the fuck is going on, Romero?" Kimball Parrish's deep blue eyes flashed to the color of a thundercloud. "What are you doing bringing her to some godforsaken drug-dealing hellhole in the middle of the night? Aren't you supposed to be protecting her?"

Alex just stared at him, ignoring the sense of doom that threatened. What the hell was Parrish doing there?

"Oliver called me and told me he'd tested you," Parrish announced with disgust. "And you failed."

Jazz propelled herself toward Alex's window. "Mr. Parrish—"

Throwing the car into drive, Parrish shook his head. "Get her out of here. I'll deal with you tomorrow." He peeled out of the lot and sped down Crandon Boulevard.

"Ollie set me up?" Jazz dropped back against the seat, her expression deflated. "Why?"

"I don't know." Alex turned toward the exit. "But we're not waiting around to find out."

"Alex!" She grabbed his arm. "Wait. He still might show. Just wait until the appointment time has passed."

He raced the engine as he pulled onto Crandon Boulevard. "Talk to him tomorrow. We're not staying here. I've fucked up enough things tonight."

"Listen, I can explain this to Parrish. It won't cost you your job. Obviously Ollie didn't tell him everything; he's up to something. Something stinks about this."

Headlights from way behind him seized his attention,

pulling out of the south end of Crandon Park. Had there been another car in the parking lot that he'd missed?

"Jesus," he muttered as he watched the lights intensify with each passing second. "This asshole must be going a hundred."

"What?" She pivoted in her seat. "Oh my God, Alex!"

"Brace yourself!"

The sound of the motor preceded the car by a half second as it bore down on them. Just as it was within a hundred yards, Alex whipped the SUV to the side of the road and the car whizzed by, a screaming blur of white.

White?

"That's Ollie!" She said it the moment he realized the car was a white Saturn. "Go, Alex. Go!"

He flattened the accelerator. The Escalade easily climbed to eighty and closed in on the little Saturn toward the end of the fingertip of Virginia Key. But he picked up unbelievable speed on the causeway—way more than the compact car was meant to handle.

The Saturn swerved and Jazz sucked in air, holding onto the dash as metal clunked under their tires and the wind sang through the window.

The Saturn lurched to the left and then the right, slowing down.

"We got him," Jazz said victoriously as they closed within fifty feet.

The white car swerved wildly, popping up and down on the raised walkway on the side of the bridge. Then he suddenly barreled into the guardrail, flipped over, and went hurtling over the edge and into the blackness of Biscayne Bay.

Jazz shrieked in horror as Alex slammed on the brakes, the Escalade fishtailing madly. All they could see was the roof of the white Saturn as the car sunk into the water.

His pulse thudded through his ears so forcefully that he almost didn't hear his phone. He held the earpiece to his cheek, looking at Jazz's bloodless face in the white bridge lights.

"This is not what I meant when I said impress the client." Lucy's voice was dead calm. "Would you like to tell me what the hell is going on, Alex?"

"I don't know, Lucy," he said honestly, staring at the annihilated guardrail and the bubbles that arose in the water below. "Maybe you should ask Kimball Parrish."

"I won't have that opportunity, Alex. He's terminated our contract. And I'm terminating yours."

CHAPTER
Thirteen

The bittersweet smell of espresso woke Jazz from a restless sleep, punctuated by the outburst of a man laughing.

That wasn't Alex, she thought, turning to the pillow that he'd slept on and pulling it to her face for a good sniff. Funny how she knew his laugh already, how she knew his smell. She closed her eyes and inhaled, trying to recapture the few hours they'd had in bed that morning, with no sex but an enormous amount of comfort.

The door to the bedroom creaked open and she emerged from the depths of Alex's pillow to see him standing there, holding a cup of liquid lead and looking at her like he wanted nothing more than to replace the pillow with himself.

Something deep inside her trembled and tingled and totally betrayed her attempt to look cool and disinterested.

"*Hola, querida.*"

"Uh-oh." A half-smile tugged at her lips. "Spanish."

He grinned. "You're safe. We have company."

"I heard." She scrambled to a sitting position, and pulled the sheets around her bare legs. She wore underwear, a T-shirt, and no bra. She remembered falling asleep spooned against Alex's hard stomach. "A wild guess . . . Bullet Catchers?"

"One of them. Dan is here." He entered the room, closing the door. *"Café?"*

She reached for the espresso cup and patted the bed for him to sit down. "Hard to imagine anyone laughing after last night." She took a taste of coffee, then cringed. "Whiskey'd be easier in the morning."

"You'll get used to it."

There was that annoying tingle again. Was that another vague reference to *their future?*

"So did he come over to hold a wake for your job, or poor Ollie?"

He brushed a hair back from her brow. "He came over to strategize the next move."

Setting the cup on the nightstand, she leaned back on the pillows. "How can he do that? I thought the Bullet Catchers lost the client."

"What we lost," he said thoughtfully, "is the principal. That would be your sister."

Her limbs went numb for a moment and she closed her eyes. Where to start? How to find her with Ollie gone?

"They're dredging the bay today to pull up Ollie's car and body," he told her. "Dan has a lead on Miles Yoder and he's going to dig around, and at the TV station."

"And what about us?" she asked, dreading the answer. *We'll lay low, Jazz. Let someone else find her.*

"We were waiting for you to get up to discuss that."

She smiled widely. "Thank you. Give me a few minutes to get dressed, then I'll join your meeting."

Leaning over the bed toward her, he lowered his head and kissed her gently. "We'll find her, Jazz. I promise."

Ten minutes later, Jazz actually downed another Cuban coffee. She sat curled on one of the great room sofas, with Alex's warm, large body just inches away. Dan Gallagher stood at the bar that separated the kitchen from the main room, nursing an American coffee and regarding her with that amused twinkle in his eye.

"So, where's Max?" she asked after they'd said their good mornings.

"Max is a rule follower," he informed her.

"Are you breaking the rules by coming here, Dan?"

He lifted one shoulder and one eyebrow in a classic devil-may-care gesture. "What Lucy doesn't know won't hurt her," he said. "Max is going to hang around the bay and see what they drag out of the water. We're not giving up on Oliver Jergen as a lead to your sister."

"I'd like to pursue Kimball Parrish," she said. "I'm the one who got Alex fired; I insisted on going to Crandon Park beach in the middle of the night. But I am not the person Parrish is paying for you to protect. He's made a gross error and the only person who can make him believe that is me."

Alex blew out a quick breath. "Jazz, I don't care about my job. I care about your sister. Let's leave Parrish out of this."

"Why, Alex? He could be a direct link to her," she insisted. "The man is either hot to have her or hot to move her into the network. Once he finds out she wasn't in harm's way last night, maybe he'll cooperate in helping to find her. He may agree to putting something out on the news."

Alex stood, running his hands through his hair in frustration. "Why would Ollie lure you out into the night, only to cause trouble with Parrish?"

"Maybe he wanted to get you fired," Jazz suggested. "Maybe he wanted me unguarded for some reason."

Dan nodded. "That makes sense. Maybe he was Jessica's stalker and he wanted Alex out of the picture."

Jazz voiced the thought that had kept her awake much of the night. "What if he's the only person who knows where Jessica is and now he's dead?" She took a deep breath and said, "What if Jessica was in that car?"

Alex simply closed his hand around hers in response. Holding his hand, Jazz dropped her head back and pictured the little white Saturn flipping over the side of the Rickenbacker Causeway.

Alex stood up suddenly. "We haven't even checked the news."

"That's right," Jazz agreed. "It's noon now. There should be a local broadcast on."

Dan's cell phone rang as Alex located the remote and aimed it at the plasma screen on the wall.

"Yo, Max." Jazz watched Dan's expression for clues to what Max was saying.

Giving into the fear in her heart, Jazz grabbed a sofa cushion and wrapped her arms around it as Dan listened to the report. As each second passed, each time he said, "I see," and nodded thoughtfully, Jazz's pulse quickened.

Finally, he signed off. Alex turned from the TV.

"You're not going to believe this," Dan said.

Jazz's nails dug into her fists.

"They pulled three teenagers from a white compact car that went off the causeway last night. Two boys and a girl, not even seventeen years old. Drunk. The car was registered to the girl's mother, a resident of North Miami. No connection to Oliver Jergen." He was quiet for a moment, listening, then added, "It was a Kia, not a Saturn."

Jazz exhaled in one long *whoosh* and propelled herself off the sofa, throwing her arms around Alex. "She wasn't in the car. And neither was Ollie." She pulled back and looked at him. "I'm going to find that man and kick the living shit out of him until he tells me where she is."

Dan started to laugh, but Alex pointed the remote over her head, toward the screen. "You won't have to look too hard," he said, easing her around to face the television.

On the Channel Five news set, a bubbly blond weekend reporter read the TelePrompTer. In the background at the circular assignment desk, Oliver Jergen worked the phones and police radio.

"Let's go," she said, already walking to the door.

"You better hurry," Dan said. "Max is already on his way there."

Jazz burst into the main lobby of the television station without changing her clothes, or applying Jessica-worthy makeup. It didn't matter; the gig was up.

But when the young guard at the front desk looked at her with disbelief, she realized she'd have to fake it one more time. She blinded him with one of Jessica's show-stopping smiles.

"Good morning . . ." What the hell was his name? Her smile froze along with her heartbeat.

"Hello, Louis," Alex said, guiding her forward without missing a beat.

Jazz shot him a grateful glance.

"Mornin', Jessica. Sir." Louis nodded to Alex as he buzzed them into the hallway to the newsroom.

Jazz hustled on, aware of Alex's warm, strong hand against her lower back, protective and supportive. Not exactly the impartial touch of a bodyguard. Then again, he wasn't her bodyguard. He was her lover . . . and partner in this. Instead of the expected lurch of distaste—especially after all the months she played second string to Elliott Sandusky's heavy-handed management of their relationship and their work—a wholly different sensation rushed through her veins.

A sensation of attraction that went beyond . . . attraction. Damn, what an inopportune time for *that* to happen. She looked up at him, but his expression was focused on their destination—the newsroom and Oliver Jergen.

She steeled herself for battle as they turned the corner into the multistory newsroom. Behind the assignment desk stood a complete stranger.

"Where's Ollie?" she demanded.

"He's in your office," the man said, pointing a thumb over his shoulder. "Doing an interview with Attila the Hun."

Max.

Alex swore softly in Spanish.

"Listen to me," she said, turning to him. "Don't get into a shouting match over whose job this is. That's all that Ollie needs to divert attention from him. Take Max outside and beat each other up if you have to, but let me stay with Ollie."

His eyes darkened. "You won't be alone with him."

"I'm fine," she said, surreptitiously pointing where his borrowed weapon was concealed in an ankle harness. "I'm armed."

His eyes half closed in disgust. "Don't shoot him, Jazz."

"I won't. At least not until he tells me where my sister is."

They rounded the assignment desk and looked into Jessica's glass-enclosed office, where Ollie Jergen sat wide-eyed in Jessica's chair, facing the human wall of Max Roper.

"Whoa, hold on, honey," Alex said, clipping a finger into her belt loop and tugging her into his chest. His forceful whisper warmed her ear. "I handle Max. Do *not,* for any reason in heaven or hell, leave that office with Jergen. Stay right there where everyone can see you."

The newsroom on Sunday afternoon was virtually deserted, and if Ollie wanted to lunge over the desk and throttle her, the only person who would notice might be the guy on the desk—if he wasn't facing the police scanners, as he was 99 percent of the time. "Sure."

He released her and they marched to the office. Alex

whipped open the door, and the conversation halted as both men looked at him.

"What the hell are you doing here, Roper?" Alex demanded.

Max scowled, deepening three sharp lines between his thick brows. "I could ask the same thing, Romero. You have no reason or right to be here." He looked at Jazz, his expression softening only a little. "Nor do you."

Jazz glanced at Ollie, who simply stared at her, his ashen complexion a perfect complement to his uncombed hair and red-rimmed eyes. Whatever he'd been up to, it didn't involve sleep.

Alex led her farther into the office. "I just heard from Lucy. We need to talk, Roper. Privately."

The big man shot Alex another dubious look, his gaze shifting questioningly to Jazz.

"Please, Max," she urged. "Go with Alex. It's important. And I want to talk to Ollie."

Reluctantly, he stood, surprising Jazz again with his height and size. He was six-foot-four inches of solid, ironlike muscle. "I'm done here," he said gruffly, giving Ollie a threatening glare.

When they left, Jazz slung her shoulder bag on the back of the guest chair and sat, fixing a stare on Ollie. The room was silent except for the hum of Jessica's computer and the soft purr of an air conditioning duct. He stared right back.

"Where is she?" Jazz demanded.

He said nothing.

"Where is she?" she repeated, her jaw clenched so tightly the words had to slide through her teeth.

He looked down and then back up at her, a contrite expression in weary blue-green eyes. "I'm sorry about last night. I hope you didn't wait very long."

So. He'd never showed.

"I left early." She narrowed her eyes at him. "Right after Kimball Parrish paid an unexpected visit."

He jerked back as though she'd slapped him. "He's in Key West."

It took everything she had not to leap over the desk and wring the truth out of his scrawny neck. "He was in Crandon Park at three thirty this morning, and he said you'd sent him there."

He opened his mouth to argue.

"I don't give a shit, Ollie," she said, holding a hand up to silence him. "I want to know where my sister is, and I want to know *now.*"

His narrow shoulders dipped in resignation. "I have no idea."

She bit hard against her lip to keep from swearing, to keep from attacking. "I think you know where she is."

"I told you, Miles Yoder is the only person who knows where she is."

"Then tell me this." Could she handle it if her sister was having a relationship with a married man?

He leaned forward, sending a whiff of something sour toward her. Alcohol?

"What is his relationship to Jessica?"

He wet his lips and glanced at the door as though he were about to divulge international secrets. Just say it. *Say it!*

"He's interviewing her for a job in New York."

She felt her air escape in a single puff. "A job? What kind of job?"

"The one she wants. Network anchor, morning show." He raked her with a look. "I don't know how much she's told you."

There were still too many unanswered questions. "It has to be more than that. Why were you so mad at me the other day, when you thought I was Jessica? What were you talking about?"

"I . . . I got pissed because I thought you were acting funny. But . . ." His face broke into a sad smile. "You were just acting. Period."

Her anger slipped a notch. "What were talking about when you said she would treat you the same? What happened between you and Jessica?"

He shifted in his seat and attempted a casual shrug. "Just a little professional competition."

"But you have completely different jobs."

"I want to go to New York, too," he admitted softly. "She arranged for me to talk to Yoder about a possible job at Metro-Net. But he doesn't want me up there. Not enough experience." He let out a long, pained sigh. "And I guess . . . some of my other problems came to his attention. I thought . . ."

"You thought what?" she pressed.

"That—that Jessica had . . . betrayed me. That she didn't want me in New York and told Yoder about . . . some issues I have."

Jazz filed that for later. "Ollie, I haven't heard a word from her except for two text messages since I got here days ago. Do you have any idea what this story she's working on is all about? Her relationship to Denise Rutledge?"

His gaze darted around the office. "She's been tracking this porn story. She thinks it has national potential—"

"What was the angle?"

"She won't tell me, which was kind of weird. She bounces a lot of stuff off me 'cause we're pretty good friends." He rubbed his hands over his unshaved stubble.

"Would Miles Yoder have known she was working on that story? Would anyone?"

"I think I was the only one. Jessica trusted me. Most of the time." He cracked a knuckle, his lips pressed together. "The station manager and news directors are both pretty much under Parrish's thumb since the Adroit takeover, and I don't think Jessica wanted Parrish to know about it."

"Why not?"

"Because of his religious beliefs."

"What do they have to do with it?"

"I'm just speculating," Ollie said, leaning his elbows on the desk, "but I think Jessica figured Parrish wouldn't run any stories on porn. He's really a right-winger, you know."

That made sense. The man was throwing shock jocks off the air and limiting play lists on his radio stations, living up to the criticisms that he was letting religion impact the media coverage. Once again, not a personality trait that would appeal to Jessica. "Ollie, is my sister dating Kimball Parrish?"

Ollie shrugged. "I don't know what you'd call it. She's

stringing him along and he's like a dog to a fire hydrant for her."

Stringing someone along wasn't Jessica's style.

Jazz gave a frustrated sigh. Now what? "So you've talked to this Yoder guy. Do you have any idea how I can get to him?"

"He's as insulated as a thermos." He laughed bitterly. "I sure as hell don't know how to get past his gatekeepers."

She still felt like she was staring at a puzzle full of missing pieces. "Ollie, if you didn't tell Kimball Parrish about last night, then what was he doing there? And how did he *get* there? He told me he was going to Cincinnati, then New York."

Ollie shook his head. "I called from here; maybe he's got the phones bugged. And he never went to Cincinnati; he's at his house down on Sunset Key, an island off Key West. He's a licensed helo pilot, and he took one of my choppers when he left. It has an on board tracking system and I saw the helo was there this morning."

She could get to Key West today. "Can you get the address for me?"

"Probably; I have a master key to the management suite. He's got a big oil painting of the place up in his office. I bet we could find the address, too." He stood and suddenly shot his hand over the desk in an awkward peace offering. "Look, I'm really sorry about last night, Jazz. I was . . . I was . . ." His face reddened. "You might as well know, because Jessica's going to tell you."

She waited for the explanation, not knowing how to put him out of his obvious shame.

"I was drunk. I get drunk sometimes and Jessica knows

it. I can get ugly, and mean. Like I was last night. Or I get . . ." He stumbled for a word, then his eyes filled. "She's trying to get me help."

"Yeah, she would do that," Jazz said.

For the first time, his smile was from the heart. "I'm in love with her."

Poor guy. She reached out and took his hand. "She has that effect on people."

His story seemed solid. She knew the call had come from this number, and maybe Parrish *did* have the phones bugged. Jessica had been adamant about not talking personal business from work. Maybe Parrish overheard their conversation last night and grabbed the helicopter to stop a rendezvous?

It was possible; Parrish was in love with Jessica, too.

Then realization slapped her. If Kimball Parrish overheard them then he knew she wasn't Jessica, and she distinctly remembered him calling her "Jessica" from his car last night.

Was Ollie lying?

Ollie stepped around the desk, and snapped his head toward the newsroom. "Come on. Let's get that address."

With the weight of her borrowed nine-millimeter pistol pressing on her leg as reassurance, she followed him upstairs and into a darkened reception area. An empty secretary's desk sat sentry in the middle of a cluster of offices, along with some chairs and coffee tables. All the doors were closed and the blinds drawn.

She glanced at the stairwell behind her. Would Alex know where she was?

He'd told her not to leave with Ollie, but now she

knew he was just a remorseful drunk with a crush on Jessica. Or *was* he?

He fumbled with keys in one of the doors before it unlocked. When he turned to invite her in, his face looked less contrite and friendly than it had downstairs. But that could have been the shadows. "God, you look so much like her," he mumbled softly.

Trepidation slowed her step. "That's what they say."

"You must have gotten mistaken for Jessie your whole life."

"No, not really." *Jessie.* Any good friend of Jessica's would know better than to call her that. "We're very different."

He nodded slowly, the hazel eyes taking a lazy trip over her body. "Well, you *dress* differently, that's for sure." *Where was Alex?*

Wordlessly, Ollie entered the office and flipped on a light. "Here's the painting of his house," he said. "Even if we can't find the address, it's not a big island. There's just one small access road and you can grab a golf cart to find this house."

She stayed in the hallway, uneasiness tickling the hairs on the back of her neck.

"Come on in, Jazz," he called. "I can't very well take the picture off the wall."

She reached down and pulled the Glock out of her ankle holster, stuffing it in her pocket. Taking a deep breath, she stepped toward the door of the office.

Ollie was staring up at the picture of a pink beach house, and Jazz's gaze followed. A thousand goosebumps flowered over her arms. That *house.* It was familiar and menacing, and just looking at it suddenly overwhelmed her with . . . *helplessness*. Something about that house was bad.

Closing her fingers over the cold metal of Alex's gun, she stepped into the office.

Max Roper was no hypocrite. Alex appreciated that as they separated in the hallway without shaking hands. They didn't like each other and never would; why fake it?

But they'd reached an understanding. Alex promised to let Jazz finish her interrogation of Ollie—who Max pronounced hungover on booze and hung up on Jessica Adams—and then Alex would do nothing more without a conversation with Lucy.

That's what Alex wanted anyway, and it appeased Max. Who would no doubt call Lucy the minute he was out of earshot, and report that Alex and Jazz were not following orders and remained on the case.

He watched Max stalk down the hall toward the lobby. Sure enough, he pulled out a cell phone before he even left the building. Pivoting away, Alex headed back to Jazz. As he turned the corner, all he could see was that empty office and Jazz's handbag hanging on the back of the guest chair.

White-hot fury and frustration ignited his blood. Why wouldn't that woman listen to him? Why wouldn't she just do what he said, stay under his wing, and—

Forget it. Trying to guard Jazz was like trying to harness the wind.

"Where did she go?" he bellowed to the near-empty newsroom.

The man at the assignment desk covered his mouthpiece and glared at Alex. "No clue, dude."

Alex spun around and scanned the two-story newsroom. The sea of computers in the middle was mostly black, the desks empty. Only one man sat across the room, on the phone. A floor manager pushed a camera across the floor of a darkened studio set. A few technicians worked behind glass in a control room near the studio, also oblivious.

All along the top floor, more glass-enclosed offices—all empty—could be seen from where he stood. On a Sunday afternoon with no newscast scheduled for hours, the place was deserted.

"They couldn't have left," he barked to the man behind the assignment desk, who just shrugged and continued a muffled conversation into a headset.

Mierda!

He peered into the hallway that ran parallel to the newsroom. The makeup studio, the control rooms, even the offices down there were all darkened. If they'd gone the other way they would have passed him, and he knew there was no other exit in the secure building. His gaze traveled to the stairs. Could they have gone upstairs?

Alex scaled the carpeted steps two at a time, his hand on his gun, his thoughts whirring. He'd left her for five minutes. Five minutes while he placated his archenemy to save her ass—and that of her sister—and buy them time and wham! She's gone. Anger and exasperation and an emotion he couldn't identify boiled in him.

Was that *fear*?

He stepped into a suite of offices, hearing only his thudding heart. What if something happened to her? What if that nutcase Jergen hurt her, touched her, *took* her?

A soft light spilled from one partially opened door. Alex resisted the urge to call out her name, willing his blood to slow so he could hear over the deafening rush of his pulse.

He heard the familiar clatter of computer keys, then an even more familiar laugh. Walking slowly toward the office, gun drawn, he listened.

"Jesus, you're good," a man said.

What the hell? He shoved the door open with his gun.

Ollie and Jazz both jerked around from the monitor, where they'd been head to head, clicking away at one of her goddamn endless databases. "Oh my God, you scared me," she exclaimed.

He scared *her*? "What are you doing?"

She pointed to an oil painting of a beach house at sunset on the wall. "Finding that house. It's on Sunset Key, about twelve minutes from Key West. That's where Kimball Parrish is."

Ollie straightened, his bleary gaze dropping to the gun, as he indicated Jazz with a tilt of his head. "She's quite the hacker."

Adrenaline gushed through Alex, leaving him pissed off and poised to slam his fist into a wall. Or Ollie's face. "Yeah, I know." He made no effort to reholster the gun that held Ollie's attention. Let the skinny twerp worry.

Jazz had returned to the keyboard, leaving Alex to stare at the back of her head.

"I told you not to leave that office," he ground out.

Jazz lifted one hand, typing with the other. "Sorry."

"You're *sorry*?" He practically spat the word at her. She defied his order, disappeared with a creep wearing a stained "Zoo York" T-shirt and scared the living hell out of him, and she was *sorry*?

"Yes!" she said with a definitive smack of the enter key. "I found it! Of course, the whole island's only twenty-seven acres, so it wasn't that hard."

She spun around in the desk chair and smiled at Alex. "How'd you unload Max?"

He didn't answer, still swamped by his physical reaction to losing her.

Utterly oblivious, she pulled a piece of paper off the printer, and then turned to the painting of a pink Key West–style beach house.

"I can find that house," she announced. "There's only one road on Sunset Key."

Alex managed a remarkably composed voice as he told Jergen, "I need to talk to her privately."

Ollie blinked in surprise, then moved from behind the desk. "I'll be downstairs. Lock the door when you leave. And turn off the computer."

She gave him a sweet smile. "I will, Ollie. And thanks."

"No problem."

When he left, Alex closed the door and stared at her. "Why the hell did you come up here with him?"

"I trusted my gut. Don't be mad." She dropped back into the chair and turned to the keyboard.

"I'm way past mad, Jazz. I told you not to leave that office with him."

"He's harmless."

"You don't know that."

She continued to scroll through something on the computer. "He's just a . . . Oh." She paused for a moment, tapped a few more words out, and leaned closer to the screen. Irritation prickled over him with each click of the keys.

"He's another guy with a wicked crush on my sister, who drinks too much to forget about it," she said absently, her attention focused on the computer.

So she and Max had come to the same conclusion.

"I've known a million like him," she added. "My shoulder's practically broken from all the fools who've cried on it over the years."

She tapped and the screen changed, and he watched her enter a password. "And you buy that?"

She shrugged, concentrating.

His gut clenched with every second he stared at the back of her head. "Damn it, turn around and look at me."

Her fingers froze. "Excuse me?"

"Turn. Around. And look. At me."

She deliberately tapped a key, demolishing the last shred of control he had. In three steps, he'd rounded the desk and twirled the chair with way more force than necessary. "Why are you doing this to me?"

"To you?" She shot up indignantly and he pushed her right back down. Sparks flared from her platinum eyes and her delicate nostrils puffed in fury. Taking slow, even breaths of self-control, she stood. "Don't you *ever* push me back into place again, Alex."

"Jazz—"

"I am *not* your little sister." She stabbed his chest with her index finger to emphasize every word. "And you are not some macho Cuban dictator who can tell me what to do and when to do it and who to do it with."

He inhaled sharply, closing his eyes for a second. "Ollie is an unknown quantity, Jazz." He kept his voice as low and modulated as possible, willing his temper to disappear. "He could have hurt you, killed you—"

She slammed her right hand into her pocket and whipped out his pistol, holding it by the butt so he could see the safety was on. "I can take care of myself, Alex."

He stared at the weapon, a thousand thoughts at war in his brain. But the only one he heard was the one that screamed from his heart. "I want to take care of you."

"What?" The word mixed with a disbelieving snort. "You want to take *care* of me?"

Carajo. Why did he say that? "It's my job."

"First of all, you were fired. Second, I don't *need* you to take care of me." She searched his face, her expression intent. "And I don't *want* you to take care of me. I am capable of handling that myself."

And that, he knew, was the root of this ache in his body, this odd emotion that rocked him inside out. Of course she was capable of taking care of herself. Of course she didn't need him. Of course she didn't want him to step in to guard, protect, and defend her.

But he didn't know any other way when he felt like this. When he felt so . . .

"Easy, boy," she said with a light laugh, stashing the

gun back in her pocket and regarding him closely. "I
don't like that look, Romero."

"What look?" As if he didn't know. *You're so deep into
her you can't see straight.* Shit. He *hated* when Roper was
right.

"This is . . . this is just sex, Alex," Jazz said softly.
"Don't delude yourself that it's anything more than that."

Just sex?

He buried his fingers into the hair at the nape of her
neck and pulled her even closer, so they touched. "I
thought he hurt you."

"I'm not stupid. I knew I could handle him."

"I would have killed him."

She smiled. "You're sweet, honey." She tipped her face
toward his, and placed her lips right over his mouth,
whispering, "But I'm not in the market for a hero."

"I'm no hero," he admitted, closing the millimeter of
space between them. In an instant, he channeled all the
whirling frustration and fear and fury in his head and
heart into a hard, hungry kiss.

She slid her tongue between his teeth, levering her
hips against an erection he didn't even realize he
had. One hand pulled her tighter, the other sought the
comfort of her breast.

Her voice rang in his ears as her body filled his hands.
This is just sex.

Her every movement confirmed that. Sex. Here. Now.
Why wasn't that perfect? Why did that leave him with
an empty sensation, instead of relief and the usual thrill
of the conquest? Why wasn't *sex* enough?

He pulled away, still tasting the remnants of café

Cubano on her mouth. Under his hand, her nipple pebbled and her heart thumped.

She closed her eyes, dropped her head back and opened her throat and chest to him. Kneading the tender flesh under his palm, he pushed her onto Parrish's desk. With one knee, he spread her legs and eased his body on top of hers, his hard-on pulsing against her.

She sucked in a raspy breath, her fingers pulling at his hair.

Just sex.

If he could just take her here, now, without care, that would prove she was right. No need to protect her or watch over her. No need for anything but *lust.*

Nothing like that miserable helplessness that had nearly wiped him out when she'd disappeared.

He yanked at her top, pushing it up over her bra. She dug into his pants and enclosed him in her hand. She whispered his name in a husky voice, stroking his cock furiously.

Blood hammered in his head, rushing to his loins, seeking a release. They scratched out harsh, ragged breaths as their bodies rocked in syncopated rhythm against each other. She murmured what she wanted in lusty, scorching words.

He answered the same way. Hard, fast, *hot.* No tenderness, no emotion.

Just sex.

He pushed her pants down, and she fumbled with his belt and shoved at his trousers. Even with a sliver of silk denying him entrance, the heat of their groins burned where he slid between her legs. Hard and full and bursting with need, he yanked her flimsy panties to the side. She lifted her hips to him, the tangy smell of an aroused woman sucker-punching him with need.

She pushed him inside her.

Sweat broke over his forehead and his hair fell into his eyes. Swiping it away, he locked on her. He had to see her, had to witness this.

"Alex, now." She closed her fists around his cock and guided him farther into her, the lace of her panties scratching his swollen flesh. "I'm coming, Alex," she pleaded, her voice breaking. "Please."

"I don't have any—"

She pushed him in deeper. "I'm on the pill."

Something clunked off the desk as he thrust into her, the force of his lunge causing a little earthquake around them. Once, twice, three times he buried himself as every shred of control vanished. He came like a thunderclap at the instant she did, emptying himself with endless, mighty jerks of blinding satisfaction and a guttural groan torn from his throat.

Sweaty, dizzy, spent, he fell on top of her. But still his chest hurt, and it wasn't from strain or heavy breathing.

Carajo. She was wrong. She was dead wrong.

This *wasn't* just sex.

His heartbeat finally steadied and her warm, sweet breath had nearly returned to normal. Easing out of her, they both let out a soft moan of unwillingness to part.

He brushed his hair out of his face and pulled up his pants, unable to stop looking at her as he zipped. She was so damn beautiful, with her silver eyes all sparkly and soulful.

Did she know? Did she know this wasn't just sex, for him?

No. Nor would she ever. Slowly, he smoothed her shirt over her lacy bra and her stomach, his fingers traveling south to linger on the wet silk of her panties. "You couldn't even get your clothes off before you came."

She grinned. "And you just did it on the client's desk."

It shouldn't have, but the idea made him laugh. "I already got canned."

"I'll talk to Parrish," she said, taking his hands in hers. "We'll get your job back, I promise."

The office door suddenly whipped open, hitting the wall with a solid *thwack*. Alex had his gun cocked and ready before Jazz even sat up.

In the doorway, Ollie ignored the weapon pointed at him. His narrowed gaze slid over Jazz, deliberately halting at the pants that hung wide open at her hips.

"You're right about one thing." Revulsion trembled in his voice. "You are very different from Jessie." Then he turned and disappeared.

CHAPTER
Fourteen

Lucy's heels clicked on the polished wood of the Sastres' home, the sound echoing through the two-story entryway. Through the leaded-glass front door, she could see the extravagant utility vehicle Alex had rented as it pulled into the circular drive.

"If you would be so kind," she said to Alex's sister. "I'd like to speak to him alone." Not that their conversation hadn't been interesting. She loved to learn about her employees' childhoods; it helped her understand how to motivate them. Ileana had been generous with her tales of Alex's overprotective streak, but Lucy had been more interested in the relatives remaining in Cuba. Alex had never talked about them. But of course she knew who and where they were.

"You can have privacy in the living room, Ms. Sharpe," Ileana replied, her dark eyes reminding Lucy of Alex. "I'll be in the kitchen if you need anything."

Although the expensive cut glass broke the visual into a hundred pieces, Lucy saw Alex get out of the car and go to the woman who obviously couldn't wait to have her door opened. Their bodies came together as though no force of nature could keep them apart.

She let out a soft sigh. Poor Alex. He *was* cursed.

The front door opened and Alex didn't miss a step at the sight of her.

"Lucy," he said, that devilish half smile tipping his lips. "Imagine finding you here."

He made no attempt to disengage his arm from the woman he was supposed to be protecting. Of course, he was no longer obliged to follow Lucy's rules.

"I happened to be in Miami," she said, her attention shifting to the woman on his arm. The imposter sister was not nearly as polished-looking as the anchorwoman, with tousled spikes in her auburn hair and barely a drop of makeup to adorn her catlike eyes. Earthy, vibrant, and feminine despite the tough-girl clothes; Lucy had no doubt Alex would be attracted to her. "I'm Lucy Sharpe."

The woman reached out her hand and offered a shake, evidently as unfazed as Alex was. "Jazz Adams. It's a pleasure to meet you."

Somehow Lucy doubted that. "The pleasure is mine." She looked from one to the other. "Where have you two been?" She didn't need to ask what they'd been doing. The beard burn on Jazz Adams's creamy complexion gave that away.

"At my sister's office."

"None of your business."

Their responses cancelled each other out as they spoke in unison.

Lucy smiled, her focus on Alex. "As a matter of fact, it *is* my business. And yours, Alex." She indicated the formal room to her right, as comfortable in the house as if it were her own. "Could I speak to you privately?"

Lucy recognized the stubborn set of his jaw, the half-hooded look in his eyes that preceded a negative response.

"Please," Jazz said before Alex could respond. "Talk to her. I have something I have to do."

He looked dubious, but Jazz put her hand on his arm and added a meaningful look. "There's nothing to be gained by being obstinate."

Tough, sexy, *and* wise. Lucy hadn't expected an ally in the girl.

Alex spoke to his sister for a moment, and Lucy strolled into the living room. She chose a straight-back chair situated in front of a wide window, leaving Alex to sink into a buttercup yellow sofa across from her with the light directly in his eyes.

But he chose to stand, crossing his arms and tilting his head enough to communicate impatience and also avoid the streaming sunlight. "I thought I was eighty-sixed this morning."

"And yet you continued an unauthorized investigation."

He shrugged. "Anything you hear from Max Roper is suspect."

Someday she hoped to find out just why Max and Alex hated each other so much. Dan Gallagher chalked it up to "male pattern domination" but she believed it was more than that.

"I knew this would happen," she said, shaking her head.

"You knew *what* would happen?" Irritation darkened his tone. "You knew I'd piss off Kimball Parrish, or you knew I'd keep working to find Jessica Adams after you axed me, or you knew I'd . . ." He glanced in the direction where Jazz had been, and let the suggestion trail into the air. "What exactly did you *know*, Lucy, when you ordered me to Miami and then followed me here?"

The only thing more formidable than his libido was his temper; only the truth would calm him down.

"Alex," she said softly. "I haven't been entirely honest with you."

His expression didn't change as he fried her with an impatient gaze.

"Kimball Parrish is not really the client in this case."

She knew she'd have to tell him eventually, but she wished it could have been later rather than sooner. And she wished they hadn't lost track of Jessica Adams in the meantime; that would have made everything much less complicated.

"Miles Yoder is the Bullet Catcher client, Alex. But that is absolutely confidential information. No one is to know."

Alex dropped onto the sofa. "Then what's the deal with Parrish?"

"Since he's footing the bill to provide security to Jessica Adams, technically he *is* the client. But Miles Yoder brought the job to us, and he is also the client—on a different level."

He said nothing.

"Miles is a married to my dearest friend, Valerie Brooks. In fact, I introduced them."

"Really?" He leaned back and looked at her from under those thick lashes. "Then maybe you should be the one to tell her he's screwing Jessica Adams."

"You're wrong," she said. "He is not involved with her. He's interviewing Jessica for the highest job in broadcasting at his network."

"So I've heard." He locked his hands behind his head. "And where does Kimball Parrish fit into all of this and why was my impressing him so all-out important?"

Lucy pressed her lips together. After years of CIA training, she always wrestled with the same question: how much to reveal? "As you know, he's fairly new to the Metro-Net family. The purchase of WMFL by Parrish's company, Adroit Broadcasting, makes the station the first Metro affiliate Kimball Parrish has owned."

"And?"

"Miles Yoder is on the board of Yellowstone, the company that owns Metropolitan Networks. He has asked me to staff the assignment with someone who could offer a reliable and objective character assessment of Kimball Parrish."

Ileana cleared her throat, standing in the entryway with a tray. "Alex told me you like tea, Ms. Sharpe."

What Alex told his sister, Lucy suspected, was that he needed a *café Cubano*. Fast. "How thoughtful; thank you."

They waited while Ileana set up a platter of fruit-filled Cuban pastries, tea, and a container of inky coffee on the table, then left. Alex helped himself to a cup of espresso while Lucy poured her tea.

"Why don't you start from the beginning, Luce?"

Fair enough. "Kimball mentioned to Miles at a social function that he wanted to hire personal security for one of his employees who had been harassed by a fan. Miles saw it as an opportunity to place someone trusted near Kimball to observe him and, eventually, provide an appraisal of how he conducts business and handles employees."

"Why not just interview his employees and look at his P and L statements?" Alex asked. "It doesn't make sense."

"It does," she argued. "He would have no reason to suspect that's what you are doing."

"Uh, Luce." He laughed softly. "Neither did *I*. Imagine how much more effective I might have been had I known what you wanted."

She took a sip of tea. "I wanted you to get acclimated to the assignment, then I planned to discuss it with you." All true. "Adroit is privately held and extremely closed to outsiders. This Parrish, however vocally conservative he is in public, is also an extremely private person. Very few people get close to him."

"What is Yoder looking for? Dirt?"

"His outspoken politics worry the network, particularly the board of Yellowstone. Miles expects to be named chairman shortly and his ability to get this kind of information is one of the reasons."

Alex said nothing, no doubt formulating a million questions.

"This decision to have Jazz pose as Jessica has complicated matters," she added.

He snorted. "Sure has."

"But Miles is confident that Jessica is successfully pursuing a story that he wants to break on Metro-Net, and once she's finished, she'll return. In the meantime, there's no reason for Kimball Parrish to know that Jazz isn't Jessica, because he won't behave as naturally around her."

He looked skyward in disgust. "Just what I want to be. A pawn in their game."

"I think of it as a mole. Miles needs to understand the man who has designs on a much bigger empire than he already has. Yellowstone is as vulnerable to takeover as the next company. They didn't necessarily welcome Adroit into the family, but now they have had to accept them. They want to know what they're dealing with."

"Why did he stand Jazz up when she went looking for him the other night?"

"I told him who she was before they met," Lucy said. "He wasn't ready to trust an outsider."

Alex regarded her for a long time. She sipped her tea while she waited for his arguments.

"I'm an executive security specialist, Lucy," he finally said. "Why didn't you put someone with investigative or psychological background on an assignment like this? You've got a few ex-spies on your payroll."

"I was testing you."

His jaw visibly tightened. "For what?"

"For your next job. Something that has been brought to me by my former employer." She took one leisurely sip of tea before dropping her little explosive. "They are looking for a special ops consultant." She paused and watched his face. "In Cuba."

To his credit, he didn't flinch. "To do what?"

"I can't say." That much was absolutely true. "But you would like the exchange rate they offered."

Only one brow lifted, but she could feel interest rolling off him in waves.

"If we succeed in the operation, they will arrange for fifteen people to leave the country. Our choice of who those fifteen people are."

His dark skin paled, melting her heart a little. Sure, he was a tough, macho, Latin male. But Alex loved his family.

"I want that job, Lucy."

"I know. But it involves careful character assessment and profiling. You're not quite ready for it. I'd hoped this opportunity would provide the background you need. But—"

"Give me another chance."

"I intend to," she assured him. "I've already convinced Kimball he overreacted and that you are the best Bullet Catcher for the job. Miles is going to talk to Kimball and second that. Frankly, he thinks Kimball's antics last night were bizarre. At the very least, they reveal that the man has a short fuse and an unwillingness to listen."

"He's thinking with his—" He stopped himself, then added, "He's not thinking straight where Jessica Adams is concerned."

"Once you've been reinstated by Kimball, you'll need to make it a point to spend as much time with him as possible. Don't bring unwanted attention to yourself and don't do anything else to alienate him."

He nodded slowly, no doubt thinking of fifteen cousins and uncles and aunts who longed for a better life. "What about Jazz?"

"What about her? She should continue her role—Miles is delighted that there's no need to cover for where Jessica is. He doesn't want Kimball to know he's planning to hire Jessica. He thinks Kimball will be reluctant to let her go to the network, because of the ratings dip it would cause at the TV station. Kimball's stringing her along in that regard."

Alex's frown deepened. "Aren't you overlooking the possibility that something might have happened to her? It doesn't bother you that she hasn't contacted her sister? You don't think there's a chance she's truly a victim of a stalker?"

"Miles has convinced me that isn't the case. He's the only person who knows the nature of the story she's developing, and he's certain that it would require her to stay deep undercover. She's utterly capable, I'm told."

An odd half-smile lifted Alex's lips.

"What is it?" Lucy prodded.

"Nothing. It's just that . . . I'm not sure this Jessica is *all that,* if you know what I mean." His smile faded. "Nor am I convinced she's safe."

Lucy studied him, turning over the facts. Alex's instinct was excellent, his sense of impending trouble the reason why he was her top personal security specialist. But Miles was much closer to the whole story, and knew the players. "Just in case you're right, Dan and Max will investigate the stalker situation, former boyfriends and some other obvious sources on Jessica. You will continue to act as Jazz's—Jessica's—bodyguard. That's how I want this assignment staffed."

He shook his head and pointed over his shoulder. "You're forgetting the one-woman bloodhound. She won't stop until she finds her sister, and she isn't going to care how you want things staffed."

"You must stop her from ruining this investigation," Lucy said.

"She's planning to go to Key West today," he said. "She wants to talk to Kimball."

Lucy's eyes widened in horror. "No. If he finds out she's not Jessica, then he'll let you go for certain. Miles will be most unhappy."

He looked skeptical. "I think her primary reason for going is to clear my name after last night. After that, her next target is Miles Yoder."

"You need to stop her, Alex."

"I don't know," he said, running a hand through his long hair with a skeptical look. "She's a force of nature all her own."

Lucy leaned forward and picked up a sticky pastry, taking a bite. "Mmmm. Raspberry." She brushed a crumb from her lapel as she captured his dark gaze. "Perhaps you can think of some creative way to distract her, Alex. You've always been so good at that."

Facts, Jazz believed in her deepest heart, didn't lie. People did. Opinions were ripe for interpretation and assumptions were the enemy. Facts were dependable.

And there was a big, bad fact staring her in the face from her computer screen.

Kimball Parrish had a direct connection to Denise Rutledge. She'd seen the reference to Desirée Royalle while searching his computer files, just after Ollie had left, while Alex had fumed behind her. She'd found a data capture feature and been able to bookmark the database, but then Alex had . . . sidetracked her. And while he'd annihilated her on Parrish's desk, she'd been downloading files.

While her laptop searched those files, Jazz closed her eyes and relived the annihilation. What was this thing between them? This went way beyond physical attraction, way past the adrenaline rush that naturally led to sexual release. What had he called it, that night she'd escaped him?

A power struggle.

Oh, yeah. And Jazz was losing. Badly.

The screen flashed as she slipped through a flaw in the firewall, forcing herself to concentrate on her missing sister and not her budding romance.

Some romance it would be. Alex traveled the world protecting rich guys and she had a fledgling PI business in San Francisco. And no desire—none, zero, *nada*—to have a relationship with a man who believed in his core that the males of the species were somehow dominant and his role in life was to protect his woman.

But, Jesus. Her nipples ached and her insides twitched and her limbs grew heavy just at the thought of how badly she wanted him. This *was* just sex. Really amazing, bone-melting, incredible sex.

No one was going to win this power struggle. The only thing for her to do was concentrate on finding Jessica. And the most fascinating piece of evidence yet was staring her in the face. An e-mail to Kimball Parrish from none other than the man who fired Denise Rutledge, Howard Carpenter.

Thank God for electronic fingerprints and paper trails that people left all over their computers. E-mails back and forth from Howie to Kimball. Arranging a sexual rendezvous with a porn actress, promising she would do exactly what he'd seen her do in a movie and, most surprising of all, clearly indicating that Desirée had asked for the assignation to take place.

Was Desirée trying to get a job in legitimate TV, hoping that Mr. Parrish was her ticket to television? Or was Desirée helping Jessica on the story?

Either way, Jazz would find out. They could hop a commuter plane from Miami International and be in Key West in an hour.

She'd just finished booking them seats online when the bedroom door opened.

"I'm still employed," Alex announced with a wry grin. "We can skip the trip to Key West and spend the day—" He raked her with a very unsubtle look. "—swimming."

Why did her lower half react that way? Who was in charge of her body, anyway? "Sorry, honey. We're going to Key West. Sunset Key, to be precise. We leave in—" She looked at her watch. "About three hours. With traffic and check-in, that leaves no time for 'swimming.'"

"We don't have to go," he replied, closing the door behind him. She heard the lock switch in place, and damn if her throat didn't go dry.

"Oh, yes we do." She pointed to the computer screen. "Kimball Parrish has an unnatural link to Desirée Royalle and I want to know what it is."

"Really?" He strolled over to the bed where she sat cross-legged and settled in behind her to read the screen. His long legs wrapped around hers and the granite of his chest warmed her back as he placed a hot kiss on her neck. Reading the e-mails over her shoulder, she could feel him smile. "That looks pretty natural to me."

"Alex." She pointed at the screen, aware that his hands had already encircled her waist and were creeping up toward her breasts. "Don't you find it incredibly coincidental that Kimball Parrish knows Denise and that she arranged to have a sexual encounter with him?"

"I don't believe in coincidence." He settled his chin on her neck and began to nibble her earlobe. "But I do believe in sexual encounters."

She dipped out of the gentle grip of his teeth. "What did Lucy say?"

"I told you, she gave me a second chance. She likes you." He glided his hand up her stomach to caress the underside of her breast. "So do I."

Closing her eyes, she tried to form a coherent thought. She wiggled out of his grasp, and looked at him over her shoulder. "What caused the white streak?"

"Excuse me?"

"Lucy's hair. A shock of gray in otherwise dark hair is usually caused by a trauma." Lucy was stunning, easily six feet tall, with pale white skin and jade green eyes, but the two-inch white streak down the front of her long, black hair was her most memorable feature.

Alex shook his head. "No one knows Lucy's background. Just that she was a spook, then left and started the Bullet Catchers."

"No husband? Family?"

"Not that I know of." He pulled her closer, threatening to tip her back on the bed. "We don't have to go to Key West. Parrish will be back in Miami tomorrow, maybe Tuesday."

What had changed his mind? She turned her attention to the computer and clicked on a few more keys, trolling through Parrish's files. Most were secured, but she got through the password protection without much difficulty.

"Lucy is convinced that Jessica is fine," he told her. "She is working on a story, exactly as you suspected from the beginning."

Icy fingers of doubt gripped her. "What's the story?"

"Something the network wants." He slid his hands over her thighs.

She'd known that days ago. She succeeded in opening a new file and clicked through the pages. "Which is?"

"Not sure." His hands stilled. "Go back a page."

She hit the return arrow. "What is it?"

"One more page." She could have sworn she felt his whole being constrict. "There."

The spreadsheet listed about twenty entries down the left, mostly four-lettered television and radio stations, probably owned by Kimball. He pointed to the screen. "Look at that."

Climax.

She blew out a quick chuckle. "You have sex on the brain."

He leaned closer, peering at the screen, his scent making her dizzy. "Click on it."

She did, and it flashed with a link to another file, which was protected. Well protected.

"Climax," Alex said. "That reminds me of something."

She leaned to her left to give him a disgusted look. "You're pathetic."

"I'm serious." She could tell by the darkness in his eyes that he was. "Search all the files for the word."

Tapping at a few keys, she searched the files she'd downloaded for the word "climax." "What does it remind you of?" she asked as they waited. As if she didn't know. Desk sex. Pool sex. More sex.

"Pornography."

Suddenly it hit her. "Climax Distribution. That was the name of the distribution company on Desirée's film," she said, snapping her fingers. "You're right."

"The same film that had Jessica in it."

Her heart dropped at the thought, but her fingers flew, typing in "distribution."

More heavily encrypted files flashed on the screen. She didn't have the software or time to hack into those.

Jazz glanced at Alex. "What if Adroit Broadcasting is somehow connected to Climax Distribution?"

"For the one-man Clean Up America campaigner, I'd say that'd be pretty bad news."

"I'd say that would be *network* news." Jazz hit a few keys to no avail. *Access denied.*

"But the network wouldn't want that publicized, any more than Parrish would," Alex noted. "Parrish owns a Metro-Net affiliate station."

On nothing more than an unnerving gut feeling, she started scanning for video files.

"What are you looking for?" Alex asked.

"I'm not sure." She found a video editing program and tried a few different search words. "I'm just . . . looking."

Alex kissed her neck, the heat of his lips slowing her fingers as she worked. "I love watching you in action," he whispered, the confession sending confusion and delight through her. "It's sexy."

She started to smile, but then froze as a familiar image filled the small video screen in the corner of her laptop.

"Alex." Jazz could barely speak at the sight of her sister's face, laughing. "Look."

"Jesus." Alex pulled her into his chest as he looked at the image on the computer. "Let's go to Key West." Alex was off the bed in one move, holding his hand to her. "Now."

God, she could love a man who thought so much like she did.

Her heart landed in her stomach with a thud so loud she was surprised he didn't hear it.

Love? Now, there was the scale-tipper in the power struggle of life.

Memories came and frustratingly dissipated like scents on the wind, gone before Jessica could capture and closely examine any one. She inhaled the pungent green tea in her cup, hoping for another snippet to break into her foggy brain.

But her head felt like a crashed hard drive.

"What did he give me?" she asked, clasping the ceramic for warmth that her body couldn't seem to generate. "I can barely remember my name."

"Some liquid roofie, I bet." Denise guzzled her own tea, looking out the sliding glass doors to the dark purple thunderhead that formed over the ocean.

Liquid roofie. Rohypnol. Now, how did she know that? She closed her eyes and dug for a memory. *Anterograde amnesia* . . . she did a story on this once. She almost dropped her cup with the realization. Club drugs that erase memory for hours or days.

"Why did he bring me here?" she asked again, knowing full well Denise either didn't know or wasn't saying.

Instead of another shrug, Denise narrowed her eyes at Jessica. "How can you get my son?"

The memory that Denise had a son had come and gone twice since she'd crawled out of the bathroom. Jessica forced herself to concentrate. "We need to get to a phone."

But every telephone outlet in the house was empty. They'd found a cell phone charger with nothing attached to it. There wasn't even a television or radio. Downstairs, on the ground level, was a set of rooms built into the stilts that kept the main house elevated from storm surge waves, but the doors were locked. The only transportation—a golf cart—was missing and Jessica was in no shape to walk far.

Jessica's gaze drifted around the kitchen. Although the place was spacious and clean and decorated with simple but expensive furnishings, the rambling beach house lacked color or personality. In the kitchen, gray ceramic tiles covered the counter and backsplash, plain white cupboards filled two walls, and the stove looked like it had never been used.

Staring at the burner, another memory tickled her brain. Cooking. She'd been cooking. That was the last thing she could remember. She'd been preparing dinner for . . . a man.

She clenched her fists and tried to pull out something, anything from her brain. Forcing herself to relax, she let the images slowly take shape.

They drank wine . . . rich and robust Châteauneuf-du-Pape. Her favorite. But something happened . . . something changed. . . . She'd run to the elevator, hurried from the apartment, her heels clapping against the concrete of the parking garage.

Then there was nothing.

That was Monday, she remembered, pouncing on the fact. Monday night, she'd had plans to make dinner between her broadcasts.

"What day is it?" Jessica asked.

Denise turned to her, an unforgiving light highlighting the deep lines above her lips. "It's Monday."

Jessica's tea turned to acid in her mouth. *She'd lost a week of her life?*

"Please tell me everything, Denise. I need to remember."

"All I know is that you wanted my help to do some

news story. You wanted some files and movies. You
wanted to follow me around, and have me sneak a camera
into the studio."

Jessica gave Denise a blank look as she tried mightily
to remember.

Denise banged her mug on the counter, startling her.
"That was supposed to help you show that no one in this
fucking business has any protection against the jerks
getting rich off our bodies." Denise shot her a dark
look. "You asked a lot of questions about Howie's distribution company and the studio in Hialeah. And then
you offered me money and security if I could get some
very specific information out of Kimball Parrish."

At the mention of the name, Jessica's whole body
went on alert. "What kind of information?"

Something rumbled on the gravel that surrounded
the downstairs of the house. Denise gasped, color draining from her face. "He's home! Get back in that room.
Hurry!"

Jessica didn't move. "No, Denise. He has some
explaining to do. I want to know why I'm here and why
he drugged me."

"Are you nuts?" Denise eyes widened. "I told you.
He's putting you in a movie with me."

Jessica just stared at her and shook her head. "You're
mistaken." But as she spoke, a vivid, ugly image flashed
in her mind.

Her own face, laughing on TV. But it had been . . .
edited.

That's why she'd run out of her apartment. He'd
shown her the film that he'd made. He'd spliced together

candid images from her between newscasts, relaxed and laughing, and edited them onto a woman's body. A woman . . . having sex. At first she'd thought it was a joke—a bad, horrible joke.

But then he turned to her and gave her that sweet, disarming smile. "Let's make a deal, Jessie."

The clunk of footsteps on the wooden stairs from the beach almost erased the tenuous memory.

"Go!" Denise pleaded. "He'll kill you if you're up."

Something in her eyes, her voice, told Jessica it was true. Had she underestimated him? Dumping the cup in the sink but hanging onto it to avoid leaving a trail, she hurried toward the back room where she'd been for a week.

As she reached the hallway, the footsteps were louder, closer. Jessica spun around and stared at Denise. They needed a plan. Time. If he thought she was still asleep, maybe Denise could get help. "Get his phone or get to one. Call my sister—Jasmine Adams in San Francisco. Call her!"

She tore the khaki sheath from her body and slid under the covers like a teenager trying to fake that she'd been in bed all night. She jammed the mug under her pillow and turned over to bury her face.

She heard a man's voice, then a moment of quiet as Denise must have answered.

Sinking under the comforter, she closed her eyes. She couldn't just feign sleep; she'd have to feign a *coma*.

Her sister slept like that.

The pleasure that came with unearthing that tidbit warmed her. Her mind suddenly flooded with information about Jazz. She could picture Jazz, sleeping. That was easy—Jazz loved nothing more. Sleeping and laughing and seizing every drop of energy out of her life. That was Jazz. Not weighed down by aspirations, structure, or the clock. And utterly lovable. She welcomed the old pang of envy, just because it felt so good to remember. But then she remembered something else.

Jazz was on her way to Miami. Or, Lord, she had been there for several days. What had she thought when Jessica never showed—

The bedroom door opened.

Jessica willed herself not to move, fighting the need to scream out and demand answers.

Rubber soles squeaked on the varnished hardwood floor as he approached the bed. Her heart punched her chest, pumping blood noisily through her ears. She needed to swallow, but her throat was dry and tight and swollen in fear.

She felt a hand on the comforter and bile rose up in her as she braced her naked body for the inevitable exposure to his eyes. Her fingers closed around the mug handle under the pillow. Could she slam it against his head? Knock him out?

Jazz could have.

He tucked the soft fabric under her chin, like a loving parent saying good night to his child. His fingertips brushed her hair, and she managed not to jerk at the touch.

"Shakespeare called ambition 'the sin that fell the angels.' " The whispered words were accompanied by a low chuckle. "Isn't that true, Jessie-belle?"

Jessica concentrated on keeping her eyelids closed lightly enough to be sleeping, not clenched in anger and fear. Not flying open to confront and attack and *hurt*.

"If you hadn't been so desperate to get to the top, I could have helped you. I could have gotten you there." He stroked her head. "And now I can't."

A warm breath covered her face as he sighed, the smell of peppermint and spicy cologne. Revulsion rolled through her, tempered only by fear of that needle.

"So, instead of waltzing into the Metro-Net offices with your scathing exposé of a conservative icon that would propel you to the marquis lights you hunger for, I will hand the Yellowstone board a copy of your extracurricular activities." He tsked like a dismayed schoolteacher. "I'm sure the board will squirm in their chairs, watching you fuck for the camera."

I'm going to fuck you while you scream at my camera.

That memory was suddenly crystal clear. The threat of a fan that she'd dismissed with a cavalier wave of the hand. There had been no fan—that had been *him*.

"You laughed at my first attempt, Jessie." His voice was menacing now. "And you were right—we need the real thing. Because your little sex tape will be carefully scrutinized on the Internet, in the media, on the covers of the tabloids. It'll be everywhere, Jessie, so it has to be real." His knuckles grazed her cheekbone. "It has to show the world just what a lying, conniving little hypocrite you are. It has to eliminate any shred of credibility, so that no one will listen to you when you try to put that media glare on someone else." His vile fingers threaded through her matted hair. "We'll be sure to keep the spotlight firmly on you. Isn't that what you want, my ambitious one?"

Her eyelids fluttered and she worked to control them, to keep them still and closed. He touched one of her eyelashes. "Are you waking up, Jessie?"

She took a long, slow breath, as though to prove she was completely and utterly asleep.

"By the way," he added, "I have to thank you for making my life so much easier. What a stroke of genius to have your sister take your place. No one ever missed you. And best of all, it looked like you fooled me, too. So how could I be involved? You've added to an alibi I had already set up." He chuckled as though pleased with himself. "After we make our little movie, I'll let you wake up. And you can remember everything you want. But it won't matter, Jessie."

He touched her lower lip, and Jessica had to keep from opening her mouth and biting him.

"Because by then your climb to the top will be all over. I'll be sure that it ends in a dramatic, headline-grabbing fashion. I know how much you like that."

Nausea rocked her as his wet lips met her cheek. "You sleep now, Jessie. I'm going downstairs to get our little studio set ready. In a few hours, you'll be awake enough to cooperate." He sighed heavily. "Although I wish I didn't have to operate the camera. It's so distasteful."

She sensed him walking away, her heart pounding with every step he took. *Leave, leave, leave so I can breathe again.*

She searched her memory banks. How long had she

known this? Had she told her sister? Did anyone on this earth realize how evil this man was? And Lord, did anyone know she was trapped in a deserted beach house with a madman and an unstable woman?

As she heard the door unlatch, she dared to peek through the slits of her lids. But just then he turned and her gaze met his smoky blue one.

He'd caught her.

He closed the door behind him and dipped his chin. "You're awake, Jessie."

Instinct took over and she hurled the mug across the room, squeezing her eyes shut as he ducked and ceramic shattered against the door.

"You lied, Jessie." He seared her with a look of ruthless determination and accusation as he approached the bed again. "Lying is a sin."

Fear went to her very bone marrow, because she remembered oh so clearly that the one thing Kimball Parrish wouldn't tolerate was a sin.

CHAPTER
Fifteen

A pounding, relentless rain drenched Alex as he tried to bribe the ferryboat captain with water-logged twenties, but no amount of money would get the old man to fire up that pontoon and head into this weather.

"You could rent a motorboat," the captain said. "Try over at Seedy's. They might let you take something out in this." He glanced pointedly to the bills wilting in Alex's hand. "For a price."

Alex looked across the harbor to their destination again. God, they were so close, he could *swim* the two damn miles between Key West and the exclusive little island called Sunset Key.

Turning back to the overhang where he'd left Jazz, a hot rush nearly made him stumble when he saw she'd disappeared. Damn that woman—wouldn't she *ever* stay where she was put?

"Alex!" Her voice was barely louder than the rain that thumped around him. He spun, looking in the direction where it had come from.

She stood in the middle of the hotel and dock parking lot, waving to him. He'd have to teach her something about being inconspicuous if they were ever going to have a future together.

The thought made him choke.

"Alex! Come here!"

He jogged toward her, preparing a lecture about the life-saving importance of keeping a low profile. But then he stopped and stared. She'd adopted that hands-on-hips stance, accompanied by as triumphant a look as a soaking-wet woman with hair plastered to her head could manage. He tore his gaze from the glorious things the downpour had done for her T-shirt and stared at the car next to her.

"A Plymouth Reliant," she said, wiping the rain from her eyes. "Isn't this the car you saw Denise get out of?"

He nodded.

"What time does the launch boat leave?"

"They're docked until the weather clears."

"Then let's rent a boat."

He pointed to Seedy's sign. "Over there." Putting his arm around her, they jogged through the rain.

Fifty minutes and sixty extra dollars later, Alex had them rumbling through the rain in a shaky nineteen-foot Boston Whaler, sucking in a mix of exhaust fumes and salt water. The canopy over the center console offered little protection and they huddled together, water sluicing down the plastic ponchos Jazz had snagged from the boat rental office.

She gripped the metal railing, focused on their destination, and a wave of affection rolled through Alex with the same power as the white water that surrounded the little motorboat.

He blinked some rainwater away. Once again, he was running straight into harm's way with the one person he should be most concerned about protecting.

Yet this was the right thing to do. If Yoder wanted inside character information on Kimball Parrish, Alex had a feeling he was about to get it. And that should be enough to earn him the assignment in Cuba, and the chance to bring fifteen more Romeros to this country.

The fact that it made Jazz happy was a side benefit. Wasn't it? Or would he be on this boat in the pouring rain even if Lucy hadn't told him what was at stake?

She suddenly grabbed his arm, squinting in the wind to look at him. "Kimball knew."

"What?"

"He knew I wasn't Jessica," she said, her silvery blue eyes looking troubled. "He made all those vague comments about changes and change being good. He wasn't talking about Jessica's job. He knew I was posing as her from the moment he laid eyes on me in the newsroom."

"There's only one way he could know that for sure," Alex said, reducing their speed as they neared the dock. "And that's if he knew exactly where Jessica was." At her horrified look, he added, "Is."

"But he hired a bodyguard to protect her," she replied. "Why?"

They looked at each other and he knew by the look on her face that they'd reached the same conclusion at the same time.

"To create the perfect alibi and cover." He steered the boat toward the dock, the whole scheme crystallizing in his mind. "If he wants to do something to stop Jessica from exposing his stream of pornography revenue, what better way to cover himself than by footing the bill for her personal protection?"

"And then I showed up and made it even easier."

"Yeah," he agreed, "but Jessica was already missing when you arrived. In fact . . ." He could still hear Lucy's words when he'd first been given the assignment. "He asked that I wait a day or two so that he'd have time to tell Jessica about his plans to provide protection."

"Then he never told her," Jazz said, the worry creasing her brow. "But what would he do to her, Alex? Why not just fire her for some bogus reason?"

"Because she could take the story to another network," he said, cutting the engine as they reached a dock slip.

The rain had slowed to a fine mist and they tied up in silence. As Alex climbed onto the dock and held his hand to help her, Jazz froze and looked at him. "I know exactly what he could do. He could ruin her career." He pulled her onto the wooden planks. "A film like . . . the one we saw would ruin her career."

"But she could weather that storm. You have enough evidence on your computer to prove it was her face edited onto someone else's body." He draped an arm around her and started toward the cluster of buildings on the island.

Her steps slowed. "He's the stalker, Alex. He wrote the letters, setting it up so he could provide protection, but he's going to release that film and then . . . make it look like she committed suicide before anyone had the chance to prove they are fakes."

Reaching under her poncho, Alex searched out her hand and threaded his fingers through hers with a nice, tight grip. She wasn't leaving his sight or his side again. "Let's see if we can rent a golf cart"

But Jazz's attention was straight ahead, toward a tiny market that bore the name "Island Outpost" on a worn wooden sign. "Look who it is."

A blond woman huddled under the partial over-hang at a pay phone, digging through a handbag for change. She dropped a quarter into the phone and dialed frantically.

As Jazz's cell phone beeped from her purse, the woman spun around toward the noise, then gasped.

"Denise," Jazz said, walking toward her. "Do you know where my sister is?"

All color washed away from the woman's face as she dropped the phone with a clunk. "He's going to kill her," she sobbed. "He's going to kill her for sure."

A weaker man would take advantage of a naked, uncon-scious woman.

But Kimball Parrish was no rapist. He was no sexual deviant. And he was anything but weak.

He hadn't amassed nearly a billion dollars and an international broadcasting empire by giving in to temp-tations of the flesh. His focus had always been on his objectives, and his objectives had always been lofty.

Not unlike Jessica Adams, he thought with a wry

smile as he looked at her. They really had so much in common. It was a damn shame he felt no attraction for her because they would have made a formidable couple. But her inch-deep cleavage and fake red hair had never appealed to him; he preferred more reserved and understated women. Flat-chested, tight-lipped women like his dearly departed wife, who turned the lights out and knew better than to gasp or moan when she did her duty.

Anything else was whorelike.

Anything else was pornographic.

Jessie let out a shuddering sigh and a low groan. He pushed himself off the foot of the bed and opened the blinds to see the rain weighing down the palm trees and turning the snowy sand a brownish yellow.

He hated that he had to stab her with so much GHB, but he'd done enough research to know the gammahydroxybutyrate wouldn't kill her. The permanent brain damage it could cause wouldn't matter, because she'd be dead in another way. As soon as the video shredded her career, no one would question her suicide.

However, now he had to be extremely creative. He'd have to wait until she began to wake up, then somehow get her alert enough to participate in——his stomach rolled——a sex act with that whore he'd just sent for props in Key West. He'd tried to buy them himself, but the very act had nearly brought him to tears.

If only she'd taken his first warning. Yes, it was amateur and clumsy, but a smart girl like Jessie should have picked up the message. All of this could have been avoided if she'd given up on her exposé.

Miles Yoder would love nothing more than crushing him, ridding their incestuous board of a newcomer and a Christian. If she had succeeded, Jessica would get her promotion to Metro-Net and he would be scorned by the media. They'd never give him a chance to explain that the only reason he'd allowed Satan's filth to be distributed through his empire was to stop it. Once he controlled it, he could stop it.

And that meant letting the business flourish for a few years. He fully intended to donate the millions he'd made to the church. If he had any doubts that this was God's will, they disappeared when her twin sister showed up to provide him with the time and means he needed.

Howard Carpenter believed in the cause—that's why he helped him. At first, he thought the fat man just believed in money, but when Howard learned the truth about what Jessica was after, he'd proven himself to be a real man of God. He'd immediately informed Kimball, then helped him by feeding misinformation to Denise, who passed it on to Jessica. That dragged things out long enough for him to write the letters and cover himself by arranging for a bodyguard.

But Howard was a little too aggressive, which was why Kimball hadn't told him about the twin switch after he'd brought Jessica down here. The man's clumsy attempts to stop Jessica—running her off the road and putting a bomb in her car—were pitiful. Kimball was much more subtle than that.

Like slipping into her apartment—God had smiled down on him by putting the security guard who recognized him as a regular visitor on duty that night, after he left Jazz in the restaurant. He'd left the cell phone so that it could never be used and traced to Key West, and made it appear that Jessica had been there. More importantly, he made sure the wineglasses were thoroughly cleared of any traces of the drug he'd given Jessica the night he'd come over for dinner. The dishwasher, the phone, picking up some "wardrobe"—all graceful and brilliant cover-ups.

Then flying up to Crandon Park in the middle of the night to scare the life out of her, proving that he still cared and thought she was Jessica. More of God's handiwork to help him on his mission.

He reached down and picked up the dress Jessica had discarded. Smoothing the expensive fabric, he gazed at her. Was this why she was so ambitious? To buy overpriced clothes and *things*?

She didn't know what was important. Shaking the dress, he glanced around for a closet, then walked to the bathroom in the hall to hang the garment on the door. She didn't even take care of her expensive *things*.

Or herself.

That's why no one would question it if she took an overdose of GHB to kill her pain—permanently. And God would understand. Satan must be stopped, and Kimball Parrish was God's instrument for making that happen.

Lucy sauntered through the lobby of the Biltmore, well aware of the heads that turned as she walked by. A six-foot woman with a snow-white streak in yard-long black hair usually snapped a few necks. Add in her penchant for eye-catching colors, like today's royal purple, and the fact that she was flanked by two jaw-dropping bodyguards who had just escorted her from a limo to the door, and it was inevitable that the staff and clientele at the Coral Gables hotel would take a good, long look.

After all those years of being undercover, it felt marvelous to stand out.

She saw Valerie and Miles before they noticed her. They sat on a bench outside the restaurant, with no space between their bodies and practically none between their heads. She could see what Valerie loved about Miles, and was happy she'd been the one to introduce the high-flying executive to her best friend. Valerie said something that made Miles laugh, and with that closely cropped beard he'd grown a few years ago and his exotic black eyes, he looked a little piratelike and dashing. They made a gorgeous couple.

Miles reached over and grazed Val's cheek with his knuckle as they gazed at each other like a couple of honeymooners.

"Break it up, lovebirds."

Miles shot to his feet at the sight of Lucy, reaching out for an embrace. Then she turned to Valerie and hugged her twice as long. "You look beautiful, Val," she whispered, pulling back to lovingly pat her friend's porcelain cheek. "Happiness suits you."

This was the first time in a few months that she'd seen Valerie. Miles kept her busy with entertaining friends and worldwide travel, and Lucy could see Val had blossomed in the domestic tranquility, so unlike the life on the edge she'd led for many years as a covert CIA agent.

Lucy had tried hard to get Valerie Brooks to join the Bullet Catchers; her expertise in electronics and communications was astounding. But then Lucy'd made the mistake of having a dinner party and inviting two people who were destined to be together, losing Valerie forever.

Lucy turned to include Dan and Max in the conversation. After introducing everyone, she said, "These two gentlemen have been trying to find you, Miles. When I discovered that, and why, I decided we should sit down and discuss this in person."

"You discuss," Valerie said with a wave. "I'm headed to the boutiques on Miracle Mile."

Lucy rolled her eyes. "What self-respecting former spy chooses shopping over threat assessment?"

Valerie laughed. "A rich one."

Miles directed them to a private table in the restaurant. "It's secure," he assured them.

"We have run into a serious snag in the Kimball Parrish assignment," she said, "and we need your help."

Miles barely masked his horror as Lucy explained the situation to him. "So my staff, acting on behalf of the client, were trying to track you down for information. It appears Jessica is not safe. Not at all."

"I suspected Parrish was a bastard," Miles said softly. "But this exceeds my expectations. What do you need?"

"We need to fly into Key West. Are you capable of changing the weather?" she asked with a smile.

"No. But I'm on the board of Yellowstone, and I control the release of helicopters from the Metro-Net television station here. Get to WMFL in the next hour and you will have a helicopter and pilot waiting for you."

"No need for a pilot. Max can fly a helicopter." Lucy smiled like a satisfied cat and looked from Max to Dan, who already had his cell phone out to call Alex. "I told you he's one of the good guys."

Dan nodded, phone to ear, then he looked at it. "No signal in the rain."

"Go in anyway," Lucy instructed. "Alex will wait for you."

Max raised a dubious eyebrow.

"He will," Lucy assured him. *He'd better.*

CHAPTER
Sixteen

"He thinks I'm in Key West buying a dildo." Denise Rutledge spoke with such flatness that Alex wondered what had happened in this woman's life to steal all her joy, all her dignity. She barely resembled the sex kitten he'd seen perform for the camera; she looked old, tired, and scared.

And wet, even though he'd given her his plastic poncho to wear. None of the shopkeepers or the lone hotel concierge on the tiny island wanted three soaking wet tourists in their places of business, so they'd ended up returning to the dock and sharing the little boat canopy while Denise told her story.

"How were you supposed to get over to Key West?" Jazz asked.

Denise wiped rainwater out of her eyes. "It looked like the weather was going to let up, so I could get on the launch. It leaves every ten minutes when it's clear."

Jazz took both of Denise's hands in hers. "Are you sure

she's okay? Are you *sure?*" It was at least the fourth time she'd asked.

Denise nodded quickly. "For now. He put her back to sleep, but he's not going to hurt her. Not until he gets what he wants on tape. Then . . . I don't know. He didn't like it that she tried to take him out with a coffee mug."

Jazz looked at Alex, her eyes the color of unstoppable determination. "We have to get her, Alex."

He nodded. It had taken ten minutes to convince her not to go crashing through Parrish's front door without a plan or strategy. "But we don't want to go in blind, or give him any indication we're coming in. He'll kill her. We're getting backup."

"When will they be here?"

"All the flights have been stopped due to weather. Lucy's plane is grounded in Miami." He looked at the steely sky and blew out a sharp breath at the sight of a private helicopter hovering over Key West. Not *all* the flights had been stopped. "I don't know."

"I still think we could surprise him," Jazz insisted. "Or maybe break into the room where Jessica is sleeping."

"He could be in there," Denise said. "He goes in there to look at her a lot."

"Jesus," Jazz muttered. "The guy's sick."

Alex agreed. "Basically, we're in a hostage situation. As soon as Dan and Max get here, we'll do a perimeter and structure check, figure out how to distract him, and rescue her."

"What could be more distracting than me showing up at his front door?" Jazz insisted. "I'll knock on the door and you go to a back entrance—"

"There's only one door in that house," Denise interjected.

"Then you can climb into a window," she continued, undaunted. "You get her and . . . and . . ."

"And what?" He scowled at her. "Take her away while he fills you with bullet holes? Are you out of your mind?"

"He's going to miss me soon," Denise interjected. "And she's going to wake up in an hour or so. If he thinks something's going on . . ." She gave Jazz a dire look. "I had no idea the man was so crazy. All I wanted to do was help your sister. Then he found out and threatened me." Her voice cracked. "And my son."

"How did a tag from my sister's dress get in your house?"

Denise frowned at her. "That was her dress? Howie brought it over when he came to tell me to get down here. He told me it was wardrobe for this shoot. When I got here, Mr. Parrish said it was for Jessica to wear." Tears welled up in her eyes. "I really didn't know who to trust. I just want to do whatever I have to do to get my son. I don't care who I have to sleep with."

She obviously didn't care who had to die, either. Alex turned away to study the clouds. *Clear, damn it.*

"What will she feel like when she wakes up?" Jazz asked Denise. "Is she alert?"

"She doesn't know what's going on for about a half hour or so. She doesn't have any memory of how she went to sleep, and she won't remember what she did during that first hour or so. At least, that's the way she's been."

"Does she know who she is?" Alex asked, running different rescue scenarios through his head. "Will she know why she's there?"

"Not at first," Denise told them. "He's giving her liquid roofie or maybe GHB."

Alex felt Jazz tense next to him.

"So she's loose as a goose at first," Denise continued. "She'd basically do anything you tell her, and he told me he just wants to shoot one scene. With her at a desk, like an anchor, you know. Then . . . with me."

"With you?" Jazz asked. "Having sex?"

"And that dildo I don't have."

"I could do that," Jazz said.

"*What?*" Alex jerked back and stared at her. "What are you talking about?"

She ignored him, her focus on Denise. "If you could distract him long enough for us to get to the room where Jessica is, we could switch her out."

Alex felt his jaw drop. "No. Forget it, Jazz. It's not happening."

"Would you stop?" Her eyes flashed at him. "This is my sister's life we're talking about, and I am not hanging around while you wait for your macho buddies to show up and be heroes! If he thinks I'm Jessica, on drugs and at his mercy, he's totally disarmed. I could be the one putting bullets through him. And you," she punctuated the word with a finger to his chest, "could be the one whisking my sister to a hospital so they can pump that poison out of her body."

"You're soaking wet," he told her, his mind whirring for arguments to stop her from this train wreck of an idea. "He'll know you're not her immediately. You're putting your life in danger. You don't know what you're getting into." He'd die if anything happened to her. "You can't be armed if you're *naked.*"

She turned to Denise. "What if you told him Jessica needed to shower to wake up a little bit? Could I be hiding in the bathroom, you bring her in, put my clothes on her and get her out to Alex? Then if I show up wet, it's plausible. Is there even a chance we could pull that off?"

"No." Alex squeezed her shoulder. "There is no chance."

She pulled out from his grip and scorched him with a warning look. "Don't do this, Alex. Don't let your personal feelings get in the way."

Too late for that. "How are you going to get into that house without being seen by him?"

"Actually," Denise said slowly, "the house is built over stilts with an apartment at the bottom. If he was in the first floor apartment, where he plans to shoot this movie, you could probably sneak up to the balcony. She's in the room next to the one with a balcony. There's a bathroom in the hall."

Alex wanted to slap the woman. Why was she *plotting* with Jazz? "You could get killed, too," he told Denise.

She bit her lip and held his gaze. "I believe Jessica Adams is good for her word. She's promised to get me custody of my son."

Jazz took her hand again. "No matter what happens, Denise, you'll get your son. I promise. I *promise.*"

Denise nodded in confirmation, and Jazz beamed triumphantly.

Alex couldn't fight two women who were willing to die for their family; that trait was too ingrained in his blood.

"All right, ladies." He looked from one to the other. "Let's do it."

Before Denise turned the switch to shut off the little golf cart, the door to the first floor apartment was flung open. Kimball Parrish looked pissed off enough to shoot someone. She hoped to hell it wasn't her.

"Did you get it?" he asked.

Butterflies took off in her stomach. She was a sucky liar. She should have told them that, but then they might have counted her out. And this was her only chance of getting Grady back.

Climbing out of the cart to avoid looking right in his eyes, she said, "I can't get to Key West, Mr. Parrish. None of the ferries are running in the rain. Honestly," she added at the ugly look he gave her.

"Did you try the gift shop?"

She resisted the urge to laugh, a nervous habit she had when she was in trouble. "They had no sex toys. Sir."

He glanced over his shoulder at the sound of a loud motor on the water behind the house, then he pointed upstairs. "Go wake her up and get her dressed. I want to get this over with."

With Jazz's phone pressed against Denise's belly, all she had to do was go upstairs and press one number to call Alex. He and Jazz were waiting behind the reeds on the beach.

She prayed to God this jerk didn't want to come up

and watch. "I'll take care of everything, Mr. Parrish. Give me a few minutes to get her dressed and in makeup."

"You don't need makeup."

But she did need time. "I'll just make sure she looks good."

"She doesn't have to look good," he barked.

"But she has to look . . . real." Her voice cracked. "And so do I. Or nobody will think this is a real movie."

He frowned, then waved her off. "Hurry up."

Denise almost tripped up the wooden stairs, letting herself in with shaking hands. Wiping her palms on her jeans, she took a deep breath and ran through the kitchen toward the bedroom.

"Jessica!" she called in a loud whisper. "Are you awake yet?"

Her sneakers slid on the tile floor as she broke her run at the door to the bedroom, and she stopped her forward motion by seizing the doorknob. She twisted and flung open the door, her other hand digging for the phone. They didn't have much—

Oh, *fuck.*

"She's gone." Alex spoke into his phone, but looked at Jazz.

Gone? "What do you mean, she's gone?"

She peered through the stalks of beach grass and steady downpour to see the house. All of the windows were closed. She could see the balcony that they'd planned to climb, but she couldn't quite make out the window to the right of it.

Alex spoke into the phone. "Are you sure he's downstairs?"

Jazz ventured closer to the house to get a better look at that window, but Alex grabbed her poncho and pulled her back, warning her with a look.

"Calm down," he said into the phone. "I can't understand you." He covered the phone, and whispered harshly. "She's totally unglued. This isn't going to work."

"Tell her I'll be right there."

"Jazz, Jessica's gone. We can find her on the ground. There's no reason to go in that house." He spoke to Denise. "Keep looking in the other rooms, see if you can find how she might have gotten out. Just press one again to call back."

Jazz scanned the beach, the clumps of palms and oleanders around the yard, everything as green and thick and wet as a jungle, the house almost impossibly protected from the beach and the road. If Jessica got out, and she was truly drugged on GHB or rohypnol, then she could be anywhere. Lost, wondering, hurt. Or she could be in the downstairs rooms of the house, tied up, and being made to do unspeakable things.

"Alex," she took his arm. "I'm going to check out the house."

His black stare of disbelief damn near singed her. "Why?"

"Because she could be in there."

He took a deep breath, and nodded. "Okay, let's go."

"No." She dug her heels deeper in the sand and squared her shoulders. "You look for her out here. It could be just as dangerous outside, even if he doesn't know she's gone. Denise said she's naked, on drugs." Jazz swallowed hard and willed him not to fight her. "She could wander into the ocean, the road. Anywhere."

"You're not going in there alone, Jazz."

She squeezed his arm tighter. "Please, Alex. We have to split up to do this right."

He searched her face, frowning, struggling with whatever he was thinking. Of course, his instinct was to protect her. But his expression was more conflicted than that.

"Alex . . ." She shook her head, then pulled the poncho over her head, shoving it at him as she welcomed the air and rain on her body. "Here. Jessica might need this."

She took a step backward and pointed at him. "If my sister's out here, you find her. If she's in there, we'll go through with the plan. I'll deal with Parrish."

She started into the reeds, but she hadn't made it three steps before he grabbed her elbow and yanked her around. His eyes burned black and his mouth came down on hers so hard their teeth smacked. Hot and angry and fast, he kissed all the air out of her, leaving the taste of salty rainwater on her lips.

"And then," he ground out, "you'll deal with me."

Alex's chest tightened to a painful knot as he watched her hustle through the bushes, her camos performing the job they were designed to do. She never turned back. Never gave him a wistful, tender good-bye. Never bothered to look the least bit scared or helpless or unsure of herself.

Why the hell did he love that about her? It was totally, utterly, completely counter to what he wanted from a woman.

He leaned forward to see her shimmy up the wooden railing to the balcony.

Make that what he *thought* he wanted in a woman.

He crouched in the tall grass, gripping the discarded poncho as he sneaked toward the house in the opposite direction. In a matter of seconds he had a clear shot of the downstairs apartment, the windows darkened, the door shut.

That prick Parrish was in there. Alex could take him down with one bullet. One kick to the door, one ambush, one dead media mogul. He wasn't going to miss this opportunity to end it all.

Just as he took a step to the door, something white flashed in his peripheral vision. Turning, he squinted through the rain and trees. He heard a rustling, deep in a thicket of palmetto plants.

Moving silently, he approached, gun drawn.

And then he saw her. Huddled near the road, hiding behind a clump of pygmy palms, a soaking wet sheet wrapped around her. Despite the heat, she shivered.

Taking it slow, he approached her. *Don't run, Jessica. Don't run from me.*

"Jessica," he said her name softly, tenderly.

She gasped as she looked up, a forlorn, bedraggled woman with dark shadows under her eyes and matted hair. She looked like a caged animal. Her eyes widened in fear and her attention dropped to the gun. Standing, she attempted to run, but the sheet caught on a palmetto branch and she stumbled, her gaze darting from the bush to him as she tugged at her meager cover-up.

He stashed the gun in his pants and held up two hands. "I'm not going to hurt you."

Terror flashed in her gray eyes. Eyes that were identical to Jazz's . . . except he'd never seen this level of fear in them. "I'm here to help you."

Still yanking at the caught sheet, she looked from the plants to him. "Who . . . who are you?"

"My name is Alex. I'm here with your sister, Jazz."

Her entire face changed, then hardened again. "Who?"

"Your sister. Your identical twin sister." He nodded, taking a few steps farther. "Don't be scared. Jazz came to find you. To help you."

Her jaw dropped a little and her eyes filled with tears. "Where am I?"

"In the Keys, on a private island. Kimball Parrish brought you here." He held the poncho toward her. "Put this on and I'll get you out of here."

With a shaky hand, she reached out for it. She pulled it to her and her eyes flashed again. "Jazz?"

He nodded slowly. "Jazz is here to help you."

Her lip curled in a half smile so like the one he'd been falling in love with that his heart wrenched a little, but then her complexion paled and she turned, suddenly gagging and bending over. She dropped the poncho and threw up all over it.

He lunged toward her to help, but she jerked away. Under the wet sheet, she was trembling, her bones visible, her skin a yellowing blue. Had Parrish been starving her for a week?

"You need to get to a hospital," he said. *Fast.*

Wiping her mouth and shuddering, she asked, "Who are you again?"

"Believe it or not," he said, "I'm your bodyguard." And his first responsibility was to get her to safety. Then he'd be back for Parrish.

Jazz had scoured the upstairs rooms, the kitchen, living area, bathroom, and ended up back in the little bedroom where Denise said Jessica had been sleeping. Her breathing shallow, she swiped a clump of wet hair off her forehead, her gaze darting around the room. The sour, stale smell of human sweat and vomit turned her stomach.

What had that bastard done to her sister?

Pivoting, she jogged into the hall bathroom, determined to find a clue to where Jessica might have gone. She closed the door and saw the khaki dress hanging off a hook in the back.

Her breath seized up in her throat.

A sudden bang shook the house, and Jazz instinctively locked the bathroom door and reached for the Glock. Was that a gunshot or a door slamming? She waited a moment, then footsteps hammered down the hall toward her.

"Where is she?" a male voice demanded.

Jazz's first thought was relief. If Parrish didn't know where Jessica was, then he hadn't just shot her. But would Denise tell him that Jessica had escaped? Would that send him outside looking for her?

"Where is she?" he asked again. He sounded desperate, not at all like the confident man she'd met.

"She needed to take a shower," Denise answered in a shaky voice.

Okay. Back to Plan A. She'd be Jessica and that would buy Alex enough time to find her sister and get her out of here. Otherwise, Parrish would tear outside the minute he found out Jessica had escaped.

She dropped her head against the door, her face buried in her sister's dress, flipping through her options.

Her original plan was the smartest. If he believed she was Jessica, she could totally disarm him, get him into the studio to admit what he'd done—on camera, so he couldn't pay his way out of a legal jam—and then, maybe as she undressed for her little porn show, she could pull the gun on him and hold him until Alex got back.

Denise whimpered something, a question so soft that Jazz couldn't understand it. Then she heard a shuffle of steps and a woman's gasp. Something hard banged on the bathroom door.

"I'll be right out," she called, purposely light and weak.

She'd already started kicking off her boots, and stripping her pants and top, and unfastening the ankle holster Alex had given her.

"Hurry up," he ordered.

Again she heard a muffled cry from Denise. She slid the coat dress over her arms, buttoning it with one hand and patting it down in search of a hiding place for the Glock. There were no pockets on the form-fitting dress. The waist pinched in a bit, but if she stuck the gun in there, it could slip out. *Damn* it.

Her bra? It would show.

He slammed on the door again.

Denise whimpered. Jazz pulled up the skirt and stuck the gun in her underpants after a final check on the safety. She adjusted the dress over the slight bump on her stomach just as the door shuddered from a kick, then wood splintered everywhere as the door smashed open. She gasped and jerked back, then blinked into the face of her enemy.

Only it wasn't Kimball Parrish. A complete stranger stared at her, with sinister dark eyes, a black beard, and a Beretta 92 aimed directly at her heart.

CHAPTER
Seventeen

"We . . . land . . . Sunset Key."

Scooting Jessica's limp body higher in his arms and cradling the cell phone between his ear and shoulder, Alex shouted into the wet speaker. "Did not copy, Gallagher."

"We cannot . . . Sunset Key . . . you . . . to Key West."

They couldn't land on the little island. Son of a bitch. He'd have to take Jessica by boat to Key West, and let them get her there. In this downpour, it would be another ten minutes until he reached the dock, then at least fifteen to get across the water.

A lot could happen in twenty-five minutes. Jazz could be dead.

Dan's voice faded in and out as he barked unintelligible instructions. With his shoulder, Alex pressed the phone tighter to his ear, but between the intermittent connection, the noise of the helicopter rotors, and the relentless rain around him, it was damn near impossible to hear a word.

"Did not copy, Gallagher. Repeat."

One short beep, then nothing. He'd lost the line.

Jessica moaned, her head lolling on her neck, her eyes half closed. He'd thrown the poncho over her, but rain poured down her face and neck.

She'd drifted into unconsciousness for a moment, and still wasn't coming out of a drug-induced fog. The bastard Parrish probably didn't care if he killed her. The right dosage could fry her brain, if not stop her heart. She had to be pumped, and fast.

Otherwise he would have stashed her somewhere safe and gone back for Jazz.

He shut the phone and stuck it between his teeth as he pressed on.

"Stay with me, Jessica," he growled around the phone. It didn't matter; she didn't know what he was saying anyway. "Do it for Jazz."

Blinking through the rain, he searched for any sign of life. There were no cars allowed on this island, and any golf carts were safely stored away.

He even considered knocking on a door, if he could get past any of the security gates, but the time it would take to explain the situation could cost Jessica her life, or at least a good portion of her brain.

Dan was right about this jungle of an island. It was all foliage and private villas; there wasn't any open area to safely land a helicopter, except the beach. And Parrish would see that. Overhead, the sky was soupy, the clouds just low enough to make any maneuver tricky.

As he reached the dock, Jessica shuddered and groaned in agony. The phone vibrated between his teeth.

Yanking it out of his mouth, he managed to open it and tuck it between his air and shoulder. "Gallagher! What are you flying?"

"A Bell two-oh-six on loan . . . TV station . . ."

The connection faded as Alex sprinted across the sodden wood planks, his cargo growing limper and heavier as an idea formed. The phone slipped between Alex's shoulder and ear, and Jessica's body threatened to do the same. "She needs medical attention. Fast."

"This is a media chopper, Romero—not a medevac helo."

"We don't have time to get her to Key West," Alex explained. "Get out here and pick her up before she dies in my arms."

"Where are you?"

"On the dock at Sunset Key."

He waited a beat while Dan and Max talked. He knew what they were discussing. A TV news helicopter wouldn't even have a sling on it, but if Roper could hover, Alex could pass Jessica over to Dan and they could fly her off.

A handoff like that was routine . . . in perfect weather.

"I can get to open water in five minutes," Alex shouted. That would make the maneuver a bitch for him, but much easier for Max.

"All Max has to do is hover over a Boston Whaler with no tower. You grab her from me. Simple and easy."

All he heard was static. Then he heard Dan's voice. "We're on the way. Get the principal out to open sea . . . pick her up . . . die trying."

"Roger that." Except no one was going to die, damn

it—not on his watch. Alex squinted into the rain at the cruise ships in the channel. He gave Dan an estimated pickup location a half mile off one of the ships' port side, and signed off.

Climbing into the boat, he tucked Jessica on the bow bench, then untied the dock lines.

As he twisted the key and goosed the throttle, the engine gasped and he gritted his teeth. *Come on.* One lousy Mercury outboard motor. If it died now, they were screwed.

But the Merc sputtered to life and Alex slammed the boat into reverse. The action and rain woke Jessica up, and she huddled deeper into the poncho, her teeth chattering.

As soon as he cleared the dock, Alex swung the boat starboard. "Hang on!" he yelled over the deafening noise. Her eyes widened as she grasped the rail. He gunned the throttle and the bow lifted out of the water, but she managed to hold on. Rainwater sluiced over his face, forcing him to wipe his eyes with one hand and steer with the other. Jessica closed her eyes and clung to the railing, her head slumping to her shoulders.

Sorry, honey. It's going to get worse before it gets better.

The little Whaler tossed and dipped in the white-caps, fighting across the normally calm waterway. All Alex could do was steer and concentrate. He could not, he would not, think about what might be happening to Jazz.

In less than ten minutes, he heard the distant whir of a Bell Jet Ranger. He cut the engine and stepped away from the center console to signal to Max. The clouds were thick and the wind strong enough to lean the Whaler starboard. Not perfect conditions, but Max could do this.

Max *had* to do this.

As the chopper dipped below the cloud line, he knelt next to Jessica, who still drifted in and out of consciousness.

"Jessica?"

Her eyelids fluttered and she tried to lift her head. He had to prepare her for what was about to happen.

"You ever been on a helicopter?" Stupid question; she was a reporter. "'Cause one's coming to get you right now."

"Don't leave me. . . ."

"I have to get Jazz."

"Jazz . . ." Her eyes narrowed at him. "Jazz is here?"

"She found you, Jessica." He squeezed her shoulders through the slippery poncho. "She wouldn't give up until she did."

A hint of a smile lifted her lips.

The wind whipped up as the chopper closed in, the engine noise and rotors making it impossible to talk. Alex looked over his shoulder, lifted her from the seat, and turned her around to face the helicopter. "Here's your ride, honey."

A blast of propeller wash pitched the boat, and they stumbled. Water spray nearly blinded him, but he managed to hold on and get her positioned for a handoff.

Max worked the nose of the chopper into the wind, bringing the passenger side door to the port side. The door slid open and Dan locked himself into position to reach for her, half hanging out over one of the skids.

Alex hoisted her forward. "Lift your arms, Jessica. Let him take you."

"It's all right, sweetheart," Dan called. "Nothing to be afraid of."

But Jessica looked at Alex. "Don't let anything happen to her," she demanded in a raspy whisper. "I love her."

He squeezed her shoulders. *So do I.* "She'll be fine. I promise."

Dan's strong grip closed around Jessica's outstretched forearms. The Whaler rose with a wave, and Dan pulled her up out of the boat to safety.

Alex didn't even wait for the chopper door to close before he threw the throttle forward and headed back to Sunset Key.

All the color drained from Jessica's face as she stared at the gun, and then met his eyes. Her silver-blue gaze went utterly dead, almost as though she didn't recognize him. But then, after what Parrish had put her through, maybe she didn't. If she realized she'd be dead in a matter of minutes, she didn't let panic show on her face.

Of course not. She was a professional. As poised facing a gun as she was facing a camera. He jerked his head toward the hallway. "We're going downstairs."

She didn't move. "Why are you doing this?"

"And I was just thinking how smart you are, Jessica." He shook his head and tsked. "Don't go stupid on me now. After all those clandestine interviews we had, I happen to know you are a very bright lady."

She wet her lips and took a deep breath. "Miles." She said his name slowly, then touched her temple. "I'm sorry, my memory is so blurred from those drugs he gave me."

Which would show up nicely on her autopsy. "Go downstairs, Jessica." He glanced at the other woman, cowering in the corner. "Kimball Parrish is waiting for you." In a pool of his own blood.

He grabbed the other woman's sweatshirt sleeve and shoved her ahead of Jessica. "Go," he said.

Then he put his hand on Jessica's arm and tugged her out of the bathroom, jamming the barrel of the gun in her lower back as he walked next to her. He didn't have much time before Lucy's men showed up, or Romero and Jessica's sister got tired waiting for them. But he had enough time to stage a horrific scene of bloodshed. Enough time to drop a media bombshell that had all the ratings-worthy buzzwords: celebrity, murder-suicide, jealousy, pornography, sex, and violence.

The advertising money his network would make when the ratings soared was really only a side benefit.

He stole another look at Jessica as they went down the stairs to the temporary studio Kimball had built. Except for her clenched jaw and shallow breaths, you'd never know she had a gun pointed at her kidney.

A shame, really, to lose such cool talent for his network.

But Kimball Parrish had been right about one thing: Ambition was Jessica's downfall. When she uncovered the revenue connection between Climax Distribution and Adroit, she should have kept her mouth shut—along with the file of information she'd snared from various sources. But she had a journalist's nose on that camera-perfect face, so he'd encouraged her. Exposing the seamier side of Adroit Broadcasting would rid him of Parrish.

It would have been much neater than what he'd done downstairs. That hadn't worked out quite as he'd planned, but he was flexible; thinking on his feet was a hallmark of his success.

At the bottom of the steps, Miles instructed Denise to open the door to the apartment. He heard her gasp and whimper at the sight of Parrish's body. He shoved Jessica in.

"Shut up!" he said to the woman who'd doubled over and started sobbing.

Jessica stared at the body, her face even paler. "Why did you do this?" Her voice cracked, but the fire still burned in her eyes.

"Don't ask questions." He glared at both of them. "Just shut up before you look exactly like he does."

Denise sucked in a huge, loud breath and clutched her stomach, falling to her knees. "Please don't kill me. Don't kill me. And don't kill her. She's not even—" She stopped, staring at Jessica. "She hasn't done anything wrong," she finished weakly.

"Let's do this fast," he said. "You." He pointed the gun at Jessica. "Go over there, directly across from him."

She didn't move.

He lifted the gun to her face. "Go."

"Not until you tell me why."

"Because you need to be on your mark, just like in the studio," he said.

She still didn't move. "Why did you kill him?"

Miles angled his head and looked at her. "I had to make an adjustment in our plan. A shame, because it was brilliant, really. I loved you going undercover to a studio with a hidden camera. And it might have landed you the Metro-Net job you crave, dear, and relieved Yellowstone of the headache of Kimball Parrish. But when he discovered what you were doing, he decided to get rid of you himself."

"And covered by hiring a bodyguard."

He nodded. "Very sly of him. He even came to me for a recommendation and I sent him directly to Lucy Sharpe."

Her eyes widened. "Is she in on this?"

"God, no." He laughed. "My only original goal with Lucy was to be sure I had someone near Kimball who could observe his behavior." He'd wanted a mole, and who better to recommend one than a former CIA agent? Without his wife's entrée, he could never have scaled the wall around Lucy Sharpe. Valerie was a very handy accessory for an executive to have. "But he screwed everything up with his elaborate scheme to make you a porn star and ruin your career."

She met his direct gaze. "But why kill him, Miles? Why not just expose him for what he is? That would have been enough."

"Because he really did plan to stop the flow of revenue from Climax Distribution." He grinned at her. "I *own* Climax Distribution. I like the relationship with Adroit

Broadcasting. It keeps my wife in diamonds and yachts."

"But you're a rich man. You don't need money from porn movies."

His laugh was dry, even to his own ears. "You can never be secure enough, Jessica." He couldn't have cared less if the world found out that Climax was associated with Yellowstone. Stockholders weren't stupid; they wanted to make money, and exporting cheap porn did that. When he realized Parrish's real goal was to stop it altogether, that hit him in the wallet.

He paused to listen to the rain. Good, it was slowing a bit. He could get out on the Donzi and disappear long before that helicopter showed up. The one he had on the roof of the Biltmore had been much faster, getting to the Keys long before the Bullet Catchers ever made it. And now it waited for him on top of the Key West Hilton, ready to take him back to Valerie who, if he ever needed an alibi, would vouch that he'd been in Miami all day.

"He's got to stay there because of the blood," he said, more to himself than to her. "So you have to stand over there. Go." He pointed with the gun to a desk Parrish had set up to look like a newsroom for his stupid little movie. "Go!" he barked at her.

She took two steps toward the desk. "What about Denise?"

"You're going to kill her first, because she walked in on you."

Jessica's jaw dropped. "No, I'm not."

"Fine," he shrugged. "I'll kill her." He turned the gun away and heard Jessica's gasp. "But not until she's in the right position." He paused to look around the little living area again. "This has to pass the forensic tests."

"It never will."

Her certainty pissed him off. "Yes, it will, because I've thought this through. Now, stand over there—because I have no problem killing you first and dragging you there if I have to."

"It won't work. Forensics will expose your scheme in five minutes."

A little white light of anger began flashing in his head. "Why is that, Jessica?"

"Because I'm not Jessica."

He stared at her, dumbfounded.

She gave him a tight smile and lifted her chin, pointing to a spot along her jawline. "See? No beauty mark. I'm Jazz. Jessica is long gone, Miles. And she still has the story." She crossed her arms slowly and looked at Parrish's body. "Which just got even juicier."

He frowned. Was she telling the truth? She looked identical to Jessica. Which one was she?

"If you're Jazz, then where's the bodyguard?"

"He took Jessica away."

Fury spurted through him as his mind spun through the options. If she really was Jazz, would the double murder-suicide still work? Even if he escaped, Jessica would make the connection to him.

So this little bitch thought she held the trump card. But after all the heart-to-heart discussions he'd had with her sister over the past few weeks, he knew there was one thing that could stop Jessica Adams's ambition: her love for her twin sister.

Without taking aim, he turned the gun toward Denise and shot. She doubled over and slumped to the ground. Jessica—Jazz—charged at him, but he turned the Beretta back at her, recocking it as she dug into the front of her dress.

"Don't move," he warned. "Move your hand another inch and you'll be as dead as they are."

She held her arms out.

"What do you have in there . . . Jazz?" Reaching for her collar, he ripped the dress open from top to bottom, his gaze dropping to a little Glock stuck in her underpants. He laughed softly as he dragged the gun over her flat stomach. "Perfect."

He aimed the Glock at her as he stepped backward to where Denise lay. He wiped his prints from the Beretta, thanked God it wasn't registered, and placed it close to Denise's hand. "A murder-suicide. She'd had enough of this life." He snuck a glance at Parrish. "Of this hypocrite."

Jazz's eyes turned to silver slits. "Jessica will figure this out in five minutes, Miles. You'll never get away with it."

"We're going for a boat ride, Jazz." He indicated the door with his head, still pointing the gun she'd so conveniently provided. "If Jessica thinks your life depends on it, she'll kill her story fast enough."

Or else he'd kill Jazz.

Alex convinced the owner of the Island Outpost to let him borrow a golf cart, then he floored the cart down the road, getting it to the house in under five minutes.

Standing in the shadow of a thick pygmy palm, he watched and listened. All was eerily quiet, almost deserted. No sound or sight of life.

His heart flipped as he moved closer and a soft moan reached his ear. The distinctive low-pitched rumble of a high-end speedboat drowned it out, but as the boat became more distant, Alex heard the moan again. Like an injured animal . . . or *woman*.

Jazz.

Drawing his gun and holding it with both hands, he made no noise approaching the downstairs apartment. He heard the groan of agony again, and with one solid kick, he busted the door open.

He smelled blood, turning his veins to ice. Kimball Parrish lay covered in the stuff, his eyes staring straight ahead. Across the room, Denise was curled in a fetal position. In two strides, he was close enough to see she was still alive.

He kneeled next to her, his gaze darting around, and he saw a Beretta next to Denise.

Jazz hadn't shot anyone here.

He touched Denise's shoulder, and saw that a bullet had ripped into her stomach. Her eyes glazed, she faded in and out of her misery.

Where was Jazz? There wasn't a single sound but for the hum of that now distant boat motor.

He stopped and listened to it. Swearing, he ran back outside to look at the water. Would she run from him . . . or to him? Damn, she never stayed put.

He jogged up the steps for a better view of the water. He could see a Cigarette-style speedboat, with red and black racing stripes on the side, tearing across the channel, and his whole being turned to lead. She was in the boat, but she wasn't alone. And they were going too damn fast for a pleasure cruise.

Running back downstairs, he dropped next to Denise and gently turned her over. Her eyes opened, then rolled into her head as she lost consciousness.

He had Dan Gallagher on the phone in less than fifteen seconds. "Send medical assistance to Parrish's beach house. And the police. Fast."

"Roger. Wait there."

"No, I can't." But could he leave Denise? He pushed the material of Denise's shirt aside to examine her. The injury was serious, but she was holding on. "Tell them to hurry. A woman's been shot."

"Jazz?"

"No. As soon as you get Jessica to the hospital, head back to the channel in that chopper. Southwest toward the Gulf. Look for a black and red go-fast."

Alex pressed the fabric of Denise's shirt against her wound and her eyes fluttered open. "Hold on," he told her. "For your son."

She managed a nod, then he left.

His fishing boat was no match for a race boat with twin engines that could chew up the water and fly like the wind. But, maybe, just maybe, whoever had Jazz Adams was no match for her.

CHAPTER
Eighteen

The Donzi slammed over the whitecaps with such force it cracked Jazz's teeth against each other. The duct tape Miles had used to bind her wrists cut into her flesh, and her hands tingled with the lack of circulation.

Still, she was alive, which might be more than she could say for Denise. And Jessica? Oh, God, she hoped Alex had found her.

Yoder hadn't bothered to tie her down or keep her quiet. Her loudest scream would never be heard over the deafening engines, and if she stood, she'd fly out of the boat from the wind and speed. And with her hands tied, she'd drown . . . or he'd be sure the engine props sliced her to ribbons. Tucked low in the captain's chair next to him, she turned to see how far they'd gone.

She guessed that they were a mile from land, headed southwest, probably into the Gulf of Mexico. The water was murky from the storm, but it was shallow and Yoder seemed to navigate skillfully around the reefs.

Who *was* this man?

A man who clearly relished control. A man Jessica had trusted with her dreams and ambition. A man so evil, he double-crossed and murdered the man who'd planned to blackmail Jessica.

The man who had "changed" her sister's life, and who had a heart of gold.

So much for Jessica's flawless character judgment.

Her heart squeezed so hard, she nearly cried. She could die in the next few minutes. She'd never see Jessica again, or her parents, or Alex.

She blinked back the tears. This was no time to cry; she needed a *plan*. She had to disarm him—literally and figuratively. She scanned the giant bowsprit, pointed halfway to the sky as the mighty engines dragged the back end of the boat deep into the water. Behind her there were two more seats. The door to a below-deck salon was right in front of her, closed.

Could she drive this thing? Possibly. She could certainly work the radio that occasionally crackled next to him.

Without warning, he slowed their speed to almost nothing. She turned to see the tiny dot that was Sunset Key, and Key West just beyond it. Two massive cruise ships blocked the storm-darkened channel between the two islands.

In the opposite direction, there wasn't another boat from there to the horizon.

Alex would never look for her out here. The sickening finality of that thought spurred her. She had to save herself, but how?

"Where is your sister?" he demanded.

"I have no idea," she said honestly. "She escaped from the house."

He swore. Whatever his plan was, it was unraveling fast. Which didn't make her feel at all safe.

"I'll work with you," she said in a tone she hoped sounded conspiratorial. "I'll cover for you. Jessica can get the job she wants, and I'll just go along with it."

He gave her a skeptical look.

"I'd do anything for her success," she added.

For a heartbeat, she thought he fell for it. Then the sound of a distant motor made him turn and glance over his shoulder. She didn't take a second to think. Diving out of her chair, she slammed her duct-taped wrists on the gun to send it flying.

"Shit!" He tried to lunge after the Glock, but she threw her body on the hard fiberglass bottom, her breasts slamming against the gun. He stomped on her back, shoving the air out of her lungs.

Jazz squeezed her eyes at the pain, and tried to slide her hands under her. If she could just get her fingers around that pistol—

He slammed his foot into the side of her head, sending fireworks from one ear to the other. Grabbing her shoulder, he tried to pull her up, which freed her hands enough to jerk them down to where the gun poked her breastbone.

Her fingers closed around the rough finish of the grip. With a grunt, Yoder managed to flip her over and grab her hair, yanking her head backward. She had no idea where the gun was aimed and couldn't see. He'd have the gun out of her hand in a second.

With one powerful thrust, she threw her arms up and let go.

She heard the splash as the Glock hit the water.

"You stupid bitch," he growled, kicking her in the side.

She sucked in a painful breath as she curled up, tensing her legs to leap up and attack. She'd die trying to kill him. She'd die before she gave in.

He suddenly froze as the sound of the motor amplified. She couldn't see anything but the man above her and the gray sky. But she could hear that motor, and it was getting closer.

Something whizzed overhead and Yoder fell on top of her. "Son of a bitch," he cursed.

He crawled off her to the captain's chair, rising to his knees, but keeping his head low. Something hit the side of the boat with a deafening thwack.

A gunshot. Jazz inched up to her elbows and tried to turn over on her stomach to see behind them. As she did, the engines of the Donzi thundered to life. Yoder pulled himself up to the driver's seat and thrust the throttle forward. The massive bow rose out of the water like the mouth of a great white shark, throwing Jazz straight back, thumping her head against the bottom of the leather seat. She managed to grasp an armrest and heave herself up.

And then she saw Alex. Just fifty feet behind them, bouncing wildly in the curl of the Donzi's wake, his hair snapped straight back in the wind, his face dark with determination. One hand was on the throttle, the other aimed his Glock at Miles Yoder's head. Relief and euphoria replaced the terror that had gripped her.

He jerked the gun up and down, trying to tell her to get out of the line of fire. Falling to her knees, she obeyed. But how could he catch them in that little Whaler? This thing would be out of firing range in less than a minute.

Pivoting on her knees, she crawled to where Yoder stood, holding the throttle with one hand and the wheel with the other. He faced forward, but he'd turn to see how much distance he'd made any second.

Raising herself to her feet, she jumped behind him and slid her bound arms over his head in a lightning fast move, seizing his neck in a chokehold. As he jerked around, she moved with him and saw the fury on Alex's face.

No wonder he was pissed. The throttle remained at the highest speed, and she was attached to Yoder's back. She had to slow the boat down.

As Yoder spun around like a dog chasing its tail, she lifted her right leg, hooked her heel over the horizontal bar of the throttle, and pulled it toward her with every ounce of strength she had. The speed plummeted and their bodies flew forward, whacking the door to the cabin with so much force, she thought they broke it. The Whaler roared closer.

Yoder hollered and tried to duck out of her arms, but she smashed her duct-taped wrists into his nose, then sank her teeth into the cartilage of his ear. He howled and twisted again, crushing her against the windshield.

Alex pulled up next to them, his gun aimed at Yoder. "Get off him, Jazz," he screamed over the engine noise.

Before she could move, Yoder reached up and encircled her head in his arm, yanking her neck until she heard a crack. Fiery pain shot down her spine.

"Drop the gun or I'll break her neck."

Oh God, he could paralyze or kill her with a single twist of his elbow. Her heart hammered wildly as he tightened his grip. *Shoot him, Alex. Shoot him.*

Alex's face was distorted with rage and the agony of a difficult choice; her face and body were just centimeters from his target.

Take the risk, Alex.

Yoder pulled again and sparks of agony almost blinded her. She couldn't breath. Couldn't think.

Shoot him, she mouthed, and gave Alex a pleading look. Then she closed her eyes and let his image fill her mind. Would that be the last thing she ever saw?

The bullet whizzed so close, she felt the air move just as she heard the slug crack Yoder's skull. Warm blood splashed on her face. His grip relaxed. His arm dropped. He stumbled backward and fell on top of her, slamming her against the fiberglass.

In a matter of seconds, Alex was on board, releasing her from Yoder, biting away the duct tape, wiping her face with his shirt. He pushed Yoder's body to the other side of the boat and scooped Jazz into a tight embrace.

His body was trembling as much as hers, his breathing ragged, his heart throbbing. *"Querida,"* he whispered. *"Pensé que te perdí."*

"Did you get Jessica?" she asked.

He nodded, just as his lips came down on hers for a shaky, desperate kiss.

She pulled out away and looked at him. "What took so long?"

"I had to get her into a helicopter, out at sea—"

"To shoot," she clarified with a half punch on his arm. "I thought you'd never pull the trigger."

"I was aiming." He tunneled his fingers into the nape of her neck and drew her face closer. "I generally catch bullets, not fire them at . . ." He kissed her hard.

"Your principal," she spoke into the kiss.

He pulled away to look at her. "Yeah, that, too." He kissed her again and and held her tighter. *"Pensé que te perdí."*

She wiped the wet hair from his face, lingering over his cheeks and lips. "What does that mean?"

Inside his shirt pocket, his phone hummed, just as the first thumping hum of a helicopter forced both of them to look at the sky.

He pulled the phone out and flipped it open, holding her gaze with a sexy, smoky look of relief in his eyes. "You're late, Roper." Then he flipped the phone shut.

He kissed her forehead, her hair, and her eyes. "I thought I lost you."

She searched his his strong, gorgeous, achingly handsome face. A mirror of the heart and soul inside. A protective, passionate lover who made her stronger, not weaker.

Never, she whispered in her head. *You'll never lose me.*

And the realization that she loved him hit her with the force of a bullet to her heart.

The story that the two men told her began to take shape in bits and pieces in Jessica's mind. Sort of like her memory, which felt like a jigsaw puzzle with completed borders, but gaping holes in the middle.

"Do you need a little more?" Dan, the one with mint-green eyes and a kissable mouth, gently touched the IV pouring saline into her dehydrated system. "Something for the pain?"

She managed to shake her head, but it hurt like hell. "No drugs of any kind."

"Let her sleep," Max ordered, his serious tone undermined by his inability to take his eyes off her, as if he couldn't believe she was real or something.

"I don't want to sleep," she insisted, swallowing against the horrific pain in her throat where they had inserted a tube to pump her stomach. "I want to see Jazz."

"She's on her way," Dan assured her, placing a strong hand on her shoulder to tuck the loose-fitting hospital gown into place. "Do you remember what Max told you?"

Yes, blessedly. Jazz, who could do things Jessica couldn't even dream of, was alive and well and, following a debriefing with police, would be on her way here. Jessica's lips lifted in a smile of pride. And Denise, the actress who had helped her, was alive. In surgery, but still alive.

They'd also told her a little bit about Kimball, and Miles, much of it conjecture on their part, she decided. She was unable to believe that kind, intelligent Miles would actually shoot someone. Kimball Parrish? Absolutely. But Miles . . .

The door burst open and the room was suddenly full of that distinctive energy that emanated from Jazz. Jessica nearly leaped off the bed with glee, but Jazz closed the space between them in a heartbeat, engulfing Jessica in a gentle, precious embrace.

Jessica just wanted to inhale her sister, to press her cheek against the one that matched her own, and hold the strongest body and bravest heart she'd ever known.

As Jazz finally released her, Jessica's gaze dropped to the ugly scrape along the side of her sister's face. "What happened?"

Jazz shrugged. "That asshole Yoder kicked me."

Jessica coughed a little laugh at the typical Jazz response. "Are you okay?"

"Me?" She gave Jessica a cocky grin. "Please. I have my own bodyguard. Now how the hell did you get out of that house? It's killing me to figure it out."

Jessica searched the wonderfully familiar face. Funny how she could see flaws in her own, but could never find any in Jazz. "I pretended to be you."

"What? And Parrish believed you?"

Jessica shook her head, and smiled. "No. I pretended to be you in my head. A 'what would Jazz do?' sort of thing."

Jazz gave her a dubious look. "You know, those drugs, J—they can do things to your brain."

"My brain is fine." She took Jazz's hands and closed them between hers. "I thought I was going to die." Her voice cracked, and Jazz closed her eyes for a second. "And when I woke up, you were the only memory I had. You." She squeezed Jazz's hands tighter. "And you're the strongest person I know."

Jazz let out a breath of disbelief.

"Seriously, Jazz. You would never let yourself be a victim; you would have clawed and scratched and fought your way out of that mess."

"That's probably true," Jazz admitted. "But only because I never had your ability to charm my way through life."

Jessica rolled her eyes. "A lot of good that did me. So this time I did exactly what you would have done."

A smile tilted Jazz's lips. "This I gotta hear."

"I walked out the front door." She grinned at the look she got in return. "Honestly. No one was around. So I just grabbed a sheet and left."

"Good plan," Jazz said with a note of respect. "As plans go, that's an A-plus."

"A C, if you hadn't sent in a team of angels to whisk me off to safety."

Jazz leaned closer for another hug. "I can't take credit for that. I've got a guardian angel of my own."

Over her shoulder, Jessica saw the tall, long-haired man who'd rescued her. She remembered him immediately. "You must be Alex."

Jazz's whole body tightened in Jessica's arms at the mention of his name. She sat up straighter, and turned to look at him. When she faced Jessica again, her eyes were shining.

"He's your bodyguard," Jazz said. "But he's done a great job of protecting me instead."

"Thank you, Alex," Jessica said, taking in his dark good looks and his potent aura. "You must be the lead guardian angel."

Max snorted, as Dan's cell phone played "Lucy in the

Sky with Diamonds." The three men exchanged a silent but meaningful look. "Juicy Miss Lucy on the line," Dan said.

Alex scowled fiercely. "She better have a helluva good explanation."

"Want to ask her?" Dan held the phone toward Alex as it played the melody again.

"No thanks." Alex moved closer to the bed. "Let Roper do the honors."

The other two men left the room as Dan answered his phone.

Alex's olive-black gaze glimmered over Jazz, then he spoke to Jessica. "Jazz is your real guardian angel, believe me. She's one dedicated sister."

Jessica's eyes filled as she nodded. "I've always known that."

"Nothing could stop her," he added, his smile full of pride and admiration. "I've never seen anyone so single-minded or determined."

"Stop," Jazz said, waving a dismissive hand. "We were a team."

Alex's grin disappeared and his expression softened. "Yeah," he said softly. "A good one."

Jessica looked from one to the other, and realization flashed through her. Stop the presses . . . *Jazz is in love.*

As soon as Dan and Max marched back in, Alex knew what they were going to say.

"We're leaving, Romero," Max told him, confirming his suspicions. "Lucy's taken Valerie Yoder back to New York on her plane, and she wants us on the next commercial flight."

He wasn't ready to leave yet. Not without another night with Jazz. Another week. Another month. No, even that wouldn't be nearly enough. "Have a nice trip. Give her my regards."

"You can do that yourself, 'cause you're coming with us," Max told him, turning his attention to Jazz. "Lucy's arranged for you to stay here in Key West until the hospital releases Jessica, then she'll send her private plane to take you both back to Miami."

"I'll take them to Miami," Alex said through clenched teeth. "Lucy doesn't owe anybody anything except an apology. And I'm not going anywhere." He looked at Jazz, who remained on the bed holding her sister's hand, her gaze on him. "I'm staying right here," he assured her.

Max crossed his arms across a massive chest. "Get real, Romero. Lucy already has your next assignment lined up."

"Then take my place, Max. You can probably handle it—or think you can."

"No, I can't."

"Why? Does it require sensitivity, brains, *and* good looks?" Alex asked as innocently as possible.

Dan laughed a little. "Actually, Alex, it requires Spanish. The job's in Cuba. Lucy said she talked to you about it."

Alex felt the blood drain from his head. So Lucy was going to reward him after all. She must feel pretty guilty about trusting Miles Yoder.

And that meant when it was over, fifteen people could leave that hellhole and live in Miami. With family. And opportunity. And security. Fifteen people who were tied to him by blood. Fifteen people who needed and *wanted* his protection . . . a helluva lot more than Jazz Adams did.

He looked at Jazz. "I have to go."

"I know," she said quickly. Much too quickly. "I mean, I knew you would."

"Come outside with me," he said softly, reaching a hand to her. "Talk to me for a minute."

Just a minute. Just one stolen kiss in the antiseptic hallways of the Lower Keys Medical Center. But he wasn't going to leave without telling her. . . .

Damn. He'd rather say it in Spanish.

Max blocked his way to the door. "No time, Romero. We're leaving for the airport."

Alex's lip curled. "Move the hell out of my way before I shoot you."

"Come on, man." Dan gave Max a light punch. "Give them five minutes."

Max took one step to the right but kept his gaze locked on Alex, who closed his hand around Jazz's and tugged her out the door.

They didn't speak a word until they were outside. The sun had finally decided to make an appearance, drying the greenery and washing the medical center in blinding whiteness.

Jazz blinked into the sky as they walked toward a bench. Was she fighting tears, or the sun? Who was he kidding? Jazz didn't cry; she was too tough.

"So. Cuba, huh?" she said, leaning against the back of the bench to face him. Her voice had an unnatural brightness, sounding more like her imitation of Jessica than her real self. "That should be . . . fun."

"Guess that depends on your definition of fun."

She seemed to tighten her grip on the bench behind her, looking up at him with a saucy smile that almost hid the sadness in her eyes. "Want to know my definition of fun?"

He couldn't resist. "Night swimming?"

"This."

"This?" Saying good-bye? In front of a hospital?

"This adventure. With you. Dodging bullets, chasing bad guys, arguing and . . . *not* arguing. This has been fun."

A new wave of affection washed over him. "You're a natural at it." He put a finger on her lips, loving the softness of them. "Except you have to be careful with that rear end."

"Excuse me?" She inched back and looked perplexed.

"When you're attacked from behind, don't stick your butt into your attacker. I've been meaning to tell you that since we met."

She laughed. "And you just remembered now."

"I thought we had more time." He slid his hands around her waist and tugged her into his chest. "I'm not ready to leave you."

She dropped her head on his shoulder and sighed. "Me neither."

"When I get back——" he started.

"I'll be in San Francisco." She lifted her chin again. "And then, you'll go to . . . Paris or Prague or Geneva."

He laughed lightly. "I'll probably bypass Geneva for a while."

"You be careful, okay?" He could have sworn there was a crack in her fearless voice. "And stay away from your client's wives."

"I'm not interested in them, Jazz."

She winked at him. "But they are—"

"No." He shook his head. "No jokes." He dipped his head closer to her. *"Querida,"* he muttered against her mouth. *"Mi amor."*

She slid her hands up his arms and locked them behind his neck. "Then no more Spanish, either. I hate that I can't understand you."

"Just ask. I'll tell you what I said."

"Okay. What did you say the first time we made love?"

He exhaled with a laugh, and shook his head. "I don't remember what I said."

"You said, *'Tenemos todo eternidad.'* "

We have all eternity. Of course, that's not what he meant when he said it. It was an expression, a sensual, lyrical way of slowing your lover down so you don't explode too soon. But she wouldn't understand that. Or the fact that he couldn't promise eternity any more than he could promise when—or if—he'd be back from Cuba.

"It doesn't have a literal translation."

"Of course not. Because we don't have eternity." At his surprised look, she added, "I found Spanish phrases on the Internet."

Of course she did. "Jazz . . . I never . . ." What could he say? He'd never met anyone like her? He'd never felt like this? He'd never meant to fall in love?

"Take risks," she finished for him, a mix of tease and disappointment in her expression. "And you are looking straight into the face of the biggest risk you've ever known."

She was right. He had no response for that.

"And I never want help," she added. "And that's what you live to do."

Right again.

The hospital doors *whooshed* open behind him, and Max Roper marched outside to suck up the sunshine with his very presence. Alex groaned in frustration, and Jazz glanced over her shoulder to see who'd caused it.

"Why do you hate him so much?" she asked.

He just shook his head. "Doesn't matter. What were you saying?"

"I was saying *tenemos todo eternidad.*" She threaded her fingers into his hair. "Not."

Right then, more than anything in the world, he wished they did have eternity. But life and responsibilities and commitments made eternity seem impossible.

Jazz tightened her hold around Alex's shoulders. "Good-bye, Alejandro."

Longing made him ache inside. Or was that ache caused by the idea of taking a risk with her? She was the one who insisted she wanted no one to take care of her, and he was a man who knew no other way to express his love.

The power struggle would never end. "Jazz . . . I have a very strange life, an unpredictable, insane, dangerous—"

She silenced him with her fingertips to his lips. "I know all that." Reaching up on her toes, she replaced her fingers with her lips. "I'll never forget you. You're my bodyguard."

He hated the pain in his chest almost as much as he hated Roper's unsubtle throat-clearing. He lowered his head and captured her mouth for one long, last soulful taste of her sweet, soft mouth. He could feel her heart hammer against his chest, their rhythm, as always, utterly in sync.

Reluctantly, he broke the kiss, then grazed her cheek with his lips and settled his mouth in the warmth of her ear. "Jasmine," he whispered, purposely using the Spanish pronunciation of her name. *"Te llevo en mi alma."*

He would carry her in his soul. That was the closest he could come to admitting how he felt, and how he felt could only be expressed in Spanish.

Her eyes darkened with a question, and her own emotions. Without waiting for her response, he followed Roper into the parking lot. He didn't look back. Because if he had, he would forget his family, his promises, his responsibilities. And then he'd probably take the biggest risk of his life—and tell her he loved her.

CHAPTER
Nineteen

Valerie Yoder was one of the few people who'd ever seen Lucy cry. She'd been there during the dark times. It was Valerie's hand that Lucy squeezed when the first shovelfuls of dirt were dumped onto the tiny casket . . . and Valerie's three-inch designer heel that had crushed the prescription bottle that contained Lucy's only escape from pain and guilt. Lucy owed Valerie Yoder her very life.

That was the only possible explanation for her flawed character judgment and blind trust of Miles Yoder.

She fluffed a small cashmere blanket around Valerie's bare feet. "Get under the covers, Val. You'll feel better."

Valerie just shook her head, curling into a fetal position, blinking at nothing. "What was I thinking when I married him, Luce?"

Lucy remembered the rapturous look on Valerie's face as she'd floated down the aisle to wed her prince. "You weren't thinking. You were feeling."

"I had no idea he was so . . . controlled by wealth."

"Fear," Lucy corrected.

Val let out an unladylike snort. "Miles wasn't afraid of anything."

Not true, Lucy thought as she crossed the guest bedroom to adjust the drapes and bring a little sunshine into Valerie's world. Death made things so . . . dark. "He was terrified to ever be poor again. He told you about his childhood. We should have known." Her world was built on her ability to read people, yet she'd misread Miles so badly. She'd gotten past the initial anger, but guilt still tightened her chest.

"He told me he worked so hard so I could have everything I wanted." Valerie shook her head. "That very day in Miami, right before we met you at the Biltmore, he said it again."

"Then you went shopping to get everything you want, and he stole off on his helicopter to make sure it happened." God, why hadn't she seen behind his mask?

She couldn't afford to make mistakes like that ever again. Last time, it had cost her everything that mattered in the world.

Valerie released a long, pained breath. "What am I going to do, Luce? I pulled away from almost everyone I've ever known to live in his world. He loathed everyone. But he always said he loved you."

He used me. "For now, you'll do what you have to, Val. The old one foot in front of the other, as you know." Lucy sat on the edge of the bed and smoothed Valerie's silky, golden hair. Despite her sorrow, Val looked as strong and bright and young as ever. Neither one of them had yet hit forty, but they'd been through two lifetimes already.

"Maybe you'll reconsider my offer to join the Bullet Catchers."

"You'll actually forgive me for convincing you to help Miles and hire someone to spy on Kimball Parrish? You would never have taken that job if I hadn't persuaded you."

"I won't let you take the blame for my shortsightedness. I need brilliant, committed people more than ever in the Bullet Catchers. I'm expanding the business to include covert surveillance, and you're a genius at gaining access and getting information."

Valerie smiled sadly at that. "But not character assessment."

"We all make mistakes, hon. Come work for me and we'll have fun."

Valerie pulled the cover higher, but her mouth curled into the first smile Lucy had seen in hours, if not days. "We'll see. Now go, Luce. Those men are in your library waiting for you."

"They can wait."

"You're procrastinating and that's not like you. Go, tell them you made a bad call. They deserve to hear it from you."

Oh, she'd made more than a bad call. She'd risked their lives, and others. "I hate it when you're right." Lucy leaned over and kissed Val's forehead. "Think about my offer. You're a rare talent, Valerie Yoder."

"Brooks."

Lucy chuckle softly. "Didn't take long to unload that name."

"I never liked Yoder." Valerie gave her a push off the

bed. "Go face your troops. Own up to your mistakes. Be their fearless leader."

Lucy left the room with a wry smile. *Fearless?* Hah.

In the library, each of the men was occupied as his personality dictated.

Dan roamed between the massive picture windows, drinking in the late autumn views that painted the Hudson River Valley in indigo and fiery gold, his gaze farther away than the horizon.

Max stood stone still, his arms across his expansive chest, staring straight ahead; his expression revealed nothing.

Alex lounged on her Napoleon III salon settee drinking coffee.

"Thank you for coming so quickly," she said, striding toward her mammoth-sized writing table. Her heart hadn't thumped like this in years. Six years, to be precise. "I made a grave error in character judgment," she continued as she pulled out her chair, looking at each of them. "I'm very sorry."

Alex sat up, clattering his cup and saucer onto the side table. Leaning forward, he casually rested his elbows on his knees, belying the ferocity that bubbled just under the surface.

"Nobody's perfect, Luce." His voice was rich with irony and accusations. "Even you."

She acknowledged the dig. "I trusted him. And, worse, I entered into an arrangement with him and—"

"Didn't tell me." Alex finished the sentence. "The breach of trust isn't between you and Miles, Luce. It's between you and me. And all of us."

For once, Max didn't contradict him. And Dan stood perfectly still.

Lucy swallowed, nodding. "My friendship with Valerie Yoder is deep and full of . . . history." She closed her eyes. "I did something I rarely do. I let myself be guided by my heart and not my head. I hope it's a lesson to all of you."

She'd only done that once before. Absently, she smoothed her snow white strand of hair.

They were all silent. She looked at each one, lifting her chin in defiance. They were angry, disappointed, disillusioned. She knew how to manage those emotions. Yet all she wanted to do was move on. Lord, she hated talking about feelings.

"I will never make that mistake again," she promised softly.

"And what about us?" Alex demanded. "Do we trust you again, Lucy? Or do we have to wonder, every time you dole out some high-profile job, that you and your buddies have ulterior motives?"

The only sound was the steady swish of the pendulum in her longcase clock. As the seconds noisily ticked away, no one said a word. Even Dan stood still, waiting.

"I will never," she said slowly, looking from one to the other, "lie to you again."

Max nodded once. Dan smiled his acceptance. Alex knocked back his coffee, stood up, and left the room.

"Forget him, Lucy," Max said quickly. "He's being his moody self. Move on. What's next?"

As much as she loved Max's attitude, she had to ignore the advice. "Excuse me," she said, getting up. "I need to talk to him."

She found Alex on the patio, his gaze on the vista that spilled for miles, gripping the balustrade as he inhaled a breath of chilly air.

Calm that temper, Alex.

She approached him without making a sound. "Are you going to leave me?"

He started and glanced at her. "You're such a spy, Lucy. I never hear you coming."

"I'll teach you the tricks," she offered. "If you don't leave me."

He turned to her, the fire in his soul evident in his eyes. "I had to shoot right at her. You have no idea how hard that was."

Oh, yes I do. Lucy closed her fingers over his. "Sometimes you have to take huge and unimaginable risks to save your principal."

He looked hard at her. "This wasn't just my principal, Lucy. This wasn't just another job."

"You love her," she stated simply.

He didn't answer.

"Why are you fighting that?" she asked. "I have no rules against happiness in my organization."

"What makes you think I'd be happy with her?"

"I've seen the way you look at her."

He snorted. "Hey, you called it. 'Gorgeous, smart, and built like a centerfold.' How else am I going to look at her?"

"It's much more than that. You've met your match."

"That I did." He gave her a humorless smile. "And for a match, we couldn't be more different."

"Same with my match."

"Who was that, Lucy?"

"He's dead." At his look of sympathy, she squeezed her hand over his. "I'm fine." Of course she was fine; she'd killed him.

"My point is," she continued, keeping her voice strong and steady, "when you meet your match, you can't walk away from her."

"I'm going to Cuba," he said softly. "At least, I assume that's where you're sending me. And after that, who knows? London? Tel Aviv? Tokyo?"

"And your point is?"

He gave her a get-real look. "That's hardly the foundation for stability."

"Alex," she said softly. "Who says she wants stability?"

"Luce, you don't—"

She took his hand and tugged him toward the door. "Come on. I have a surprise for you. I can't give you any more of a mea culpa, but I can give you something else."

When they returned to the library, she sat behind her desk and the three men resumed their previous positions.

"And now we move on, to Cuba." She looked at Alex and described the job, which included guarding a high-level Cuban executive who had also been set up to appear to be part of a money laundering scheme.

"Obviously, the principal in Cuba requires exceptional personal protection. I'd like you to handle that, Alex."

He nodded and took the dossier she handed him.

"I'd also like to launch an investigation into some of the allegations against this man, and I'm going to need someone who can dig into the laundering situation and figure out what's going on." Lucy looked at Max and Dan, then her gaze returned to Alex. "You'll need a partner."

"I don't need a partner," he countered with a scowl.

"You do. I've given this a great deal of thought." Again, she looked at Max, then back to Alex, who looked ready to leap across her writing table and choke her.

"I have someone in mind for this assignment already, Alex. Someone you can trust," she continued. "Someone as strong as you, but willing to work with you and not against you. Someone very smart, capable and intuitive."

"Thank God," Alex said dryly. "You've ruled out Roper."

"You might not realize it, but Max possesses all those qualities. However—" She held up her hand before he protested. "I also need someone with unparalleled computer hacking skills."

The first light of understanding glimmered in his eyes.

"I envision a partner who is an equal to you." She gave into the urge to smile. "Someone who is relentless, inquisitive, unstoppable. Someone who is truly . . . your match."

Dropping back against his chair, he laughed softly.

"I'm willing to hire an outsider on a consulting basis." She picked up another file. "If this works out, we can add her to the permanent Bullet Catcher staff."

"Are you serious?" The hope in his eyes touched her. Oh, yes. Jazz Adams was a very lucky, and loved, young woman.

She held the dossier toward him. "I like what I've seen on this candidate. All the qualities I'm looking for in a Bullet Catcher are there." As he took the folder, their hands touched. "Do you trust my judgment, Alex?" she asked.

"I trust *you,* Lucy."

She accepted his absolution with a single nod to the folder. "Can you teach her Spanish?"

He grinned. "We've already had a few lessons."

He opened the file and let out a low, slow whistle. Dan leaned over his shoulder and looked at the picture. "You'll have your hands full with that one, Alex."

"You have no idea."

And even Max laughed at that.

"I just want to let you know I'm leaving now." Jazz felt Jessica's soft kiss on her cheek. "Ollie's downstairs to pick me up, Jazz. You can sleep for a few more hours."

Jazz refused to open her eyes. "When will you be back?"

"A day or two. However long it takes to gather Denise's son and start the paperwork up there." Jessica pulled the blanket higher and rubbed Jazz's shoulder. "I have to mend fences with Ollie. He's been a good friend to me. And still is, considering he's willing to fly to Minnesota with Denise and me."

Jazz nodded, unwilling to pull out of sleep to discuss Jessica's friendships. "Call me."

"I will," Jessica promised. "Now go back to sleep."

Jazz curled deeper into the bed and inhaled. The guest room bed hadn't been changed yet, and it still smelled like Alex. Wrapping her arms around the pillow, she snuggled into the down, listening for the soft beeps of Jessica setting the security alarm. Once she heard them, she let herself get lost in that heady, masculine scent that seeped into her pores and even deeper into her heart.

Would she, could she, ever forget a man like Alex Romero?

Sleep descended again as she breathed evenly, loving

the memories that went with his scent. He'd slept in this bed, warmed it with his strong, long body. The ache to hold him was so sharp, it threatened to wake her.

So she settled on the memory of his lips, his laugh, the sound of his voice. *Querida. Querida. . . .*

"Despiértate, querida." In her dream, she remembered his touch on her cheek, the feel of his breath on her ear. *"Estás tan rica que te quiero comer."*

The memory of his provocative wake-up call curled her toes. The blanket moved, the bed dipped, the sheets rustled, the scent intensified. And Jazz was suddenly awakened from the deepest sleep to the most startling reality.

Alex. Next to her. In bed. Wearing nothing but that sinful smile. He propped himself up on one elbow and a lock of his hair fell over one eye.

"Jessica let me in on her way out," he said, touching the fading bruise on her cheek.

She remained perfectly still, buried deep into her pillow, staring at him. "Good thing, because we changed the alarm code."

"It's about time." He dipped closer and touched his lips to her wounded cheek. "I missed you."

The whispered words sent a shudder through her, tightening her tummy and every muscle below that. She stroked the hair off his forehead. "I thought you were on your way to Cuba."

"I am."

Her heart plummeted. "Today?"

"It depends." He slid his arm around her and pulled her into the granite of his muscular body. "How quickly can you be ready?"

For a moment she thought he'd spoken Spanish, because the question certainly didn't make sense in English. "Ready? For what?"

"To go to Cuba."

She lifted her head, searching those black-coffee eyes. "Why would I go to Cuba?"

"Because Lucy Sharpe has extended a provisional job offer for you to join the Bullet Catchers."

"She has?" Maybe she was still dreaming.

He nodded, sending the wayward hair over his eyebrow again. "And I really need you on this job, Jazz. It'll be fun," he teased softly, leaning to kiss her lips as he draped a bare leg over her.

Her eyes widened. Her jaw dropped. Her heart sang. "You need me?"

"Constantly." He winked at her. "Even though you don't need me."

The admission washed over her like warm air. "You need me. On this job." She sounded like an idiot repeating his words, but they just didn't make sense.

"I need a partner," he said, tracing her cheek and lower lip with his fingertip, slowly easing his body against hers. "On this job . . . and in this life."

Her chest ached with the breath she held. What was he saying? "I . . . don't understand."

"Would you prefer I say it in Spanish?"

She turned on her side to line their bodies up, feeling his heart hammer at the same crazy rhythm as hers. "Say it . . . in any language."

He moved closer. "*Te deseo* . . . I want you." Turning her onto her back, he eased on top of her. "*Te necesito* . . . I need you." Then he took her mouth in a long, sensuous kiss. After, he whispered, *"Te quiero."*

"Te quiero," she repeated. *I love you.*

"And I want to spend the rest of my life with you."

Jazz closed her eyes and let the euphoria envelop her. "That's quite a big risk for a guy like you."

"Open your eyes and look at me, *querida.*" When she did, he held her gaze. "I'm not afraid of risks, Jazz. I'm afraid of you believing that we shouldn't be together because you don't want someone to take care of you. I know you can take care of yourself—and all the people you love—and I would love nothing more than the honor of coming along for the ride."

She tried to smile, but her eyes filled with tears.

"Aw, Jazz." He laughed and kissed her eyelids. "I've never seen you cry before."

"Don't get used to it," she said, her voice cracking.

He kissed her cheeks, her mouth, her throat. "I'll never get used to you."

Arching into him, she knew she'd never get used to this—happiness so intense it hurt, and contentment so real it numbed her.

Love. Love so wild and strong and inviting that she could barely breathe.

"Tell me again, Alex. Tell me you love me."

And he did, using the universal language they both spoke fluently.

POCKET BOOKS
PROUDLY PRESENTS

ROXANNE ST. CLAIRE'S

next Bullet Catchers novel,

FEATURING MAX ROPER

COMING NEXT SUMMER FROM
Pocket Books!

TURN THE PAGE FOR A PREVIEW...

"You know what I hate most about you, Caroline Peyton?"

Caroline turned to drink in the sight of her closest friend descending three stone steps to the lower lawn, moving in beaded evening pants as gossamer-like as her nickname. "I'm sure the list is long, Breezy, but what is it now?"

"That death becomes you."

Caroline drew back at the statement. "That's not funny."

"I'm not, for once in my life, going for humor." Breezy slid a well-toned arm around Caroline's waist and tugged her closer. "I watched you work that party for the last hour. You manage to exude grace, class, and radiance, with just the appropriate amount of grief and ennui."

Caroline couldn't help but smile. "I'm willing to bet, oh, everything I have, that you have no idea what the word *ennui* means."

Breezy looked insulted, but recovered. "That's a sizeable bet, since you now have plenty."

"But I don't have William," she said softly.

"See? See what I mean? How do you *do* that?"

"Because I really do miss him. Even after six months, and especially on a night like this." She swept a hand toward the dazzling uplighting surrounding her sprawling tropical estate, the vast pool and pavilion area trimmed with stately royal palms and littered with overdressed guests and obsequious waiters. "I just expect to turn around and see him wearing a tux and that expression of . . . awe he saved just for me."

"I'm going to be sick."

Caroline prodded Breezy's ribs gently. "Did you come out here to abuse me or just ruin my one moment of peace in a sea of curious, probing eyes?"

"They may be curious, but they are generous, too."

That they were. Miami's wealthiest socialites would pour $200,000 into the Peyton Foundation account during this one cocktail party, and darling Breezy had done all the work to make it happen. "I could never have pulled off this fund-raiser alone." Caroline leaned her head toward Breezy's thin but always supportive shoulder and sighed. "I'd be so lost without you."

"Don't mention it. I had fun. My goal was to make it so that all you had to do was slide your sexy self into that eye-popping Valentino and show up to answer the one question on every collagen-enhanced lip in Miami."

"Which is?"

"Did he die in the sack?"

Caroline couldn't help but laugh at Breezy's tasteless humor. "You know he did. But in his sleep." She found the star she'd been looking for, hanging above a blindingly white ninety-foot yacht anchored across the wide canal that surrounded her Star Island home. "What they really want to know is if the trophy wife has turned into a merry widow."

"Screw 'em. You never were a trophy wife." Breezy pulled a cigarette out of her tiny bag and shot a glance toward the house as she lit and inhaled sharply. "Anyway, I came down to tell you that you have a guest."

Caroline stepped away from the cloud of blue smoke. "I have two hundred of them. Is there one in particular I'm ignoring right now?"

"This one claims to be your bodyguard." Breezy blew out in the opposite direction, her green eyes narrowed by smoke and accusation. "So you really did it, huh?"

"I had to," Caroline said. "That little scene up in Bal Harbour convinced me."

Breezy nodded knowingly. She hadn't been shopping with Caroline the day a menacing black Jag swiped her so close the side mirror knocked her handbag to the ground, but she'd shared the post-event trauma just the same.

"Where'd you find this guy?" Breezy asked. "He's smoldering hot."

"I didn't find him. A woman who was at William's funeral owns a security firm that Peyton Enterprises has used on occasion. I called her and asked her for someone intimidating and visible."

"He certainly qualifies."

"I want to send a message to that weasel that I'm not afraid of him."

Breezy snorted. "I notice that weasel hasn't made his appearance yet."

Caroline silently thanked God. The last thing she needed on her first major social outing as the widow of William Peyton was a run-in with the *son* of William Peyton. "After serving papers to my attorney contesting the will? I doubt even he has the audacity to show up at my house tonight."

"If he does, you've got one sizeable stud up there to

protect you. Here, he gave me his card." She snuffed the cigarette in a planter and reached into her bag to produce a business card.

Caroline started toward the steps. "I thought he was coming tomorrow. I guess I have to deal with him."

"Trust me, it won't be painful."

"No thanks, not interested."

"You might change your mind when you see Mr. . . ." Breezy tilted the card toward the light to read it. "Max Roper."

Caroline's foot slipped off the limestone step and dipped back into the grass. "Excuse me?"

"Executive protection and personal security. Max Roper."

Caroline seized the card, the blood draining from her head so fast the letters danced. "Oh, Lord, the universe could not be so cruel and twisted."

From the top of the stairs, a shadow eclipsed the glittering party lights. She didn't have to look and he didn't have to speak. She couldn't smell the saltwater or even the sweet oleander anymore.

She could only smell *him*.

"The universe is most definitely a cruel and twisted place." From the shadow, a sinfully deep baritone rumbled right through her. "You of all people know that, Mrs. Peyton."

She looked up and swayed a little. But that was surely from her high heels sinking into the lawn, and not from the impact of a man she had loved and hated at the same time.

God in heaven, it *was* Max. "What are you doing here?"

"I'm with the Bullet Catchers. Lucy Sharpe sent me."

"You?" She injected a healthy dose of disgust and dismay into the syllable, letting her heels submerge further into the earth for stability.

"Me." He took two steps closer, but that did nothing to diminish the sheer size of him. Maximilian P. Roper III was six feet five inches of unforgiving muscle and man. No doubt he made an excellent bodyguard.

Only he wouldn't be hers. Never, never, never.

"Caroline, do you know this man?" Breezy closed in as though her one-hundred-and-one pounds could actually keep Max Roper at bay.

"We met years ago." Max said. "In Chicago."

"I lived in Chicago years ago," Breezy insisted. "I never met you."

Caroline put a hand on Breezy's arm and hoped her friend didn't notice that she was shaking. "I'll talk to him alone, sweetie. Then he'll be leaving." *No matter what.*

Breezy shot a warning look at Max as she left, but his gaze never wavered from Caroline, slicing her with those black-diamond eyes that refused to reveal anything as mundane as an emotion. An expensive sports jacket covered what she knew to be a Herculean chest, and in that chest pounded a heart that she'd once considered her most treasured possession. Long ago.

"There must be a mistake," she said. "I arranged for a bodyguard, not a DEA hunting dog."

The corner of his mouth quirked—for Max Roper, a full-blown grin. He reached out a hand for a formal shake. "Max Roper, here to offer you unparalleled personal security."

She backed away, more willing to wrap her fingers around a charged lightning rod than touch Max again. "You work for Lucy Sharpe," she said, finally thinking clearly enough to snap pieces into place. "You're one of the Bullet Catchers."

"Yes."

"And she sent *you* to protect *me*."

"I suppose there's some irony in that, but Lucy has her reasons and we rarely question them, Mrs. Peyton." The emphasis on Caroline's married name wasn't lost on her. Of course, he'd believe what everyone else did: Caroline had married an older man for his money and won the lottery when he died in their bed, leaving her an heiress to a two-billion-dollar estate and controlling interest in Peyton Enterprises.

But wouldn't Max, of all people, know her better than that? Maybe not. And she wasn't about to stand out here in the merciless Miami humidity and explain it to him.

"I'll call Lucy and make other arrangements," she said simply. "Obviously she doesn't realize we have . . ." Her voice trailed off.

"A history?"

Her mind flashed with the memory of soul-flattening kisses and heart-cracking tears and gut-wrenching accusations, all delivered in a dingy hallway of a hundred-year-old building in Chicago. Yeah, that was certainly *history.*

"A conflict of interest," she concluded.

"That assumes . . . interest." His eyes glittered, but of course he didn't smile.

"I have no intention of playing word games with you." She'd lose. "If you don't call your boss, I will. You're not . . . what I had in mind." Now there was an understatement.

He pulled out a cell phone and held it toward her. "Just press one. It's programmed to her private line."

He was a world-class bluff caller. She remembered that from the nights she'd played poker with him and her father and a couple of other DEA agents. Max loved nothing more than tempting her into higher bets, his impassive expression never revealing his cards. Or his feelings.

She'd bet everything on him, all right. And lost.

She took the phone, her heart finally calm enough for her to remain steady as she regarded him. He really hadn't changed at all. If he'd spent the last eight years chasing evil drug lords, the job hadn't ravaged his handsome face; if anything, he looked better. Older. Wiser. Scarier. His dark hair was just as thick as it had been back in the days when Caroline's fingers explored it endlessly, although he'd grown it longer, letting it touch his collar and fall over one ominous-looking brow. A brow that still knotted at the sight of her, as though he could never figure her out but refused to stop trying.

"Are you going to call or just stare at me?" he asked.

Max was the bluntest human being she'd ever met. The bluntest, brashest, coldest human being, who once brought her to orgasm using nothing but . . .

She almost choked on the memory. "I just can't believe you're here."

"I understand." He crossed his arms, pulling the fabric of his sports jacket across that endless chest. "I've had some time to get used to the idea."

"You knew who I was when you accepted this assignment?"

"The whole world knows who Caroline Peyton is." He dipped his head closer to her. "And, by the way, my deepest sympathies on the loss of your husband."

There was no indictment in his voice. None of the veiled resentment at her fortune. In fact, she heard that underlying gentleness he loved to hide, and her heart just about stopped. Max could always get her with softness. No matter how big and tough and mean and bad he was, when he turned soft, it killed her.

No, she reminded herself sharply, it killed her *father*.

She opened the skinny silver phone and pressed the talk button. As the screen lit up, she squeezed it tighter to cover the tremble in her fingers. "Did you say press one?"

He flipped the phone closed. "I'm the best she's got, Caroline."

She looked up and met his gaze. "I understand the whole Bullet Catchers force is the cream of the security crop. I'm sure we can find a suitable replacement."

He reached for the phone, but she tugged it toward her chest.

He relented and let her have it. "Before you call, why don't you tell me exactly what the problem is," he suggested. "Then I can help Lucy pick the right bodyguard for you."

A shatter of glass and metal reverberated from the patio. In one split second, Max whirled around, blocked Caroline with his massive body, and whipped out a handgun.

"I just want to talk to her." The strident voice echoed across the lawn, loud enough to hush two hundred inquisitive guests who peered at the scene from around the pavilion and on every balcony. "I don't need a fucking invitation to my own house."

Oh, God. *Billy.*

"Don't shoot him, Max," Caroline said, stepping away from the human wall he'd made. "He's my stepson.

And that's"—she added with a quiet sigh—"precisely what the problem is."

Billy Peyton easily pushed past Breezy's ineffective arms and ambled across the expanse of the lawn, drawing every eye to the luster of his platinum blond hair. Caroline knew the cellular buzz from South Beach to Coral Gables tomorrow would be that Billy Peyton was wasted. But that wasn't exactly news.

She squared her shoulders, bracing for the worst. She'd become adept at acting as though his behavior was normal, a trick she'd used to keep William from getting enraged over the antics of his only son. "I'm right here, Billy."

As she took the steps to the upper lawn to meet him, she sensed Max right behind her.

Billy stumbled as he approached her and she reached out to steady him, but made it look like a stepmother's cool greeting. No need to throw her arms around him and air kiss. Their animosity was no secret and Caroline was no phony.

"What do you want?" she asked.

He leaned back and even in the dim party light, she could see his enlarged pupils and pink-rimmed eyes. What was it tonight? Weed? Coke? Ecstasy?

Those battered eyes swept over her. "That's a pretty stupid question, *Mom.*"

Disgust roiled through her, but she kept her tone modulated. "I received the papers, and my attorney will contact yours. There's really nothing else to discuss. Especially not tonight. This is a critical fund-raiser for the Foundation. Please. Do me a favor . . . and leave."

He dropped his head in a bull-like gesture that might have been threatening if he wasn't just this side of throwing up and his floppy surfer locks didn't ruin the whole effect. "I don't want to discuss shit and I couldn't give a rat's ass about your Foundation. Where's the bar?"

"It's closed."

"Open it."

"I would very much like you to leave," she said through gritted teeth, vaguely aware that Max had moved from behind her to behind Billy. "Without making a scene."

He opened his mouth to continue the argument, but before a sound came out, Max seized him into a headlock. Billy lunged away, but Max overpowered him, effectively paralyzing him with one unyielding hand.

The other hand rose slowly, holding a sleek black gun.

"Holy fuck—" Billy's eyes widened in terror and he jerked again, but Max immobilized every muscle with one squeeze.

"Watch your language around the lady," Max growled, pointing the gun straight up. Caroline's limbs grew numb as she stared at the pistol, but she forced herself to look at the horrified expression on Billy's contorted face.

"Who the hell are you?" Billy grunted, twisting his head to see Max. "Get your fu—"

Max yanked tighter. "I said, watch your language around the lady."

Caroline took a step toward them. "Billy, I've hired a bodyguard. And you know exactly why I've done that. I will not be intimidated or threatened by you or your sluglike friends."

He snorted. "You are swimming in delusions of grandeur, Caro. No one is trying to hurt you. I just want what is mine. Just because you got flat on your back for—"

Max wrenched his neck, maybe a little harder than necessary. "The lady wants you to leave, Mr. Peyton."

Fury flashed in Billy's pale blue eyes and he tried to shake his head. "This is my house and I'm—"

Max cocked the gun. "Let's take a walk."

Billy stared at the weapon, beads of sweat forming over his upper lip.

"Is there another way out besides the front?" Max asked Caroline.

She indicated the north lawn. "You can take him around there to the gatehouse."

Billy narrowed his eyes at her and all she could see was the blackness of his dilated pupils. "Whore." He mouthed the word at her so Max didn't hear it.

"He shouldn't drive," she said quietly. "I'll meet you in the front and get a cab for him."

"I'll take care of him," Max said, walking away with Billy tightly in his grasp. "Billy and I are going to have a little talk."

Caroline watched them disappear in the shadows and stared into the darkness. What would he do? What would they talk about? Billy hated her, but Max wouldn't believe his lies.

Would he?

Maybe Lucy Sharpe did have someone else just as good in her stable of bodyguards, but there was a certain comfort in knowing it was Max Roper responsible for her life. After all, who owed her more than Max?

Breezy appeared at her side with two glasses of champagne and a sly smile. "Well, I'd say you made the right call on the whole bodyguard thing."

Caroline reached for a flute and let out a soft gasp. "Oh, I still have his cell phone."

"How clever of you." Breezy chuckled and raised her drink in a mock toast. "An absolute guarantee that he'll be back, even if you do try to get someone else for the job." She took a sip and winked. "Which, we both know, you won't."

*A love like you've never known
is closer than you think...*

Bestselling Romances from Pocket Books

The Nosy Neighbor
Fern Michaels
Sometimes love is right
next door...

Run No More
Catherine Mulvany
How do you outrun your
past when your future is just
as deadly?

Never Look Back
Linda Lael Miller
When someone wants you
to pay for the past, you can
never look back...

The Dangerous Protector
Janet Chapman
The desires he ignites in
her make him the most
dangerous man in
the world...

Blaze
JoAnn Ross
They're out to stop a deadly
arsonist...and find that
passion burns even hotter
than revenge.

The Next Mrs. Blackthorne
Joan Johnston
Texas rancher Clay
Blackthorne is about to
wed his new wife. The only
question is...who will she be?

Born to be BAD
Sherrilyn Kenyon
Being bad has never felt
so right.

**Have Glass Slippers,
Will Travel**
Lisa Cach
Single twenty-something
seeks Prince Charming.
(Those without royal castles
need not apply.)

www.simonsayslove.com

12909